KARISSA LAUREL

SERENDIPITY AT THE END OF THE WORLD

Serendipity at the End of the World
Red Adept Publishing, LLC
104 Bugenfield Court
Garner, NC 27529
https://RedAdeptPublishing.com.

Cover Art by Streetlight Graphics[1]

---

1.   http://StreetlightGraphics.com

For Erica Lucke Dean and Kim Husband

Chapter 1: A Mysterious Rescue

Boxed in on all sides—how had I let that happen? I'd known better than to go out alone, unarmed, unprepared. When I left the vault at sunup, I hadn't intended to stay out so late. Sunset signaled the beginning of the definitive countdown, the ticking time clock warning the quick and the breathing to get behind closed doors. Fast. The staggering, groaning figures shuffling toward me would hear no pleas for second chances, and they never forgave mistakes, especially the stupid ones.

I reached into the deep front pocket of my leather blacksmith's apron and clenched my trusty stiletto's handle. The slim blade was the only weapon I'd brought with me. Neglecting to stock up on more firepower was not my only error today, but I'd have to save enumerating my many failures for later... if I survived. Spreading my feet wide for balance, I raised my arm like a constable stopping oncoming traffic then bent my wrist, fingers up, palm toward me. I flicked my fingers twice in a come-hither gesture.

It was all bluff. I wasn't that brave, and by no means did I want to face my death. Not like this.

The winds changed, swirling loose curls around my temples and driving the sickly-sweet ammonia scent of rotting flesh up my nose. My stomach rolled, and bile climbed up my throat. I choked it back. Tears welled, and I was tempted to let them blind me. *Don't really want to see what's coming for me, do I?*

The first one, the most eager and ravenous, shambled close enough to catch a slash from my knife. A cut wouldn't do it, though. I needed to sink the blade in deep, damage the brain or spine. I'd killed the nasty critters plenty of times but with a rifle or a handgun from several yards away. Hand-to-hand combat had never been my forte, but neither was having my guts ripped out by a mouthful of putrid teeth.

Drawing in a deep breath, I tensed for a lunge, but at the same instant I shifted to strike, an arm snaked around my waist. A hand as strong as steel clamped around my stiletto. I shoved and struggled, kicked and clawed, but the hands were too powerful, the arm too binding. I screamed loudly enough to shred vocal cords.

See? Told you I wasn't all that brave.

"Quiet," a male voice whispered harshly in my ear—not one of the dead because they never spoke. "Follow me. Quickly."

"But there's nowhere to—" I said, but the figure that had materialized at my side had already dashed away, his wool coat swirling like a black cape. After several long strides, he flung himself over an iron railing behind me and landed—*thunk*—at the bottom of a stairwell. I'd known about the stairwell, but it led to the access door for an unfinished subway tunnel. Those doors were solid steel and, in my experience, never unlocked. I'd failed to consider the subway as an escape route for that reason, but I swore to never make that mistake again along with all the others I had already committed today.

Without hesitation, and with the undead's hot, pestilent breath following me, I cleared the railing and landed gracelessly at the bottom of the stairwell, taking the brunt of the fall on my tailbone. Rolling to my feet, I rubbed my bruised rear end and muttered curses under my breath. The stranger was no longer near enough to hear my complaints though. He had opened the access door and disappeared into the darkness on the other side.

"Hey. Wait for me!" I said, calling into the subway's shadows.

A hungry growl slithered down the stairs. Turning, I recoiled and backed away from the creature leering at me from the top step. Something resembling a woman wearing a mink stole and a pale-pink gown took her first clamoring step. She was nasty, missing at least half her jaw. *How did she intend to bite me without it?* But yellowed nails at the tips of her skeletal fingers clawed at me, eager and hungry, promising to inflict the damage her missing teeth could not.

Spinning around, I scurried toward the subway's darkened doorway. As soon as I cleared the threshold, a cool breeze blew past me, and the steel door slammed shut. In the draft, I caught a faint whiff of sandalwood and male sweat. A spark from a lighter sputtered, and a flame erupted from the fist of a gloved hand. He touched the flame to a lantern wick, bringing to life a warm, yellow light. Before he turned away, the glow revealed a striking profile: dark hair, sharp cheekbone, high brow, lush-lipped mouth. He was young, possibly my age, but certainly no older than Bloom.

In a city bereft of the living, I was confident I'd never seen him before, which was odd. Not impossible but certainly improbable. There weren't so many of us left alive that we didn't all recognize each other, even in passing. And almost all human relationships in this city were passing.

"Follow me," he said in a gruff voice.

"Where are we going?" I asked.

He declined to answer. Instead, he led me down subway tracks, laid but never used. We dodged the occasional puddle when possible and plowed through them when it wasn't. He moved fast enough to discourage conversation, and we raced the distance of several city blocks before he stopped at an open doorway. A warm draft wafted over us, and the lantern's flame flickered.

"There's a ladder at the end of this hallway," he said. "It'll lead you to a storm drain. That storm drain ends a block from your place. You can find your way from there."

"How do you know where I live?" I asked.

He ignored my question and shined his lantern down the hallway, keeping his face averted to the shadows. I stepped forward to get a better look at him, but he must have sensed my intentions because he backed away.

"You can't show up out of nowhere like that and tell me nothing," I said. "Who are you?"

"I'm the guy who just saved your life."

"That's it?"

His silhouette shrugged. "Yup."

I snorted and rolled my eyes, although the darkness had probably concealed my gesture. If he wanted to be a mystery, who was I to argue? I glanced at him once more before turning for the ladder.

"Wait a sec." His hand flashed out and hooked my elbow, stopping me mid-step. "Take this."

He dumped something into my palm, something hard, dense, and warm from his touch. My thumb swiped a rough engraving on the object's flat surface. I leaned closer to the lantern, and its light reflected off a small square of rustless steel: a lighter. Before I could say thank you, my rescuer doused his lantern and dissolved into the gloom, disappearing like a ghost.

Chapter 2: Get Lazy,
Pay the Price

I climbed the ladder at the end of the short hallway, and exactly as my rescuer had said, it brought me through the floor of a storm drain. I stopped and flicked the striker of my gifted lighter, and its small flame illuminated a long, narrow tunnel of brick. Something skittered beyond my small ring of light. Maybe it was only rats, but no point in waiting to find out if I was wrong.

I moved on, making my way in a slow, steady shuffle, my boots scraping over a mostly dry floor. *Thank God it hasn't rained in a while.* The night sky illuminated the storm drain's exit, where murky purple light oozed into the darkness. I crept forward, trying to make no sounds or attract unwanted attention. Rotters loved the night, and their activity increased as the darkness thickened. Maybe the black of night reminded them of the safety in the graves they'd left behind.

The end of the storm drain emptied into a refuse pond at the bottom of a gully. I leaped diagonally and landed beside the pond in a soft, marshy patch of mud that smelled like mildew and sour milk. My boots withstood the wet and cold, however, and lent me traction as I fought my way to solid ground. After climbing the gully's steep embankment, I stopped to catch my breath and gather my bearings. Sharpening my ears, I listened for the presence of the undead—groans, gnashing teeth, or scraping footsteps—but I heard nothing to rouse my worries.

Pale moonlight illuminated the familiar landscape of a park I used to play in as a small child. Bloom and I had lived in a large townhouse then, one in a row of homes adjacent to the opposite end of the park. Their dark and empty skeletons blotted out a patch of night sky. No one had lived there in years. I knew where I was, and I knew how to get home. My stranger had been right—I was no more than a block away.

For the past five years, my sister, Bloom, and I had lived in a bank vault, one in the basement of what used to be the Savings and Loan. The vault was cramped and claustrophobic, but only Bloom and I lived there, so we made do. We could also seal it up at night and sleep without worrying that we might wake to a horde of hungry, rotting corpses snacking on our livers and spleens. The bank building had suffered a lot of wear and tear during the Dead Wars. Somewhere along the way, an explosion had torn a chunk from the offices on the upper floors and cracked the vault's roof. The crack let in enough air to breathe and leaked something awful in a rainstorm, but it was a reasonable price to pay for our security.

"Serendipity Blite, where in hell's blue blazes have you been?" When she was angry, Bloom sounded a lot like our father. She looked like him too—long, lanky, and pale as milk with dishwater-blond hair. Physically speaking, she was a stark contrast to me—short, curvy, and auburn haired. I favored our mother, who came from an indecipherable blend of backgrounds and ancestry. As for our personalities, we were complete opposites as well.

Perched in an upper window of the Savings and Loan building, Bloom's dark silhouette watched me creeping along the sidewalk. I suspected she wore a deep scowl, but the light from the dim lantern beside her failed to reach her face.

"The King of England asked me for tea," I said, "and I thought it rude to decline." In truth, King Edward was probably a hungry corpse by now. We didn't get much news from across the pond these days, though, so I couldn't be sure.

A ghastly howl from somewhere nearby raised the hairs on the back of my neck. An answering moan had me shifting nervously from foot to foot as I waited for Bloom to lower the ladder from the fire escape. The moment it touched down, I scurried up, quick as a lizard.

"You weren't supposed to be gone so long," she said as she hauled the ladder back into place.

"Someone found our stash." I grabbed Bloom's lantern and led us through a broken window into a dusty office. "There was nothing left when I got there, so I went looking for another cache."

The probability of finding food decreased every year, but Bloom and I had lucked out about a month back and found a mercantile with a basement smorgasbord of canned foods, coffee, and crates of flour, cornmeal, and sugar. We should've hauled every ounce of it back to our place a long time ago, but Bloom and I had seen no one—no one *living*, anyway—in our part of town in weeks. It had been a dumb mistake, because our number one rule for survival was "Take nothing for granted." We got lazy, and we paid the price.

Bloom noted my empty hands. "Did you find anything?" She turned a gear that lowered sheet metal shutters over the broken office windows. Then she brushed her palms on the seat of her pants. Bloom loved devising mechanical things like those shutters. She would have done something really amazing with all her smarts if the Dead Disease hadn't ruined everything.

"I did, but I had to dump it and run when the Rotters caught my scent."

"We haven't seen anyone in weeks, Sera." Bloom guided us from the room and paused while I held the lantern over the stairwell leading to the basement. We both held our breaths and listened for sounds of movement. Ever since a Biter had found its way in through an air vent we had overlooked, Bloom and I always double-checked.

Bloom exhaled first and moved toward the stairs. "Who do you suppose it was that took it?"

"I don't know," I said. "But they got the whole stash. There wasn't even a coffee bean left on the floor." My thoughts flickered back to my strange savior. *Who was he, and where did he live? More importantly, was he the one who'd found Clawson's Mercantile and its store of dry goods?*

"Damn," Bloom said. "Cleaned out."

"I found a place a little farther away that had sugar and some old, musty coffee. That's what I was bringing back when I ran into the Rotters."

"Did you fight any of them?"

"No." I thought of the desperation I'd felt as I stood there, waiting for the inevitable. I would have fought them, but it would have done me not one lick of good.

"Are you hurt anywhere?" She sounded like a concerned sister, but she mostly had her own self-interest in mind when she asked that question. It was okay. I also had my own self-interest in mind whenever I asked her the same question after she'd been out foraging. Early on, people figured out the Dead Disease traveled through a bite. The knowing didn't help. The only remedies involved decapitation or a bullet in the brain, and that wasn't much of a cure, in my opinion.

"No, they didn't get close enough to bite," I said.

"So, no dinner tonight, I guess."

"Won't be the first time."

Bloom answered as always, "Won't be the last."

In the vault, Bloom plopped onto her canvas cot and reclined, exhaling a noisy sigh. "We're going to have to get out of the city before long. There's nothing left, and I'm tired of scrounging so hard for the little we can make on our own. If we stay here, we're going to starve to death. Or worse."

There had once been a time when I'd believed nothing could be worse than death. I had since amended that belief. "I don't want to leave," I said. "This is our home. I'm attached to it. We've had this discussion before."

"Everyone's gone, Sera. What reason do we have to stay?"

I had no reason other than that the city was a part of me. Leaving it would have been like chopping off an arm or something. "We'll look tomorrow," I said. "Both of us. We'll find some more stuff."

We had to.

Chapter 3: Mint Jelly and Little Green Peas

Bloom and I always waited until the brightest part of the day to do our foraging. The dead shied from direct sunlight, and that gave us our only advantage. While they were uncoordinated and easy to kill, there were at least twenty Rotters for each living person, and the dead liked to roam in packs.

"Find anything?" Bloom asked as she searched the storeroom of a little Italian restaurant we had discovered miles away from the Savings and Loan. We'd never needed to go so far for supplies before.

"I found some crackers." Crumbs sputtered from my lips as I exited the kitchen.

"What else?" Bloom peered into the dining room and glanced out the restaurant's front windows. In one hand, she clutched her Colt Walker, a .44 caliber revolving pistol. In the other, she carried a .22 Bloomington rifle. Both guns had once belonged to our father, who had spent most of his life working as an engineer with the Bloomington Arms Company. If you haven't caught on by now, Bloom's name was no coincidence. Neither was my affinity for firearms.

I remembered how Father's slim, calloused hands had guided my smaller, paler ones as, together, we broke apart one of his many, many rifles. We oiled and swabbed the chamber and pin and polished the barrel until it shined blue. "Always wipe off the excess polish, Sera," he'd said. "Don't gum up the works."

He would watch me buff the walnut stock to a warm, rich gleam. I reloaded the cartridges and raised the stock to my shoulder as if to fire, finger resting beside the trigger. Peering down the sight, I admired my handiwork. Then we broke the rifle apart and did it again.

"Unless we're practicing, never fire it unless you mean to kill someone," Father had said. "And, darling, I hope you never have to..."

Bloom wasn't the only one packing heat. I carried the sister to her Colt, and my trusty stiletto rested in the pocket of my leather apron. I kept the knife as backup only. Despite my mistakes the day before, my number-one goal was to never get close enough to one of the rotting Bone Bags to have the need to use it.

We might've had a hard time finding food, but guns and ammunition were plentiful enough. People had hoarded them when their neighbors started falling to the Dead Disease. Not many of those people had managed to survive since then, but their guns and bullets sure had.

"Got some more tea," I said as I crammed another stack of crackers between my teeth.

Bloom scowled. "Quit stuffing your face, and let's go. You know I don't like standing around in one place too long."

I shoved five boxes of saltines into my canvas duffel and buttoned it closed before joining my sister in the dining room. "Let's go on a little bit farther." She kept her attention on the plate windows framing the empty street outside. "I'd kill for a tin of sardines."

We searched for a few more hours and found several more boxes of tea in a basement apartment. Then, with delirious relief, we stumbled upon a tin of dried fruit almost entirely free of mold. I inhaled the sweet perfume of shriveled apricots and currants and longed for the summer, when we would keep a container garden on the Savings and Loan's roof. We grew tomatoes, squash, cucumbers, and whatever else we could convince to take root in buckets and empty wine casks.

Occasionally, Bloom and I braved the lengthy walk to the river to fish. We resorted to roasting squirrel and pigeon when we were hungry enough, but I longed for a nice beef rib roast. Bloom was wrong. We wouldn't starve to death if we stayed in the city, but the question came down to what we were willing to do, or eat, in order to survive.

The sun was sliding fast from the sky, slinking toward the horizon. If we stayed out much longer, we risked walking home in the dim light of dusk. We'd seen no signs of Flesh Eaters so far, and that made it a good day. But I didn't want to foul our good luck with unnecessary risk-taking.

"What I wouldn't do for a hot cherry pie." Bloom licked her lips as she stuffed a dried apricot between gum and cheek. She held it there like a plug of tobacco.

"I'd like a meatloaf," I said, holding out my hand. She plied it with an apricot, and I followed her lead, packing the fruit against my gum to slowly dissolve.

"Meatloaf?" Bloom pursed her lips. "Why not a rib eye? Or a lamb chop?"

"With mint jelly?"

"And little green peas."

"And whipped potatoes?" My mouth watered, and the apricot turned to mush. Most days, I missed real food more than I missed people.

"And gravy," she said. "Don't forget the gravy."

"What about dessert?"

We played this game frequently, and it never grew old. You might say we were torturing ourselves. You might be right.

"Lemon meringue pie," Bloom said. "With a glass of cold milk."

I suspected the memories of what used to be were harder for my sister because she'd had five more years to collect them than I had.

She remembered our mother better than I did as well, but she never talked about her, and I never pressed.

"Well, we've got crackers and tea," Bloom said. "We'll have to use our imagination."

"At least we won't go to bed hungry."

"My stomach might not growl, but I wouldn't call that being satisfied."

"Maybe tomorrow we should try shooting pigeons again." I adjusted the straps of my rucksack and steadied my grip on my guns as we stepped onto the sidewalk, heading for home.

Bloom scrunched her nose. "They're just rats with wings."

"When you're hungry enough, even rat tastes like prime rib."

Once we reached our building, Bloom laced her fingers together and waited for me to give her my foot. She hoisted me into the air, and I caught the bottom rung of the fire escape. I hung there until my weight pulled the ladder down. She and I had practiced this routine so many times, we could've performed an acrobatics show. So far, the undead hadn't managed to figure out this trick. Cooperation was not a concept that lingered in their putrefying brains.

"To the roof?" I asked.

Nodding, Bloom motioned for me to lead the way. I climbed the ladder, and Bloom followed, our boots softly clanging on the wrought iron stairs.

We kept cisterns on the roof to collect rainwater, and over the past few weeks of spring, we'd managed to save up a lot. Bloom had also built us a cookstove that ran off firewood. The city provided plenty of wood as long as we didn't mind busting up some disappeared family's bedroom suite. And trust me—we didn't mind.

"Get some water boiling, would you?" Bloom said as she packed fuel into our stove.

My sister had made our cookstove out of industrial parts we'd hauled to the roof one piece at a time. I had never understood quite how she made it or what the bits and pieces used to do before they became a stove, but I was thankful to have it. I filled a dipper with water from one of the rain barrels and poured it into a pan covered with cheesecloth to filter out small bits of trash.

When the water finally boiled, Bloom poured us both a cup, dunked in our newfound teabags, and sat down beside me to wait while it steeped. I wished we had sugar, but we had run out a few days before. The search for sugar was what had kept me out later than usual when that ravenous horde had trapped me. Thinking of my mysterious rescuer again, I opened my mouth to mention him to Bloom, but a desperate shout from the street below cut me off.

"Oy, Bliters, let us in. Quick!"

That shout was answered by a distant cacophony of undead shrieks and roars. After a relatively uneventful day of scrounging and foraging, it seemed our evening was about to get a lot more interesting.

Chapter 4: Hot Cha-cha

Bloom glanced at me and rolled her eyes. Only one person referred to us collectively as the Bliters.

"John Brown," she and I said at the same time.

Folding my arms over my chest, I scowled. "I'm not in the mood for him."

"He's a distraction." Bloom's mouth quirked into a sideways, apologetic smile. "I love you, Sera, but sometimes I get tired of the quiet."

"John doesn't know the meaning of quiet."

"That's my point." She shuffled to the roof's edge and peered over.

"Hey, Blite," John shouted. "There's a load of Nasties on our heels."

"Our?" I asked.

"He's got Timber and Honey with him."

I nodded. "Timber's all right."

"Well, it doesn't look like we've got much choice. There's a herd of dead rounding the corner behind them." Bloom started for the stairs. "You give them some cover while I let them up."

I never turned down a chance to practice shooting, so I grabbed a loose chunk of rubble from the roof and used it to prop up my rifle barrel. I was a flawless marksman at about fifty yards. Much farther than that and my accuracy declined exponentially with each extra yard. Fortunately, the dead were in range.

"Come on, Bloom!" John shouted again. "You're cutting it close, and it ain't funny."

She hollered back at him. "It's not my fault you come calling this close to dark, John. Don't get your stays in a bind. Sera's got them covered."

"Sera's with you?" The obvious interest in his voice made my skin crawl.

Bloom glanced at me, an exasperated look on her face, before she yelled down to him. "If you weren't sure she'd be here, why'd you take the risk of coming all this way? You're lucky we were on the roof and heard you shouting."

I considered feigning a misfire just to give John a scare, but like I'd said, Timber was all right, and getting your brain sucked dry by something that smelled like the trash heap behind a leather tannery was no way to go. I lined up my gunsights with a dead man's head. Most of a long, droopy mustache clung to the livid skin of his upper lip, but one of his ears had gone missing as well as a large hunk of flesh from his neck. He stumbled ahead of the pack, making himself my prime target. I exhaled and squeezed the trigger.

Blam!

The explosion roared in my ears. Contrary to what you might think, I found the sound comforting. Mustache Man's head exploded like a ripe melon. "Hot-cha-cha," I said and lined up my sights for the next one, a short woman wearing a ridiculous plaid nightgown and a lacy nightcap. She lacked most of her right arm and shoulder, so I felt none too bad about taking her head as well.

Blam!

"Bull's-eye," I whispered.

"Keep it up, Sera," Bloom called from somewhere several stories below. "The ladder is sticking for some reason."

Turning my attention back to my gun, I peered down the barrel, searching for another target. A head full of gold ringlets appeared in my sights. The curls belonged to a little girl in a yellow dress with crinoline and lace. Pausing, I let my barrel dip down. The girl wore a hungry, empty look on her face like all the rest, but her hair was less matted, her face less bloodied. Most of her body remained intact. Once upon a time, she must have looked like a baby angel.

"Sera?" Bloom asked when she heard no gunshots from me.

"Sorry. Had to reload." I moved to target the young man behind the little angel. He might've been around Bloom's age and wore a round bowler hat. *Why does a dead guy need a hat?* I removed it for him, along with most of the top of his skull. By the time Bloom returned with our guests, I had picked off three more Rotters.

"Maybe you can give Honey some shooting lessons." John Brown crossed the roof and squatted beside me. His beefy, ex-boxer frame strained the seams of his tweed waistcoat and trousers. His red hair was parted in the middle and slicked down flat, and he smelled like lavender and something caustic and sharp. *Turpentine?*

Timber ducked under the access doorway and joined me and John. I'd never known his real name, but everyone called him Timber because he was so tall that if he ever fell over, someone would have to call out *Tiiiiimberrrr!* in warning. He carried a parcel wrapped in brown paper and winked at me as he set it beside the cookstove.

Honey scooted up next to Bloom. Because her temperament was usually more sour than sweet, I figured she'd gotten her nickname from the color of her lovely gold skin. Honey was obviously sweet on my sister, but Bloom said Honey had little to offer other than a pretty face, and no one could afford to get by on just their feminine wiles anymore. Honey had more womanly charms in her little pinky than I had in my whole body, but I shot better than most men, and I wasn't afraid to go out in the city on my own. She was probably jealous of my survival skills, and I was a little envious of the way she filled out a dress, but you'd never catch me telling her that.

"Hey, Sera, let me give it a try." John reached for my gun, but I jerked it away. "Those half-dead freaks have followed us since Third Avenue. I'd like to give them a proper send-off."

I never liked people touching my rifle. It had belonged to my father, and it was about all of him I had left.

"I ain't gonna hurt it," John said, wheedling in a whiny voice. He looked like an overgrown toddler, even though I suspected he was well over thirty years old. "Just let me knock off a couple of them Rotters."

I exhaled and handed over my rifle, though it pained me to do so. He lowered himself flat to the roof and took careful aim. We all watched, breath bated, as he pulled the trigger. His shot missed the horde and took out a chunk of brick from a wall across the way. "Damn," he muttered as he aimed again. With his next shot, he managed to hit a thick fella right in his sagging gut. The revenant rocked back on his heels but kept his balance as he shrieked a hateful sound. I believed they felt no pain, but even the dead had to hate taking a shot in the belly.

"Give it back." I scowled, hoping John could read disapproval in the lines on my face.

He gave me a dark look in reply, but he didn't resist when I tugged the gun from his grasp. Balancing the barrel on the piece of rubble again, I steadied my breathing and put the wretched beast out of its misery in one shot.

I often wondered what would have become of me in the Time Before. This strange new world suited me. *Maybe it suits me just a little* too *well.*

Chapter 5: A Slice of Heaven

"You two are wasting your time." John crossed his arms over his wide chest. "Why do you wanna live down here in this part of the city all by yourself, scrounging for food and the means to get by? It don't make no sense." Turning to Bloom, he pleaded his case. "With the skills the two of you've got, you know Moll would give you a job and plenty to eat."

"We're not working for Moll." My tone was firm, unequivocal. We had this argument every time John visited. "Bloom and I will make it on our own, thank you very much."

"Eating pigeons and scavenging for whatever you can find that ain't rotted or spoilt?" He wrinkled his crooked nose. "That's not making it, if you ask me."

"We're not asking you," Bloom said.

Moll Grimes was the boss in the central part of the city. She had once been the girlfriend of a notorious gangster who ran "private security" for politicians and union bosses before the Dead Wars. She had caught on early to what was happening and encouraged her beau to use his considerable influence, strong arm, and general lack of morals to make preparations. That meant stealing, looting, and storing anything he thought might have a use. Then Moll killed him and took his place.

"So maybe we have to eat stale crackers," I said, shrugging. "At least we don't have anyone telling us what to do all the time."

"You got your stomach telling you what to do. And your fear of the dead. You live with Moll, you ain't got none of that."

Moll might've provided her people with fresh food on a regular basis, but she took payment for it in blood, sweat, and tears. Mostly blood.

In the years following the Dead Wars, Moll had built a compound centered around a high-rise building Bloom and I liked to call Grimy Towers. The high-rise sat on the corner of the city's largest park. Moll Grimes named the area Mini City, and her goons erected razor-wire fences around the park so she could turn it into a farm. A big herd of cattle grazed there alongside well-stocked chicken coops and a pigsty. She set up booby traps all over the place, and guards patrolled at all hours. No one got close to Moll's part of town without an invitation. Even the dead didn't like going there.

"You sound like a campaigner, John." Bloom snickered. "Is Moll running for office?"

Glowering, John spat a wad of phlegm on the roof. "I'm just looking out for my friends is all."

"Come on, Johnny." Honey scooted to his side and slipped her fingers around his massive biceps. "Have a drink with me."

John's thick red eyebrows—the left one was bisected by a scar—knitted together, and he glared at her down his flat, twisted nose. In the Time Before, John was supposed to have been a wunderkind, training to join the professional boxing circuit. Moll's boyfriend had dipped his fingers in a bit of everything back then—government, business, gambling—and John Brown was going to be his next big thing. Turned out the next big thing was actually the Dead Disease.

Honey unearthed a flask from a pocket in her skirt and held it out. John's glower slid into something more amiable as he wrenched the cap free. He tipped back his head, and his thick throat worked, swallowing the flask's contents. I smelled it from where I sat, and it reminded me of the spirits I used to clean my guns.

"Here, Bloom, take a swig of that." John pushed the flask to her chest. She tried to hide her displeasure, but her eyes went hard in a way only I seemed to notice. Putting the flask to her lips, she gave it a quick sip. She tried not to cough, but her eyes watered until she gave in and cleared her throat.

"Sera?" John offered the flask to me.

"No thanks." I stood and moved closer to the cookstove. The sky had gone fully dark, and the chill of a spring evening sifted over us. Honey tightened her coat around her shoulders while John rambled about one of his latest escapades. Timber, on the other hand, sat as silently as a stone statue at the edge of the roof, watching the affairs of the remaining dead below.

"You wanna take a shot?" I asked, lowering into a crouch beside him. His thick, dark eyebrows flexed upward, and I nodded toward where my rifle lay nearby.

A slow grin unfurled across his long face. I didn't know how old Timber was—probably somewhere around Bloom's age if I had to guess, but sometimes he seemed a lot older. Maybe because of how solemn and serious he always seemed to be.

"No." His words rumbled from deep in his chest. "But have you got any more tea?"

I smiled at him. "Sure, I do."

He opened the parcel he had brought with him, and it turned out to be a loaf of sweet nut bread. I nearly cried at the sight of it. After dividing the cake five ways, he passed it among our group. Then he and I took our tea and cake back to our seats at the edge of the roof, leaving John Brown's sensitive ego in my sister's capable hands. She was naturally a better diplomat than me, always trying to make nice. Bloom and I had no love for Moll Grimes, but we weren't interested in making enemies either, so we had to take care not to offend when her emissaries came to visit.

"It's nice to have guests," I said to Timber, trying to think of something polite.

Timber chuckled. "There's not much nice about John or Honey, but I appreciate you saying so."

"Well, it's nice to see *you*, anyway. What have you been up to?"

"Moll has a bunch of us working down at the river. She's got plans for a steam turbine she wants to build. Says she can make electric current." Timber shook his head as though he couldn't quite believe or understand what he was saying.

"What does she want that for?"

"Says she can do all kinds of things with it. Run lights, run machines."

"Wow." I blinked slowly, trying to comprehend the possibilities. "Yeah... wow."

The best thing about Timber was his knack for idle chatter, but if you just wanted to sit quiet with him, he was good at that too. Our tea had finished steeping, so we sipped it under the stars in the comfort of each other's quiet company. And in case you were wondering, the nut cake tasted like a little slice of heaven.

I WOKE AT FIRST LIGHT, still wrapped in Timber's massive coat that covered me like a blanket. A few feet away, Bloom was curled around the cookstove that had almost burned out. At some point in the night, our visitors had left, but I didn't remember their departure or when Timber had tucked me into his rough wool coat. It smelled of mechanical grease and something distinctly masculine. Most likely sweat, if I had to guess. I rose, shrugging Timber's coat tighter around my shoulders, and stoked the stove's fire, throwing on more fuel.

My scrounging must have awoken my sister because she sat up and rubbed her eyes. "G'morning," she said, her voice roughened by sleep.

"Morning, love." I pointed at the pot on top of the stove. "Want tea?"

Nodding, Bloom shifted into a crouch at my side. Before long, we were warming our hands at the fire and watching the rising sun illuminate the city. When it reflected off the windows of taller buildings downtown, the light momentarily brought the city back to life. I closed my eyes and imagined the rumble of carriages, wagons, foot traffic, and voices on the streets below.

"What's on the agenda today?" Bloom asked, breaking into my reminiscing.

I grunted. "More of the same, I guess. Foraging."

"Want to go fishing?"

Her suggestion perked me up, and I glanced at the patchy clouds in the sky. "Will we have enough daylight?"

It would take us most of the morning to hike to the river, but it would be worth it if we caught anything. Rumors said Moll Grimes stocked the ponds in her park with all kinds of fancy fish, even a few pink salmon. In the Time Before, a deli near our townhouse would pile thinly sliced lox on a bagel smeared thick with cream cheese. And what I wouldn't have given for a basket of fish and chips from the stand near my father's office. You'd think after all these years, the cravings would have subsided. Bloom and I had accepted things would never again be the same as they used to be, but that didn't stop us from wanting it anyway.

"If we get moving," Bloom said. "We can stay for an hour or two. We ought to be able to catch something."

At the thought of catching something, I shivered. If we were lucky, the undead would stay in the shadows, and the fish would be the only things getting caught. But this world had stopped being lucky for me a long time ago.

Chapter 6: Guess I'll Go Eat Worms

Bloom and I fished from one of the big industrial docks where cargo ships used to unload. From our position, we could make out the distant shapes of Moll Grimes's generator construction site, the one Timber said he was working on. The smell of industry had dissipated over the last five years, but the ammonia stench of fish still permeated the air. Shad ran in this river. So did sturgeon, herring, and catfish. In my opinion, catfish were the rats of the underwater world, scarfing up whatever fell to the bottom. On a human scale, Bloom and I probably also counted as bottom feeders. The Living Dead were the sharks.

If I could ever manage to choke down a worm, I'd never go hungry again. But while I couldn't stomach the thought of swallowing something so cold and slimy, the bluegill loved worms, and I loved the bluegill, so it was a win-win situation. This early in the spring, though, the fish stayed hunkered down deep, and that probably explained our bad luck.

Bloom and I managed to fill one measly stringer with a few skinny breams. If we picked around the tiny bones, we might've had enough meat to make a half-decent meal. Our harvest was barely worth the effort, but at least it had broken up the monotony of fruitless scavenging.

In the early afternoon, we put away our equipment, wound up our lines, and started for home. Bloom and I stayed to the middle of the street, shunning the dark places where the Rotters liked to hide. No matter where we walked, though, we couldn't avoid Mother Nature, and she must have had it in for us. We'd awoken that morning to a clear sky, but throughout the day, the clouds had gathered as if conspiring to blot out the sun. We picked up our pace as I caught the first whiff of rain.

The wind swelled and licked at our necks. Bloom turned up the collar of her coat, an oiled duster like the cowboys wore. She also sported a wide-brimmed hat that reminded me of the one Keen Jane Colt used to wear in the posters advertising her Wild West shows.

I raised my voice over the roar of a nasty gust of wind. "Think we should run?"

"I guess we should," Bloom said. Our cane poles, gear, and fish stringer made running a tricky task, but our fear of encountering the deceased and hungry motivated us. The clack of our booted feet striking the cobblestone street echoed off the buildings around us. In my ears, the clatter sounded like forty feet instead of four, and a sinking feeling chilled my gut. Reluctantly, I peered over my shoulder. *Damn.* So it wasn't just my and Bloom's footsteps I had heard, after all.

"Uh, Bloom—"

"Don't say it. I can already smell them." She picked up her pace, and I ran faster, trying to keep up with her. "How many?" she shouted, raising her voice over the pounding of our feet and the thudding of our hearts.

"I don't know. Can't count that fast."

The fresher they were, the faster they ran, and the older bodies shambled and hitched at a surprising rate when motivated, sort of like a donkey loping after a carrot. They didn't run quietly either. The dead sent up a cacophony of grunts, moans, and shrieks that raised hairs on my neck and sent chills slinking down my spine. I pictured a gray, decomposing hand reaching for me and stifled a squeal.

"How many more... blocks do you guess?" Talking and running was more of a challenge than I was up to.

Bloom was panting heavily too. "Four... or five."

My legs burned, and my lungs heaved like bellows. I practiced my shooting all the time, but I should have added running to my regular training regimen.

"We'll make it," Bloom said. "We have to."

If we kept up our pace, we would outrun the dead, but four blocks was a long way on a mostly empty stomach. Plus, Bloom and I had to stop long enough to bring down the fire escape ladder. I said a little prayer, even though my belief in a benevolent and merciful God had severely deteriorated over the past few years.

The Bible said the dead would rise in the end times, and some people believed what had happened was the fulfillment of prophesy. The Bible also said there would be trumpets and angels to escort believers to Heaven. I had heard plenty of cries and screams and sirens and whistles, but no trumpets. I never saw any angels, either, and I shot Bishop Carmichael in the head when I caught him trying to eat a little boy in the middle of Fifth Avenue. He was still wearing his clerical collar when he went down. That was no kind of Rapture if you asked me.

A block away from the Savings and Loan, Bloom stumbled and dropped hard to one knee. The fishing poles flew from her grip and clattered to the ground. I heaved her up to her feet, and we left our equipment behind. That pause gave me a chance to look behind us. The calls of our pursuers must have awakened their brethren because what might have been twenty when we first started running now looked closer to forty.

My heart sank. *We're never going to make it.*

"Come on, Bloom." I tugged her arm. The fall must have hurt her, because she limped every time her right foot hit the ground. Her injury slowed our progress, and the dead gained ground. "We're almost there."

"Go on ahead of me," she said through gritted teeth.

"Don't be a dummy. I can't get the ladder down without you." What if we couldn't even make it to the ladder? Either way, I'd go down swinging before I'd leave my sister behind, sacrificing her to that mindless swarm of gnashing teeth and clawing fingers. With dread rising inside me like a storm-surge flood, I reached for my knife.

A heavy footstep clunked beside me. Yelping, I turned toward the sound, my knife drawn. Every muscle in me froze with surprise as the gears in my brain whirred, trying to make sense the sudden, unexpected arrival of the person now standing beside me. "Where..." I coughed and tried again. "Where in the undead hell did *you* come from?"

Chapter 7: Can't Be Coincidence

The stranger ignored my question, same as he had when I'd last seen him in an abandoned subway tunnel. He'd saved my rear end then, and he was saving it again now. How did he manage to be in the right place at the right time so often? *It can't be just coincidence.*

Instead of answering, he fired a pair of pistols into the mêlée behind us. The sunlight brought out indigo highlights in his inky hair and drew warm undertones from his deep-amber skin. A jagged lock of hair swept across his forehead, hiding most of his face from view.

"I'll hold them off," he said in his raspy voice. "Get your sister home as fast as you can go." He paced backward beside me, firing a steady shot on every other step. I didn't stop to judge his accuracy but shoved a shoulder under Bloom's armpit and carted her the rest of the way home.

After Bloom and I brought down our ladder, Bloom scrambled up the steps, and I turned back to watch our mysterious rescuer's progress. He had laid down enough bodies to build a stumbling block for the pursuing hordes, and the ungainly dead tripped and fell over the bodies piling beneath their feet. When one managed to get past, Mysterious Rescuer volleyed another shot and brought it down.

I hadn't come out unarmed, by the way, not after what happened the other day, but it was impossible to run fast and get off a decent shot at the same time. Running and helping Bloom had been my first priority. But now, with my home at my back and Bloom tucked safely away, I whipped my Colt from my apron, braced myself, and took aim.

The Colt had a mean kickback. Bloom said the pistols gave me such a hard time because of my small frame, but I'd never let my stature keep me from doing anything I put my mind to. My rifle accuracy far surpassed my Colt shooting, but I supposed no one would bicker over body counts at the end of the day. After taking a deep, calming breath, I raised my gun, gave the trigger a firm squeeze, and...

Bang!

I dropped an emaciated man wearing a pair of saggy red long johns. "Right in the kisser!"

"Quit showing off," Bloom said, calling down from the fire escape. "Get your rear up this ladder, right now."

Ignoring my sister, I squeezed off another round and socked a tall guy in the shoulder. He wore a soldier's uniform—likely fought, and died, in the Dead Wars, poor schmuck. He stumbled back but kept his feet. My mystifying, black-cloaked stranger finished him with another shot.

"That's it." He kept his back to me, and his black coat billowed in the rising winds. "I'm out of rounds. Get up the ladder, Sera."

How does he know my name?

He stood close enough to touch, but my hands were filled with guns, and I wasn't going to put them away just so I could feel up a stranger—not even one who had a nice jawline and a sturdy set of shoulders. He kept a close watch on the progressing herd, which had slowed to a shamble since we'd gone on the offensive. There was no better way to ensure a Rotter will chase you than to take off running. I'd heard the same was true for wolves and other natural predators.

Without another moment of hesitation, I flew up the ladder rungs and stopped to catch my breath on the landing while I waited for M.R. to join us.

"Where'd he go?" Bloom asked, squatting next to the ladder opening in the landing's grated floor.

"Who?"

"The guy who helped us. He's gone."

I peered over the railing, and a horde of undead stared back at me. M.R., however, had disappeared into the same thin air from which he had appeared. Bloom and I scanned the encroaching multitude, but there was no sign of a living soul among them. *Not totally convinced M.R. is a living soul. He behaves more like a ghost.*

"Who is he?" Bloom asked, obviously baffled.

I told Bloom about the day M.R. had rescued me by leading me through the subway tunnels and giving me his lighter. After tugging the lighter from my apron pocket, I presented it to Bloom as proof of my story. The engraving on one side showed a logo for one of the Sandhog unions, the guys who dug the subway tunnels.

"Weird," Bloom said and wound the ladder up from the street with another of her geared mechanisms. She locked it in place with a combination padlock and gave everything a good shake to make sure it stayed in place.

"You can say that again," I said as I followed her through the office window.

"I was really looking forward to those bluegills for dinner."

My stomach grumbled. "Me too. And we lost our tackle."

"At least fishing poles don't rot. We can find more. Quackenbush's had a ton of them last time we checked."

If you couldn't eat it or kill half-rotted corpses with it, then there was a chance you could find whatever you needed easily enough, clothes especially. I'd found my beloved leather apron hanging on a peg in a blacksmith's shop on the edge of the city. Its giant front pocket kept my guns and knives handy, but I had first started wearing it to add a layer of protection between my vital organs and the dead's gnashing teeth. Under the apron, I wore a heavy pair of canvas pants like the ones gold miners preferred. I also wore leather work boots with thick soles. Considering how much time I spent running for my life, a good pair of boots made all the difference, especially when broken glass, rubble, and debris littered so much of the city's streets. The outfit suited me—I never liked petticoats anyway.

We were safely ensconced in our basement vault by the time the rain hit. Leaks dripped into buckets placed strategically around the room. Later, we'd use that water for sponge baths. Bloom lit a lantern and leaned back on her cot. She pulled her harmonica out from someplace and tooted out a slow, rambling version of "Yankee Doodle."

"Sounds like a funeral dirge." I stretched out on my cot with a tattered copy of my favorite dime novel—a Western about a lady gunslinger named Bullets Boyette. "Did Yankee Doodle die or something?"

Bloom paused her song. "Didn't you hear? Yankee Doodle's a Rotter now." Bloom heaved a sigh. "I'm mourning the loss of my supper—and the loss of beer. That stuff John Brown makes tastes like cleaning spirits. I want a mug of stout so thick you can stand a spoon in it. I want beer with a head so foamy it leaves you with a mustache."

"I want a strawberry shortcake," I said. "With lemon curd and whipped cream."

And that's how we fell asleep, as we had many nights, torturing each other with all the things we missed the most.

Chapter 8: Corpse Bait

Like a pair of wraiths, Bloom and I crept toward the center of the city. The moon shone like a gigantic lantern, so I expected high activity among the Flesh Eaters. They avoided the sun, but a moonlit night brought them out in droves. Maybe Bloom and I were idiots for taking such a chance, but boredom and monotony were our enemies just as much as the Not-Quite-Dead.

Several blocks from our destination, I caught a hint of movement in the shadows ahead and stopped, mid-step.

"What?" Bloom whispered. She peered into the gloom, training her eyes in the same direction as mine.

"Shhh." I stilled my breath and sharpened my hearing. Adrenaline streamed through my veins, and my muscles clenched, ready to fight or run, whichever tactic increased my chances of survival.

Boot soles scraped over cobblestones a few yards away. A match flared, igniting the cherry of a cigarette. I heaved a sigh, and my shoulders slumped. The Mortally Challenged avoided open flames, as they tended to be highly flammable, especially the older and more desiccated they became. Whoever had struck the match probably had a pulse, although that didn't necessarily make him or her an ally.

"Who is it?" Bloom raised her voice above a whisper, just loud enough for the smoker to hear.

The smoker chuckled and stepped closer. Moonlight glinted over his brass breastplate, and he clutched a matching helmet under his arm. A long, thin cigar smoldered from between his fingers. "What are you two doing this far outside the Forces' patrol zone?" The Forces were Moll's security guards assigned to roam the perimeter of Mini City. "You ought to get inside."

"We're Solo Practitioners," I said. "Independents."

He snickered. "Nah, you're just more of the dead, only you don't know it yet. Corpse Bait is what we call you."

Bloom stepped up and offered her hand. The moonlight shined brightly enough so that the stranger noticed the gesture. He stabbed his stogie between his teeth and shook Bloom's hand. "Bloomington Blite, and this is my sister, Serendipity."

"The Bliter siblings," he said, talking around his smoke. "I heard of you from John Brown."

A growl buzzed in my throat. I'd kick John Brown next time I saw him. If you didn't work for Moll, then it was best to stay invisible, and that was hard to do with John throwing our names around.

"And who might you be?" I asked. Whoever he was, his friendship with John was certainly no character reference.

Our new acquaintance shrugged. "Corporal Baumgartner, but you can call me Shep."

Good name for a guard dog. I snickered but tried to cover it with a cough.

"Where are the two of you headed this fine evening?" He blew a stream of smoke into my face. On purpose, I was certain. "What's worth taking your chances against the Usurpers of the Grave?"

"Wow," I said, honestly impressed. "Now that's a name for my collection."

Shep's chest puffed out. "Made it up myself just now. It's a hobby."

Ah, so Shep and I had something in common, after all. "Living Impersonators," I said.

"Bone Biters."

"The Perpetually Decaying."

"Morbidly Alive."

"Brain Lickers."

"*Okay*," Bloom said, whispering harshly. "We're going to stand around in the street and wait for them to chase us down, or can we move on to safer quarters, please?"

"Where are you headed?" Shep asked.

"Livestock," she said.

"You properly armed, or do you require an escort?"

I flashed my Colt at him. "Don't need an escort. Brought my own. Besides, won't Grimes bust you for leaving your post?"

Shep shrugged again. "I'm due for a replacement any minute now. I figure I've earned some refreshment."

Bloom and I agreed to keep the corporal company until his replacement arrived. Then we walked the last few blocks to Livestock together while Shep entertained us with stories of life in Mini City.

"So, how's it you know John Brown?" I asked when the conversation lulled.

"You live in Grimes's world long enough, you get to know everyone—whether you like it or not."

"I don't like John Brown bringing up our names around Moll and her people."

Shep's dark shadow nodded. "I know what you mean. It wouldn't matter much though. You'd be famous anyway because of who your father was."

"What about our father?" Bloom had been quiet, but she must have found this turn in our conversation interesting. So did I.

"Cardinal Blite," Shep said. "Master engineer with the Bloomington Arms Corporation. One of their top guys."

"Yeah, so?" I said.

"Moll Grimes hasn't got a gun in all of Mini City that doesn't have Card Blite's stamp on it. He was the best. He made the best."

"Yeah, so?" I said again but with less impertinence than before. Shep was talking about my father. In my mind, he might as well have been talking about a god.

"Word is that his genius didn't die with him. Word is your sister's got a brain just like her daddy."

My heart sank into my gut, and my voice quavered when I said for a third time, "Yeah, so?"

"So... Grimes is interested in mechanical minds. She's got big plans for bringing this city back to life, literally speaking. There is no America anymore, not like it was. But if there's going to be anything like it ever again, then Moll aims to be the woman to make it happen, and she's going to need good help."

"Is she trying to be the president or something?" I asked.

"Yeah. *Something*."

So, Moll Grimes knew about my sister and her "mechanical mind." I didn't like it, and Bloom's talk of getting out of the city sounded more like a good idea than it ever had before. My stomach churned at the thought of leaving the place I had called home for the past nineteen years, but I'd do it.

I'd do *anything* to keep us away from Moll.

Chapter 9: Off Her Rocking Horse

Several armed sentries patrolled the streets around Livestock, and gaslights burned brightly enough to chase away gloom and ghouls. I contemplated those gaslights as Shep ushered me into the Livestock's main room. Bloom probably understood how the lights worked, but I wouldn't ask her to explain it. Talk about B-O-R-I-N-G.

I also wondered where the gas supply came from, but like I'd said, Moll Grimes's boyfriend had stuck his fingers in a whole lot of pies in the Time Before (before she killed him in his sleep, if you believed the rumors). If you paid her enough, Moll might let you stick a thumb in one of her pies too.

"What'll you have?" Shep asked. He talked to me in a familiar way, even though we had met only minutes before. How did I feel about that? Before I could make up my mind, Bloom had recognized some other Solos in the corner and left Shep and me on our own.

"I don't really know," I said to Shep. "I've only been here once, and Bloom would only let me have tea."

A gleam lit in Shep's blue eyes, and he dragged me closer to the bar. "Rocking Horse for the lady." He jammed a thumb in my direction. "A pint for me."

The bartender nodded and slid us a mug of beer and a tin cup, the contents of which smelled like hair pomade.

"What's this?" I motioned to my cup.

"Rocking Horse? It's the house special."

"But what *is* it? What's in it?"

Shep grinned, revealing several crooked bottom teeth but no apparent holes. He wasn't half bad looking if you go in for the big, blond, German type. "It's wine... sort of."

"I don't like the sound of 'sort of.'" I peered at my drink as if it might jump up and smack me. It smelled strong enough to put up a good fight.

"They take a bunch of fruits—cherries, crabapples, blackberries—whatever they can get their hands on—mash them up, stir in some sugar, and then let it sit in its juices until it ferments."

"It's sweet!" I said after an experimental sip. Then I tossed back the cup for a longer drink. The wine fizzled on my tongue, and in another few minutes, I suspected it would fizzle in my brain.

"Too sweet for me." Shep grimaced. "But the ladies seem to prefer it."

I had never liked being lumped in with the "ladies," but I had tasted beer enough times to know I had no palate for it. The wine, however, went down like candy. "Why's it called Rocking Horse?"

"Because if you drink enough of it, it'll rock you off your horse. It'll give you a rotten gut and a thumping brain in the morning, too, so go easy." Shep guided me to a table near the one Bloom occupied with her friends. She had ordered a pint of her own—no Rocking Horse for her. Bloom liked her beer thick and dark. "You have a right to worry about John Brown and Moll." Shep pulled out a seat for me. "They're not the type a couple of kids like you and your sister ought to get mixed up with."

"Bloom's no kid." My sister was five years older than me, and if Shep was a day older than Bloom, I'd lick his boots. "And anyone who's survived as long as we have on our own has lost most of whatever once made them children."

He inclined his head toward me in a gesture of concurrence. "Maybe you got a point, but you are still a little naïve. Naivety and brains are the best combination in Grimes's eyes. She could use you up, and you won't even know any better."

"I know better than to get mixed up with her."

He drained the rest of his beer and held up his mug, gesturing to the waitress. She shuffled to our table and collected the empty cup from him without a word. "Moll can make a pretty attractive offer."

"Like what?" I peered into my emptying mug and considered asking for another despite Shep's warnings.

"Security, uncommon comforts, food. And I mean good food too. Moll has convinced many a stubborn man to come work for her with nothing more than a plate of ribs and a side of baked beans."

My traitorous mouth watered. "Barbecued pork ribs?"

He chuckled. "With all the trimmings."

"Well, that's not fighting fair at all." I frowned into my wine.

He chuckled again. "Moll has hot-water plumbing fixed up in her high-rise building. You can take a hot bath with the turn of a handle."

A groan full of desire and lust—things I only knew about because of the cheap novels I liked to read—seeped from my throat. "Did she send you to recruit us?"

"How was I to know I would run into the notorious Blite siblings tonight?" Shep leaned back in his chair, threaded his fingers together over his stomach, and shrugged. The waitress returned and set another beer on the table before him. He snatched it up and swallowed a long gulp. Then he scrubbed his cuff across his mouth, wiping away his foam mustache. "You're the one who showed up on Grimes's doorstep. Might appear to her that you and your sister came to talk business."

My heart skipped a beat, and a chill slunk down my spine. "Moll doesn't have to know we were in her part of town tonight."

He raised a judicial eyebrow. "See, that's some of that naivety I was talking about. Nothing that happens in this neighborhood goes unnoticed, and you and your sister are particularly interesting. Soon as you two leave, most everyone in this room is probably going to beat a path to Moll's front door to let her know you were here and what you were talking about."

I leaned forward and bared my teeth. "Including you?"

He shrugged. "We all gotta survive."

I glared at Shep before returning my attention to Bloom. She had leaned in to talk to her companions in a low voice. I couldn't make out her words, and with the way her head was turned, I couldn't hope to read her lips. She seemed serious, though, and I found myself needing to know right that minute what she was talking about.

"'Scuse me, Shep." I rose to my feet. "I appreciate your hospitality, but I'd better be getting back to my sister now."

Wearing a sardonic smile, he stood, nodded, and tugged his forelock as I left his company. "Another time then, Sera. It was a pleasure to meet you."

"Sure, sure." I flapped a hand toward him but kept my gaze trained on my sister. "Nice to meet you too."

One of Bloom's cohorts—a young man close to her age—nudged her as I made my way to her table. My sister clamped her lips into an unconvincing smile as she pushed out a chair for me. "Had enough of the corporal's company?"

"Maybe." I slid into the seat beside her. "And maybe I'm just more interested in whatever it is you've been talking about." I narrowed my eyes at her. "What have you been talking about?"

Bloom's gaze darted to the others at the table before returning to me. "Talking about the weather, garden crops, undead activity, the usual."

Her answer was too much sugar for a nickel, but I would save our inevitable confrontation for later, when we had only the four walls of the bank vault to overhear us.

"And did you learn anything noteworthy from your new friend?" Bloom asked, blinking her long, dark lashes in an innocent way. She didn't fool me. My sister was a great politician but a terrible actress.

"Oh, we just talked about the weather, garden crops, undead activity..." I smirked at her. "The usual."

My conversation with Shep had been informative but not particularly scandalous. I didn't think I could say the same for the subject of Bloom's secretive tête-à-tête. There was something she wasn't telling me, and in our world, secrets could be deadly. Or worse.

Whatever she was scheming, I hoped it wouldn't get her, or both of us, undead.

Chapter 10: Vulture Bait

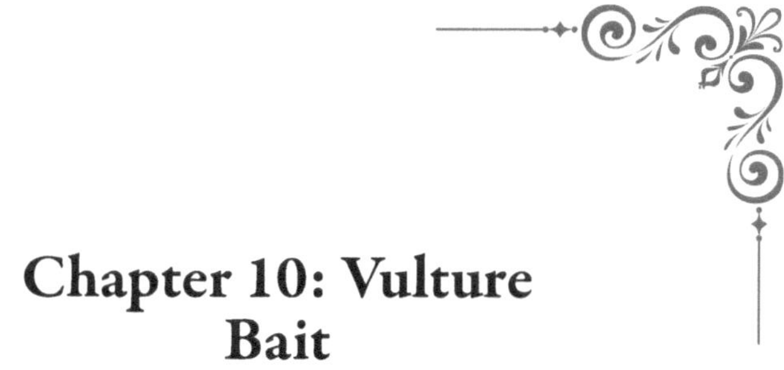

My sister and I had moved our cots to the roof as soon as the weather warmed enough to allow it. The first few blooms in our garden had opened, and I dreamed of tomato and cucumber sandwiches. Until we could pick our first harvest, though, we collected wild greens growing in the nearby parks and empty places. There were more and more green spaces each year—the natural world encroaching on the city, chipping paint, and eating cobblestone, brick, and mortar. Turning things back to the way they used to be before people invented steel and rubber and steam power.

We usually made it through the worst of winter by canning all the garden harvest we could spare. Every now and then, a deer would wander into the city. I hated shooting them, but the meat lasted a while if temperatures stayed near freezing. Whatever we couldn't eat, we traded with other Solos—*when* we could find them. We never knew from year to year who had managed to survive. Still, no matter how much storing and planning we did, by the end of winter, we rarely had anything left of the previous summer's crops.

A family of Solos lived at the very south end of the city—nearly a half day's hike—and they kept goats. Bloom and I had traded for milk and cheese with them before, but they were stingy. I didn't blame them. We would've liked to raise animals, too, but we had no good way to protect them. If anyone got word you had anything of value, you might end up with a battle on your hands trying to keep it.

Also, when the dead got hungry enough, they'd eat whatever warm-blooded thing they could find. You could wake up one morning to find your goat herd missing most of its interior bits and pieces.

The goat keepers had a big family, so they took turns guarding their treasures around the clock. Sure, Bloom and I had considered taking up with another group of Solos, but we had done for ourselves for so long that it was hard to think about getting along with anyone else or having to abide by their rules.

"I think we should try making sauerkraut this year," Bloom said as she inspected a few premature cabbage leaves.

"Aw, no, I hate that stuff." I pulled a weed from a tomato bin. How had the weeds managed to find their way to the rooftop?

"It'll flesh out our diets in the spring. You're the one who's always telling us we've got to get our vitamins." She paused and gave me a doubtful look. "You want to say you've never been hungry enough to eat your own bootlaces?"

"Okay," I said, ceding her point. "If you'll eat it, I'll make it."

"I'd like to try making pickles this year too."

The previous year, we had found dill weed growing in the park near our old townhouse—the one near the drainpipe I had come out of the night M.R. first rescued me. I hadn't thought about M.R. in a while. Neither Bloom nor I had seen any sign of him, and since we'd had no close calls with the undead, he'd had no reason to come around. In fact, things had been downright peaceable for a while.

I should have known it wouldn't last.

"BLOOM, YOU DOWN THERE?" I peered into the stairwell from the roof access and called her again. I had awoken to find the first cluster of tiny green tomatoes on our vine and wanted to celebrate, but Bloom's cot was empty. The moon had been particularly bright the night before. Maybe she couldn't sleep and had gone down to the vault.

"*Bloom*," I called again. She didn't answer.

Scuffling around the roof's perimeter, I peered at the street below, looking for signs of my sister. The street was still and silent, but the fire escape ladder hung askew, unlocked and drooping toward the ground. Not low enough to invite danger but enough to raise the hairs on the back of my neck. Bloom never left without word, without telling me where she meant to go and what time to expect her back. A cold current churned in my stomach.

"Bloom!" I shouted to the silent neighborhood.

A pigeon sitting on a nearby gutter spout eyed me and ruffled her feathers, but nothing else responded to my cry. I spun on my heel and raced down the roof-access stairs with my revolver cocked and ready. Had we suffered a security breach? I took the interior stairs two at a time all the way down to the vault and threw open the heavy door. Nothing. Empty. No Bloom anywhere.

"Bloom!" I screamed her name over and over as I climbed back to the roof, my breath heaving, heart beating as if to explode. The pigeon greeted me with an annoyed coo, but nobody else responded.

Okay, maybe not nobody if you counted the Risen Dead as somebodies. A few had braved the sunlight to investigate my outrage. I screamed all the nasty epithets I could think of at them. "You dirty bastards! You rejects of hell! I'll track down every last one of you and make you vulture bait if you've hurt her!"

They answered with unintelligible moans and shrieks. What had I expected? Admissions of guilt? A news report of her current location? I fired my Colt into the crowd, popping off round after round until my ammo gave out. As I plopped on my rear, angry tears prickled behind my eyes. "Stupid idiot. Serves you right if you go off on your own and don't leave any word. Serves you right if you get your guts sucked dry."

But I didn't mean a word of it. Bloom was the better of the two of us. Death was too disgraceful for her. She didn't deserve it, and certainly not at the hands, or teeth, of a Rotter.

"Do you really think there's something wrong with me for doing these kinds of things?" I had asked her that night we'd come home from Livestock to the pile of bodies I'd left to rot on the sidewalk outside the Savings and Loan.

"What kinds of things?" She cocked her head to study me.

"Making a game out of shooting those poor souls. It's disgusting. Maybe I'm going mad."

"I think the definition of madness has changed," she had said. "If we're not all a little bit insane, then I don't think we could survive."

Maybe her disappearance was divine justice, penance for my unholy, irreverent behavior.

When my crying jag finally ended, I paced the rooftop and didn't once think about my empty stomach. I stayed out so long, waiting for her to come home, that I got a nasty sunburn. Then the sun set and the stars rose, but they brought me no word of my sister.

Come out, come out wherever you are... Olly olly oxen free.

Where the hell are you, Bloom?

Where the hell did you go?

Chapter 11:
Jurisdiction of the Devil

After a fitful night of little sleep, I set out into the city to search for my sister. Bloom said I was always too eager to rush into action without thinking about what I'd do when I got there. I forced myself to slow down long enough to put together a pack with food: a few crackers, a couple of dried strips of squirrel jerky (just as bad as it sounds), M.R.'s lighter, an extra pair of socks, a canteen of water, and most importantly, extra ammunition. I'd have to forage for more food along the way.

The sun had crested the tallest rooftop by the time I stepped off the fire escape ladder's last rung. Giving it a shove, I sent the ladder up out of reach. *Really gotta find Bloom now. Gonna have a hell of a time getting to the fire escape without her.*

My footsteps echoed, each step like a gunshot, and I imagined a hungry mob falling in to pursue me at any moment. When the rest of the morning passed without a sign of anyone dead or alive, some of my paranoia subsided. Couldn't say the same about my worry for Bloom though.

A little past noon, I paused for lunch near the perimeter of Mini City. If you'd asked when I left the Savings and Loan, I would've said I had no idea where to start looking for my sister, but my feet must've had a plan. It made sense that Bloom's disappearance had something to do with Moll Grimes. Realizing that didn't ease my concern, though. In fact, it made me sicker. I could fight a street full of Flesh Eaters, but I had no idea how to fight Moll Grimes or her Forces.

After first checking for Rotter infestation, I hunkered in the doorway of an abandoned clockworks repair shop. From that position, I could watch Moll's guards stroll inside the perimeter of a high, wrought iron fence topped with barbed wire, a fence that bordered all five square blocks of Mini City and Moll's impromptu farm. The resources required to make such a barrier were mind-boggling and further proof of Moll's resourcefulness. It was also proof of how she was a Goliath and I was a mere little David. *A lucky slingshot strike won't be enough to take her down.*

I was too far away to discern the guards' features. If Corporal Baumgartner marched among their ranks, I'd never know without creeping closer. But making the guards aware of my presence meant risking that they might mistake me for a lone, Shambling Corpse. Or, if they didn't kill me first, they might capture me and force me into Moll's service. Neither of those outcomes appealed, so I stayed quiet in my hidey-hole, snacked on jerky, and watched.

Jeez, Bloom, what have you gotten yourself into? And how am I supposed to get you out of it?

Of course, it was possible my sister was nowhere near Mini City. She could've disappeared for a hundred different reasons in a thousand different directions. If I had to guess, though, I suspected Moll's interest in finding a great engineering mind had caught up to Bloom. But if so, then how had Moll taken Bloom away from the Savings and Loan without waking me? My mind raced with possibilities, few of them good.

I freed a cracker from my pack and nibbled it while I watched the guards and waited for inspiration to strike. It finally did when I remembered my conversation with Timber from the night he, John Brown, and Honey had come to visit. Timber had said he was working on Moll's electricity machine down by the river. Maybe Moll had taken Bloom there, and if not, perhaps I could find Timber. If he knew anything about Bloom, he'd tell me... or so I hoped.

I glanced at the sun, still high in the sky. Could I make it to the river from here before nightfall? And if so, then what? I'd never get back home alone before dark.

One problem at a time, Blite. Get to the river and find Timber. Worry about getting back home later.

THE CONSTRUCTION SITE on the bank of the Madsen River was a mostly empty mud pit when I arrived. A sparse crew of men in dungarees hauled building materials, bricks, and bags of mortar from one stack to another. One worker paused to measure a board while another used a long wooden paddle to mix something gray and gelatinous in a wheelbarrow. I had stopped to evaluate the site before I approached, but none of the workers looked anything like Timber, or Bloom for that matter.

While no one from the construction site should've been able to see me from my hiding place in the empty doorway of a nearby warehouse, I had failed to account for anyone approaching from my rear. Bloom was right—I was more executioner than planner. A footstep scraped behind me, and someone with a low, rumbling voice said, "Is that you, Sera Blite?"

Squealing, I recoiled and reached for the weapon in my apron pocket but stopped cold after realizing who had found me. My stomach sank to my feet. "Hey, John," I said in the friendliest voice I could fake. "Long time no see."

"What are you doing here, so far from home?" John Brown wore a curious smile that made him look like a cat who had found an unexpected puddle of cream. "Looking for a job?"

"No, I'm looking for my sister." Why hide it? Maybe John knew something about Bloom's disappearance.

His furry red eyebrows furrowed beneath the brim of his bowler hat. "What's she doing here? Did she finally take my suggestion to join up with Grimes?"

"I actually don't know where Bloom is. Woke up to find her missing this morning."

"Missing?" His eyes went wide and round.

"Rumor says Moll's interested in my sister. Thought Moll might have something to do with Bloom's disappearance."

John raised a shoulder and dropped it. "Bloom ain't here. Nobody's here today except a handful of workers, a few security guards... and me."

I stepped back, repositioning for a getaway should I need it. "Are you a security guard?"

Funny. I'd known John a long time without ever knowing exactly how Moll Grimes kept him employed. He might've mistaken it as a sign of my interest if I'd asked him too many personal questions.

He shoved his thumb against the breast pocket of his plaid waistcoat. "Head of security. Chief, in fact."

"So..." I eased back another step. "Do you know where Bloom is or not?"

He shook his head. "Ain't seen her, but that don't mean she's not back at Mini City. I'll take you in if you like. Escort you around. Help you look for her."

John's offer raised my suspicions. I stepped back again. "You'll take me inside Moll's place?"

He scraped his dull brown eyes over the construction site as he answered. "Sure. You can ask Grimes yourself if she knows anything."

"She doesn't strike me as the type who likes answering other people's questions."

He grinned, flashing a set of unfortunate teeth—stained, broken, and missing in several places. "Don't worry, Sera. I'll vouch for you."

His capacity to inspire my confidence was like a shark trying to convince a fisherman to come down for a swim. "Maybe you could just ask Moll on my behalf and let me know what she says."

His expression darkened as he considered my suggestion. Then his face cleared, and he shook his head. "Nope. Can't do that. You're just gonna have to come with me."

I stepped back again, and it put nearly a yard between us, but I still didn't feel safe. "I don't see why."

"Because I'm in charge of security." He tapped his chest and stepped forward. "And what I say goes."

"But you're not in charge of *me*." I bit my tongue. Not a good time for making inflammatory comments.

"But you're in Grimes's territory, ain'tcha? That gives me jur-is-dic-shun." His face screwed up as he pronounced the last word.

"Then how about I leave, and you can pretend you never saw me?"

His square head swiveled on his beefy neck. "No, Sera. You're coming with me."

John lunged, but I dodged his grasp. He might have been quick in the boxing ring once upon a time, but his middle had gone soft in a way that said he'd taken to lying about more than training.

"Grimes is going to be very interested in you, and that works out good for me."

When reasoning failed, it was time to run. It clearly had, and so I did, as fast as my feet would carry me.

"Oy, Blite!" John shouted behind me. "Get back here!" A single shrill note pierced the air—a police whistle. He must've kept one in his pocket, being Head of Security and all. "Aye, boys!" he shouted. "Fall in!"

Men from the construction site responded, whooping and hollering until they sounded like baying wolves.

"You ain't getting away, Sera Blite. You ain't got nowhere to go!" John might've been about as smart as a box of rocks, but for once, he was right. He knew where I lived, and going back there was as good as inviting him through the front door.

Over and over, John yelled and blew his whistle. Either his brain had taken one too many punches in his boxing days, or he hadn't realized how far from Grimes's territory we'd run. He should've known better than to make such a racket. To the Undearly Undeparted, John must have sounded like a ringing dinner bell.

And speaking of the devils...

Just ahead, in the heavy shadow of a wharf warehouse, a few of the Eagerly Soulless shambled into my path. I had stuffed my heavy Colt into my pack, but there was no time to stop and dig it out. Instead, I pulled a lighter-weight, single-shot Bloomington Rider from my apron pocket and fired into the crowd. Rotters scattered like cockroaches in sunlight, and I plowed through them, holding my breath to avoid inhaling their rancid fumes.

Another pair of undead lookie-loos lumbered into view. One minute, they were shambling toward me, groping fingers extended, mouths gaping like the gates of Hell, but in the next, they were falling, one after another, like dominoes. *What the hell? How did that—*

Then I saw him, standing a few yards beyond the bodies, holding a smoking gun, black coat swirling around his ankles.

"M.R.!" I shouted, not caring that it wasn't really his name. "Boy, am I glad to see you."

Before I could make out the details of his face, he spun on his heel and dashed through the dark doorway of a nearby warehouse. "Follow me," he said, echoing a familiar refrain from our previous encounters.

He and I had danced this dance before, and I didn't hesitate to obey him. It seemed an easy thing, following M.R. *He had cleared a path for me, hadn't he?* But never take such things for granted. It always ends badly when you do.

M.R. had already disappeared into the warehouse, so he never saw the grotesque demon rising from a hiding place behind several abandoned crates near the doorway. The thing stepping out before me might have been a circus giant in a previous life, and something about him seemed terribly familiar. He moved with surprising agility, leaping at me before I could change my trajectory. Momentum slammed me, full-bodied, into his surprisingly solid chest. The odor of mechanical grease permeated his death stench, and a dreadful realization struck me.

"Aw, jeez," I said, shuffling backward as fast as possible. "Oh, God, Timber, is that you?"

Of course, he didn't answer. He simply cracked open his horrible maw and leaned down, eager to sink his teeth into my fresh, pink flesh. His purpling fingers dug into my upper arms. His unnatural life had robbed him of his sense, but not his peculiar strength.

"Timber, *no*," I said as if he were a dog who'd piddled on the rug.

Something in my tone must have gotten through. The thing that once was Timber paused, a split second only, and his grip relaxed. His hesitation allowed me to pull free, but my sudden movement snapped him back into action. His massive paw shot around my neck, closed tight, and *squeeeezed.*

Blackness swirled around the periphery of my vision, and my last coherent thought was, *I should have returned his coat.*

Chapter 12: Phantom of the Subway

"Dear Lord." I put a hand to my head to stop it from rolling off my neck. My voice sounded like a scratched phonograph recording, and hot, glowing brimstone burned in my throat. Surely, if I were dead, I wouldn't have to suffer the injustice of a pounding headache and an epic sore throat. So maybe Timber hadn't killed me after all.

I blinked until the outlines of furniture, hanging drapery, and other unfamiliar housewares took shape in a low-lit room. Somehow, I had sunk into the depths of a plush feather mattress, topped by mounds of cozy sheets and velvet coverlets. Struggling up from the bedding's nebulous depths felt like fighting my way out of a stubborn cloud.

A shadow shifted in a dark corner. I gasped and recoiled from it—visions of monsters still danced in my head—but the shadow coalesced into a familiar figure. Exhaling, I shoved a loose curl from my eye. "Oh, it's you."

M.R. approached, carrying two big earthenware mugs, and the scent wafting from them was thick, rich, and heady. That store of dried goods Bloom and I had found at Clawson's Mercantile months before had included coffee—until someone had scooped our stash out from under us. I inhaled, preparing to ask M.R. if he knew anything about it, but he spoke up first.

"Coffee?" He shoved a mug at me.

The aroma, as heavy and thick as wood smoke, washed over me, and all cognizant thought fled. My brain pushed aside all other subjects and focused solely on the contents of that cup. Forgive me, but coffee and I had developed an obsessive love affair, and we'd been apart for way too long.

"What did you call me out there?"

He eased onto the edge of the bed, careful to keep his profile to me. Still, it was the best look at him I'd gotten so far, and he was lovely: dusky skin, dark lashes, high cheekbones, and a nose that would have been knife straight if not for a little hump near the bridge, possibly a break that hadn't been properly set. Having survived this long, chances were good that we had all broken something—just ask my little toe and the ring finger on my right hand.

"I called you, M.R."

I sipped from my cup. He had sweetened the coffee, probably with sugar from the same stolen stash. The heat from it eased the sting in my ruined throat, and I savored the brief relief.

"Em-Are?" He turned so I could see the quirk of one black eyebrow.

"No." I shook my head. "It's the letters, M and R. You wouldn't tell me your name, so I made one up for you."

"What does it mean?" He furrowed his brow.

A blush flared in my cheeks, and I ducked my chin. "Mysterious Rescuer."

He choked but managed to swallow his coffee without dribbling on his shirtfront. I peeked at him over the rim of my cup as he wiped a few drops from his chin.

"My sister thinks it's silly too." Speaking of Bloom brought her to the surface of my thoughts. "You haven't seen her anywhere lately, have you?"

The one black eyebrow arched higher. "She's missing?"

"You must have known I was looking for her if you knew where to find me."

He shrugged in a noncommittal way and turned, almost giving me his back.

Something about the sudden wariness in his posture raised my curiosity. "You don't know anything? Really?"

He shook his head. "I don't watch her."

"But you do watch me."

I'd figured out that truth a while ago—there was no other way to explain his timely appearances. The more I talked, the more I sounded like a croaking frog, and my throat protested the strain. Nevertheless, I intended to get answers from him. He could be secretive, but I would have bet dollars to donuts I could be more stubborn.

He shrugged again.

I narrowed my eyes at him. "Where are we?"

"My place."

"And where is that?" I tried to imagine him rescuing me from the terrible thing that had been Timber and carrying me back to his home. M.R. was tall, but under that big black coat, he probably had no more meat on his bones than Bloom or me.

He slid off the bed and moved to a plush, upholstered chair in the corner of the narrow room. The already-dim lighting fell short, leaving him wrapped in deep shadows. I sat up straighter and huffed. An errant curl stirred on my forehead.

"Did you know him—the one who was choking you?" he asked. "I heard you call his name."

The pain in my throat flared. I gulped the last of my coffee and set the empty mug on the floor by the bed. "He was a friend, I guess. We called him Timber." Shame stung my cheeks. I called him a friend, but I'd never asked for his real name.

"He's very big."

"Hence the nickname," I said. "He seemed... impenetrable. Like a fortress or something. I wonder how they got him."

M.R. shifted in his seat and leaned forward, resting his forearms on his knees. "There was an attack on the worksite a few days ago. That's why it was so deserted."

"I thought Moll Grimes kept plenty of security around her turf."

His dark figure shrugged. "She's gotten a little too comfortable, I think."

"I'll say. How many do you think it was?"

"How many undead, or how many people lost?"

"Both, I guess."

"A lot, on both sides. I didn't count. Only a few workers got away."

A light flicked on inside my head—an idea coming to life. "I wonder if that attack had anything to do with the timing of my sister's disappearance."

"Sounds like a reasonable assumption."

"But you don't know for sure?"

No reply.

"I wonder why they didn't take me," I said, mostly to myself. I pondered that question until the silence and M.R.'s shadowy presence weighed too heavily for comfort. Shifting, I threw aside my covers and settled my feet on the carpeted floor. Only then did I realize he had removed my boots. "I thank you for saving me. *Again*. But I guess I've imposed on your hospitality long enough. I'll be on my way."

His dark head jerked up, and he seemed surprised, though the shadows made it hard to tell. "Where would you go?"

"I'm... not really sure." I couldn't go home. If John Brown survived the afternoon's undead attack, he'd never accept letting me get away. The Savings and Loan would surely be the first place he'd go looking for me. And if I were him, I'd bring reinforcements.

"It's night, Sera. I think you should stay here until morning. You shouldn't be looking for cover at this hour. Your bank vault is very secure, but I promise that my home is even more so. Stay here. You'll be safe."

I started to argue, started to explain how I couldn't afford to accept too many favors—I had no way to pay them back.

Before I could form my thoughts into words, M.R. stood, crossed the room, and pushed aside one of the tapestries, revealing a doorway. He paused and glanced over his shoulder.

"My name is Erik, by the way."

Then he slipped through the doorway and disappeared into the gloom on the other side.

The tapestry swung down behind him like the curtain at the end of a play. He didn't return that evening, and strange as it was to sleep in another person's home, he had a point. I felt safe there, and for some reason, I believed him when he said his home was secure.

For once in my life, I decided I should take my sister's advice. *Don't jump into action without making plans first.* I'd stay long enough to figure out my next move. In the meantime, I'd have to hope Erik wasn't some opportunistic creeper who'd make me regret not leaving as soon as I had the chance.

Chapter 13: Hiding Something

If you thought I'd hightailed it out of there the next morning, you'd be smart, but you'd be wrong. After Erik left the room, I had drifted back to sleep despite the caffeine in the coffee he had given me. Being half-killed by an undead giant took a lot out of a girl.

When I awoke later to an empty chamber, I scooted out of bed, went exploring, and discovered Erik's room was actually a subway car. It had been abandoned in a short warren the transit authority had probably intended to use as a garage. A steel door squatted at the head of the tunnel, separating us from the track outside. The heavy door was locked tight and made the perfect undead barricade. It also made a great prison.

"How can you be sure you won't run into any Rotters down here?" I asked when Erik reappeared from the gloom and found me inspecting the door. He snatched my lantern and marched to his subway car, leaving me in shadows.

"Hey!" I scurried after him, following him to his posh compartment. "I'm talking to you."

"Who else would you be talking to?" He hung the lantern on a hook affixed to the exterior near the train car's entrance.

I huffed, blowing stray hairs out of my eyes. "How long have you been on your own? Your manners are a bit rusty."

Once again, he didn't answer but climbed a few short steps and pushed aside the tapestry he used for a door. After following him inside, I plopped on the foot of the bed and watched him fuss over a pot sitting on a brazier in the room's rear. It glowed warmly and put off an amazing amount of heat for such a small stove. He wrapped a tea towel around the pot's handle and poured hot water into the same two mugs we'd used the day before.

"You take sugar with your tea?" he asked, still keeping his back to me. Always his back, never his face. Could he not bear to look at me, or was he hiding something?

"Of course. As much as you can spare."

He dumped in two heaping spoonfuls and glanced over his shoulder at me. "Was that polite enough for you?"

Gritting my teeth, I glared at him. He chuckled and turned back to the brazier. "What are you hiding?" I asked.

He paused, but still, he wouldn't face me. "What do you mean?"

"What's all the mystery about? The appearing and disappearing, the way you won't answer a question straight. I mean, you won't even let me get a good look at you."

He fiddled with the tea things, clinking mugs, pouring sugar—nervous gestures, in my opinion. "Do you know what the word 'melodramatic' means, Sera? You've gotten me confused with some kind of dime-novel character."

I did, in fact, know the meaning of "melodramatic." I also knew the meaning of "rhetorical question."

"That's what Bloom says too."

He chuckled. "I think I might like your sister."

"Maybe you two can be best friends." I narrowed my eyes. "Just as soon as I find her."

Still keeping his back mostly to me, he passed me a mug of tea. "And how do you plan to do that?"

The tea's sweetness reminded me of the question I had never asked him the night before. If he could change the subject, why couldn't I? "You ever been to Clawson's Mercantile?"

He shook his head, and light flickered on the dark strands as they swished about. "Why?"

"It had a good stash of coffee and sugar up until a couple months ago. Someone got away with the whole lot."

"Maybe you should have taken it all when you found it."

"We hadn't seen human action in our part of the city in ages." I shrugged and shifted my weight, trying to keep the bed's lush mattress from sucking me down like quicksand. "But we should've known better than to assume it was safe."

"You know what they say about those who assume."

"No." I frowned as I tried to work out the subtext of his question. "What do they say?"

He shook his head again. "Never mind."

I harrumphed and considered slinging my hot tea at him, something to get his attention, make him react, lose his annoying cool. Fed up with his meaningless conversation, I was ready to get back up to the streets, but first, I had to put in the last word. I always did. "See?" I swiped my hand through the air, gesturing broadly. "There you go, proving my point. I ask you a simple question, and you won't answer it."

"What's your question again?" A tinge of laughter seasoned his words.

As cool and capable as he seemed, I never thought I could get one over on him. But when I flew to my feet, indignant and ready to demand his cooperation, he didn't see it coming. His fault for keeping only one eye on me. I grabbed his shoulder and jerked. He came around, off-balance and stumbling, spilling hot tea everywhere. Only then did I get a good look at what he'd been trying so hard to hide.

It stunned me to silence.

Frozen in place, he let me study him, but anger rolled off him in waves as hot as the nearby brazier. "Is this what you wanted to see?"

He sneered and jerked free from my grasp, turning his back. He held his shoulders stiff, his spine straight.

When I found my voice again, I fought to keep it steady and light. "What happened? Were you burned?"

He shook his head and answered in a growl. "No."

Gathering my courage, I stepped closer, approaching him like I would approach a wild animal. He must have sensed my nearness and tensed as if to run—or fight. If I had fallen in with a feral animal, a lion, then I was now trapped in his cage, but instead of trying to escape, I was going to ask the lion to let me put my head in his mouth. "Show me."

He'll tell me to get lost. He'll tell me to go to hell. Instead, Erik turned in slow increments, giving me time to steel myself. He swept a dark forelock over his brow, trying to hide as much of the damage as possible. I raised a hand, intending to tuck his hair behind his ear, but he backed away.

"Was it an animal?" I shoved my hands in my pockets, showing him I meant no harm.

"Not quite." His right eye refused to meet mine. The other eye, milky and barely visible under a lid and brow twisted by scars, looked nowhere. The scarring traveled down his cheekbone but faded before it reached his top lip—a lovely, full lip that was verging on the edge of a sneer. His seeing eye, dark as straight coffee, glinted with hostility.

"A fight?" I asked. "An accident?"

His head bobbed once. A muscle worked in his jaw. "A fight."

I sucked a breath between my teeth. "Whoever he was, he fought dirty."

"That's the way they all fight."

"They?"

"The undead."

I must have misunderstood. "The... the undead? What do you mean? Did you get hurt in a street fight?" In the early days of the Dead Wars, people fought not only with guns but with pitchforks, broken glass, rubble, homemade grease bombs, anything they could get their hands on. If you got in the way of a panicked mob, you could wind up beaten, broken, and scarred like Erik. Or worse.

"No, Sera." His voice sounded tired and full of resignation as he shook his head in a defeated manner. "I was bitten."

Chapter 14: Immune to the Stuff

Everything in the room jumped up and took off spinning. Weak-kneed, I stumbled back, ready to go down, but I didn't. I wasn't a fainter, but Erik didn't know that. He caught my shoulders and held me steady as I struggled for composure. He had recently hauled my lifeless carcass from the streets to his underground home and probably thought passing out was my normal reaction to stress.

"But... how? That's not..." My brain and mouth refused to cooperate.

"Not possible?" Erik said. "That's what you're thinking, isn't it? It's what I thought too. I put a gun to my head as soon as I finished killing the bastard who bit me, but I passed out before I could pull the trigger."

"But you're not a..." I gulped. *Did I really need to state the obvious?*

"Not one of them? Nope. I woke up bleeding all over the place and blind in my left eye, but it eventually healed, and I never developed a craving for human flesh."

I giggled inanely. "Well, thank God for big favors."

He still had an arm around me, supporting my weight. I made a gesture toward his bed, and he helped me to the mattress. I sat, and he pressed my mug into my hands. The tea had cooled, but the sugar in it helped steady my nerves once I'd gulped it down.

"You're not still angry with me for prying?" I asked. He hadn't kicked me out or given me the cold shoulder again. Instead, he squatted on the floor near my knee and stared off at nothing.

Blinking, his attention returned from wherever he had gone in his thoughts. "You're not disgusted?"

I looked him over again, searching for something that might repulse me. "No, I don't guess so. The rest of you is so pretty, it makes up for the parts that aren't so much."

He made a strangled noise that turned into a wry laugh. "Pretty?"

"You know what I mean." I stabbed a finger into his shoulder.

He snatched my hand and held it clenched in his own until his mirth subsided. "No one has ever accused me of being pretty before."

Other people's opinions rarely mattered to me. He was lovely, and his scars couldn't change that. "How did it happen? How come you aren't up there on the streets, moaning and groaning, stumbling around, and looking for your next live meal?"

His expression turned serious again, lips tilting down, brow furrowing. "I think... I'm immune."

I gaped at him. "Immune?"

"Yes. Immune means—"

"I know what it means." I rolled my eyes. "I just wonder what's in those things that you could be immune to."

To tell the truth, I had thought of it less like a sickness and more like demonic possession or something equally evil and otherworldly. Of course, that made little sense in retrospect. The churches might have stood a better chance if the Dead Disease had been something spiritual rather than physical.

Erik nodded and rubbed his thumb across my palm. Only then did I notice he still had hold of my hand. My blood stirred, and heat crept into my cheeks. "I think it's something like the black plague that happened in Europe hundreds of years ago," he said.

"I know about that." I nodded. "People got sick and died, but they didn't get back up again."

"I'm not saying this is the same sickness. I'm just saying that back during the plague, people got sick by getting it from others, but some people didn't get it because they were immune for some reason."

"Like when you get pox as a kid and you can't ever get it again."

"Yes, maybe something like that." He shrugged. "But I don't think I got some sickness as a kid that put me in bed for a couple of weeks but kept me from turning into a full-blown flesh eater later in life."

"No, I guess not." My shoulders slumped. Lacking further theories about his potential Dead Disease immunity, I changed the subject. "Did you grow up around here?"

"Saint Theresa's," he said in a quiet voice.

Saint Theresa's was an orphanage in the city's south side, and it had been my father's pet project. He'd donated a lot of his time and money to both the kids and the nuns who ran the orphanage. My father had often brought me along to play with the other children while he patched a hole in the roof, repaired the front porch steps, or dropped off a bundle of clothing or food or toys—whatever he thought might make the place a little more like a home, and less, well... like an orphanage.

I studied Erik again and searched my memory for a possible match from all those years ago. "How old are you?"

He let go of my hand and stood, his tall frame taking up most of the subway car's vertical space. He crossed the room and leaned against the wall near the tapestry covering the door. "You should save your questions for finding your sister."

I folded my arms over my chest and frowned at him. "Telling me your age has nothing to do with whether I'll find my sister or not."

He grimaced and pushed his way past the curtain. I jumped up and followed him. He took the lantern from its hook and went to fiddle with the big iron door at the head of the tunnel. "You got weapons on you?" he asked.

Only then did I notice my missing leather apron. He must have removed it when he dumped me on his bed. "Where's my stuff?"

He pointed to the train car. "In there by the bed. Get your things and come on."

"Where are we going?" I asked.

He pointed up and grinned. "To the surface."

Nodding, I whirled on my heel and dashed into his room to collect my possessions. When I was little, my governess had said a girl should never leave home without a proper set of foundational garments. I couldn't have agreed with her more. Regardless of whether Erik and I met any Rotters or not, going outside without my weapons was like forgetting to put on underwear. My governess had also frequently said she wasn't sure her lessons were getting through my thick skull. Guess I proved her wrong.

Chapter 15: One More Risk

"Don't the dead like dwelling in the dark?" I whispered as Erik led me through the subway's almost impenetrable blackness. Though we treaded lightly, the walls played with sound, making everything echo, making me feel enclosed in a tomb, surrounded by death. "How can you move around down here without running into a nest of them?"

He stopped in front of a thick metal door that seemed to appear from nowhere. When he turned the handle, it opened on silent hinges. Pointing to his scarred eye, he said, "I'm immune. Remember?"

I pointed to my own relatively unscathed face. "But I'm not."

He shined his lantern into the space beyond the door and illuminated a circular iron staircase. "I've never seen them around my place." He started up the steps. "I think they sense something's different about me."

My footsteps reverberated as I followed him up the winding stairs. "You aren't afraid I'll draw them in?"

"I've seen you shoot." He paused, and I caught a flash of his white grin in the darkness. "So, no, I'm not worried."

"Glad one of us can afford to be so cavalier."

At the top of the steps, Erik opened another door, and sunlight and heat spilled in. We stepped onto an unfamiliar street, but from the fishy stench in the air, I suspected we were near the river. Most of the buildings seemed industrial, warehouses and such. Many were fire scarred and soot blackened with broken windows and crushed roofs. "What are you going to do now?" I asked.

Shifting, he crouched down on one knee and adjusted the buckles of his black boots. He'd strapped a rifle across his back, and under his coat, he wore a heavy utility belt stocking a large supply of ammunition. Despite his nonchalance about his susceptibility to the Dead Disease, he looked prepared to fight off an attack. "I know some people who deal with Moll Grimes," he said. "We'll talk to them, see if they know about your sister. See if they can find out something for you."

"Now, wait a minute." I raised a hand, gesturing for him to stop. "I don't want to do anything else to attract Moll's attention."

"You think talking to John Brown yesterday didn't already do that?" Erik rose to his full height. He stood almost a head taller than me, and he stepped closer, forcing me to look up at him.

Is he doing it on purpose? Does he think I'm easily intimidated?

"Yeah, but I can avoid John Brown," I said. "He's just one man."

"Just one man?" Erik's lips twisted into a cynical smile. "Brown is head of Moll's security. He has all of Moll's Forces at his disposal. And if you can't go back home, where are you going to go? How will you keep him from finding you?"

"I haven't figured that out yet." My chin dropped as I kicked a loose bit of rubble down a street still littered with detritus from the Dead Wars: toppled wagons missing their wheels, smashed crates, piles of stone, and broken bricks. "But I'm working on it."

"You'll stay with me," he said in a dismissive tone. Before I could argue, he turned and strode away without looking back to see if I would follow.

"Mmm."

For the last five years of my life, I'd mostly made all my decisions on my own. Bloom and I had argued fiercely over my stubborn need to remain independent. Turning any ounce of control of my life over to Erik went against my strongest instincts. I considered letting him go on without me, but I was entirely too curious about him and the people he knew. Erik was my Professor Lidenbrock, and I was Alex, reluctantly following him through a volcanic crevasse into a prehistoric realm. Erik *probably* wasn't leading me on a journey to the center of the earth, but how could I be sure?

"I don't need any more enemies," I said, running to catch up to him. "I don't know how talking to people who 'deal' with Moll Grimes could be a good idea."

"This is a different kind of deal than what you're thinking about." Erik kept his gaze trained on the street ahead, obviously wary of human or nonhuman confrontation. There were plenty of places for the undead to hide. Plenty of places for the desperate and depraved—those who'd kill us just for our shoelaces—to set up ambushes too. "There are some things Moll can't get, make, or grow on her little farm. Things she has to go outside for. It puts these people I'm taking you to in a special position."

"What could they possibly have that could be that valuable? And if they trade it to Moll Grimes, then they're just as beholden to her as anyone else is."

Erik coughed a petulant laugh. "What they have, Moll can't get anywhere else. She trades with them because she's got no other choice. She's got nowhere else to go, and she'd give almost anything to have it."

The need to know had become a living thing inside me, pushing against my skin. I launched myself in front of Erik, blocking his path, and set my hands on my hips in my best no-funny-business pose. "Tell me what it is, or I won't go one step further with you."

He took a deep breath and blew it between his teeth, making a little whistling noise. "You ever heard of something called alchemy?"

"Sure. I read a novel about it. *Doctor Goldenov*. It was about a scientist who makes gold out of lead and stuff like that."

Erik rolled his eyes. "'Stuff like that.'"

"Well, that's what the story said." I shrugged.

"You can't believe everything you read, Sera."

I decided to take the mature path and did not stick my tongue out at him. "So, you know some evil scientists or something, and they make stuff for Moll Grimes that no one else can make, and they use some kind of magic science to do it."

"Basically." He shrugged. "In a nutshell. They're not evil, though."

"They don't make gold?"

"God no. Who needs it? The banks are full of it. The rich homes have gold piled up in jewelry boxes. It's useless. Would you rather have a beefsteak right now or a bar of gold?"

"I get your point." I folded my arms across my chest and huffed. "So, are you going to tell me what it is, or are you going to keep making me ask questions until I guess?"

"You'd never guess."

I stomped my foot and issued a silent scream, something Bloom and I had learned to do in a world where keeping quiet meant the difference between attracting Rotters and going about our business unmolested and uneaten. "Were you born this way?"

His black eyebrows drew together, and he frowned. "What way?"

"Why can't you just answer a simple question? And why do you have to act like such a know-it-all?"

He glanced at his feet and had the decency to look chagrined. "You'd be surprised by how much I don't know." Stepping around me, he picked up his pace, and I hustled to keep up with him. In a jarring non sequitur, he said, "Your father was Cardinal Blite."

"How is it practically everyone knows that?"

Erik slowed long enough to gape at me, wide-eyed and blinking. "He was as good as a celebrity, Sera, especially during the Dead Wars. The guns he designed were about the only ones that stood up to the fight. Most rifles, when you use them a lot, they get overheated. The barrels warp. They jam, backfire, or worse. Blite's guns kept going long after the others wore out. Most people who have survived say that a Blite rifle saved their life."

Still marching forward, he shoved his hands deep into the pockets of his long black coat and furrowed his brow. "I know one of them saved mine."

I thought back to the day of my father's death, and a rough, brown anger swirled into my thoughts. "Well, they sure didn't save *him*."

He slowed his pace again, nearly stopping. "How'd he die?"

I stormed past him. He didn't like answering personal questions? Well, neither did I. Two could play the Avoid the Painful Topic game. "How about you tell me about your parents. How'd *they* die?"

This time, his expressive brows shot toward his hairline, both eyes widening big and round. "Now who's the one who can't answer a simple question?"

"Tell me something about yourself, first." Maybe I sounded like a brat, but talking about my father did funny things to my emotional restraint. "Tell me something private."

"I already told you about my scars and that I came from Saint Theresa's."

Putting a hand on his arm, I pulled him to a stop. "Nope. I want to know something about who you are. What makes you tick?"

He blinked at me. "What do you mean?"

"Tell me why you're helping me. Why you watch out for me and come to my rescue all the time."

A shadow crossed his face, masking his expression. Apparently, my question had touched a sore spot, but my father was my sore spot, so fair was fair.

"Forget it. Never mind." Shaking his head, he stepped away. I reached out to stop him again, but he jerked free. "We're almost there," he said gruffly. "You better let me do the talking."

"Oh, sure... because you're so good at conversation."

Why was I following him? Was I trusting him? He had evaded nearly every one of my questions, and yet I trailed after him like he was some kind of pied piper. But no one else was offering to help me find my sister, and I was out of ideas on my own. Surviving in this world meant taking risks. Following Erik was one of those risks. *Please, God, let it be a good one.*

Chapter 16: At the Heart of All Things

Erik led me to a part of the city once populated by clusters of emigrants: Russians, Eastern Europeans, Irish, Portuguese, Greeks, Indians, Chinese, Japanese, and Koreans. The various cultures had staked invisible boundary lines throughout acres of tenement buildings, and the numerous languages, religions, customs, and cuisines rarely intermixed. Erik turned into an alley threading through an area that locals and visitors had called Little Delhi.

The Dead Wars had affected this area, too, but many signs, in both English and Sanskrit, had survived. I recognized fading images of Hindu deities, mandalas, and the other commercial images still adorning the few intact storefronts and doorways. When I said I read a lot, I wasn't lying. It wasn't always dime novels, either.

The sun's rays fell in thin, watery streams between the closely packed buildings, and the gloom heightened an already thick atmosphere of dread and doom. Occasional sets of stairs descended from street level to basement entrances lining both sides of the alley. Erik trooped to the bottom of one of those stairways without looking to see if I would follow, as though he knew that curiosity had me hooked. If that was what he thought, he was entirely right. He stopped before a heavy basement door and rapped on it in a peculiar rhythm.

"Secret code?" I asked, intrigued. Earlier, he'd accused me of reading too many sensational novels, but here he was, acting out his very own mystery caper.

He put a finger to his lips in the universal gesture for quiet. When nothing happened, he rapped on the door again. After another brief pause, something on the other side of the door responded, scraping and clicking. A small square peephole opened at eye level. Two dark eyes set in brown skin peered at us from beneath a pair of white, woolly-worm eyebrows.

"Hello, Cy," said the man behind the door. He spoke with an accent that sounded like a blend of nationalities. British and Indian, I supposed. "It has been a while since we have seen you."

"May we come in, Doctor Dwivedi?"

The dark-brown gaze on the other side of the door shifted toward me. "Who have you brought with you?"

"This is Serendipity Blite." Erik waved at me. "You might've heard of her father, Cardinal Blite."

"Serendipity? What a remarkable name," Dr. Dwivedi said, but he made no response in regard to my father.

"Mostly, I go by Sera," I said.

Dr. Dwivedi studied me, and as he did, the longer hairs of his eyebrows twitched like antennae. I returned his bold stare as he debated letting us in. Finally, he chuckled, and a friendly spark glinted in his eyes. Charmed by his expressive eyes and warm laughter, I smiled at him. Until he closed the peephole with a sudden and decisive *clunk*.

"What happened?" *Had I offended him somehow?*

But no, the door clinked and clacked as the locks disengaged. Apparently, Dr. Dwivedi had decided to let us in. "Why did he call you Cy?" I whispered as we waited.

Erik motioned to his seeing eye. "Cyclops."

Before I could respond to that, the door opened to reveal a small, brown man with a shock of white hair and a thick mustache that complemented his furry eyebrows. "Welcome to the College of Kimiyagari, Miss Blite." He tilted his head in a polite bow. "Tell me if you've ever heard of such a place."

Dr. Dwivedi led us into a dark basement, and his dim lantern illuminated a dank, empty space reeking of mildew and soured water. Nothing in the basement lent a clue about what kind of place or what kind of people Erik had brought me to meet. I shook my head in answer to Dr. Dwivedi's question. "The majority of my day, so far, has been mostly a mystery. This place is yet another one."

Dwivedi offered a kindly smile. "Kimiyagari is the study of the making, the elemental creation, at the heart of all things. It is the exploration of the unknown processes that sustain both this world and all the others we haven't yet discovered. A seemingly magical process of transformation, creation, or combination, but there is nothing magical about it. Magic is only science that is not yet explained or understood."

"Are you talking about alchemy?" I asked.

Dwivedi frowned and glanced at Erik "This word brings too many closed-minded associations with it. The things we study here require openness to every possibility."

Afraid of offending him further, I refrained from saying anything and simply smiled and bobbed my head.

Dr. Dwivedi led us up a flight of stairs to a landing and through another door into a cozy lobby full of blazing sconces and chandeliers. More gas lighting. Had the residents of this place traded Moll Grimes for the fuel, or had they found their own source? I put that on my growing list of questions that probably wouldn't be answered that day.

The wizened alchemist stopped us in front of a strange brass door with no handle, and he fiddled with a lever on a tall switch attached to the floor. Something mechanical clanked and groaned behind the walls. The floor beneath us shook. "An elevator?" I asked, not a little bit awed.

"Yes." Mr. Dwivedi bobbed his head. "This one was designed by the original inventor, Mr. Otis himself."

A pair of brass doors slid apart, and Dr. Dwivedi shoved aside a folding gate. He motioned for us to enter the tiny chamber. When the three of us had squeezed in together, Dr. Dwivedi rotated another lever on the interior wall, turning the indicator as far as it would go. Number ten, the top floor, I presumed.

"Where are you taking us?" I asked. "We haven't even told you why we've come."

"I am taking you to the heart of the college. Whatever it is you have come for, that is where we begin."

Chapter 17: A Misplaced Sister

The elevator shook and shimmied as it rose. I gritted my teeth and tightened my grip on Erik's arm. What a way to go. Survive the undead Armageddon only to die in an elevator. But we didn't fall to our deaths. Instead, the elevator shuddered to a stop. Mr. Dwivedi pulled back the gate and led us out into an open room that resembled a combination café and library. "Before we begin our business," he said, "we will pause for refreshment." Dr. Dwivedi clapped his hand and called out. "Parvati?"

A moment later, a girl about my age swirled into the room. Her gorgeous gown wrapped and folded around her body in a single piece of shimmering, bright fabric. The sari's soft-pink hues brought out the rosy undertones in her dusky skin. "This is my niece, Parvati." Dr. Dwivedi gestured toward the girl then bent and whispered in her ear.

Parvati nodded and disappeared but returned moments later carrying a laden tea tray. She had prepared it so quickly, almost as if she'd been expecting visitors. Gold bangles glinted on her wrist as she arranged cups and pots. I had never really coveted jewelry—too impractical—but she wore the accessories in a way that stirred a strange longing in my heart. Most of the time, I didn't dwell on the loss of luxury and conveniences. Waking up each day to find myself still alive was usually enough to satisfy me. But sometimes... sometimes I missed the comfort of soft, shiny, ridiculous things. I missed the lost world they signified.

Dr. Dwivedi motioned toward the low table, and Erik stepped forward. I mimicked his actions as he lowered himself to his knees and eased onto an overstuffed pillow. Only then, in the warm lighting of the café, did I notice more details about our host. Dwivedi wore a dark-green jacket hanging nearly to his knees. Elegant stitching adorned its banded collar, and mother-of-pearl buttons dotted the length of his coat's placards. In fact, almost everything about Dr. Dwivedi and his home was more elegant than anything Bloom and I had stumbled across in all the years of our lone survival. High-dollar homes in the city had managed to retain an air of stylishness, but whenever Bloom and I stopped in to raid them, those abodes had felt like empty husks, leftover skins shed by a snake. This place, however, felt vital—alive and thriving.

Dr. Dwivedi poured from his teapot as another man entered the room. He slid a slim volume onto one of the abundant bookshelves lining the walls. Then he paused, one hand braced on his hip and the other stroking his bearded chin, as he pondered his next selection. Questions flooded me, so many I couldn't decide where to start, but Erik must have sensed my unrest because his strong fingers clamped down on my knee. He didn't let go until I stopped fidgeting.

Dr. Dwivedi blew into his teacup then sipped. Smacking his lips, he sighed, obviously satisfied with the brew in his cup. "Now that we have a proper setting for it, please tell me why you have come."

Though Dr. Dwivedi had directed the question to me, Erik answered. "We hope you can help us find something that has gone missing."

I scowled at Erik for speaking on my behalf, but he ignored me.

"Is this something that belongs to you, Cy?" Dwivedi asked.

"No." Erik flushed. "No, this is Sera's loss."

"Then why do you not let her tell me about it?" Dr. Dwivedi's gaze turned to me. "Tell me, Miss Blite. What have you misplaced?"

"It's not so much of a what as a who." Tentatively, I sipped my tea. Flavors of cardamom, cloves, anise, and cinnamon flooded my senses. Milky, hot, and spicy, the stuff in my cup resembled nothing of the teas Bloom and I had brewed in our vault.

Dr. Dwivedi chuckled. "What who?"

"My sister, who. Bloomington Blite. I call her Bloom."

"You've misplaced your sister?" He blinked like a surprised owl.

"I didn't misplace her." Heat scalded my cheeks as shame, anger, and dread washed through me. "She's just up and went missing."

"And where was the last place you remember seeing her?" he asked, as though Bloom were a set of misplaced house keys.

"We fell asleep on the roof of the Savings and Loan—that's where we live. It was the night before last. When I woke up, she was gone. I haven't seen her since."

The scientist's brow folded into a field of deep wrinkles as he considered my story. "I suppose her behavior is unusual, then. She does not regularly disappear without first telling you of her intentions?"

I shook my head. "No, sir. Never."

"At this juncture, I would be disinclined to believe there is any assistance that anyone here might offer you. We are not regularly in the business of rescuing lost souls, at least not the physical bodies containing them. I suspect, however, there is more to your story."

"I think Moll Grimes has something to do with Bloom's disappearance." I took another careful sip from my cup. Beside me, Erik also seemed to be enjoying his tea. In between sips, he stared at it as though it contained the answers to all of life's deepest mysteries.

"Moll Grimes?" Dr. Dwivedi's nostrils flared. His mustache twitched as his full lips thinned into a hard line. "I should have suspected."

After I explained about Bloom's mechanical aptitude and how the attack on the generator at the river coincided with Bloom's disappearance, Dr. Dwivedi urged us to finish our tea. Then he led us back to the elevator and directed the car to lower us deep into the bowels of his college, even below the basement level where Erik and I had first entered.

"We have made many improvements to this building," Dr. Dwivedi said. "Most of which the city council would have never approved in the Time Before." He must have noticed the worried expression on my face, because he patted my shoulder. "Oh, everything we have done is structurally sound. Do not worry for the safety of your lovely head. It is simply that the city would have required permits and inspectors, which would have elicited too many of the wrong kinds of questions.

"If the library, where we just were, is the heart of this college," he continued, "then the place to which I now conduct you is the brain."

The elevator settled with an audible thud, and Dr. Dwivedi opened the brass cage. He conducted us into a room furnished with row upon row of flat wooden worktables covered in glass jars, beakers, tubes, and other mechanical whatnots I couldn't put names to. Colorful potions bubbled and steamed from some containers while others rested dormant in racks and shelves, looking somehow ominous in their stasis. Large wooden cases lined the perimeter of the room, stacked with books, scientific equipment, and other things utterly unfamiliar and foreign.

Like a ringmaster in a circus presenting a daring new act, Dr. Dwivedi bent at his waist and executed a wide, dramatic wave that encompassed the entire room. "Welcome to the laboratory."

Chapter 18: Let's Make a Deal

Dr. Dwivedi tucked my hand into the crook of his arm as he escorted me around the large, open laboratory. Erik followed like a silent shade. He kept his eyes pinned on me and seemed unimpressed with our surroundings. Obviously, he'd been there before.

"What do you make here?" I asked, trying not to gape or stumble over my own feet.

"We make a lot of mistakes." Dr. Dwivedi stopped beside one of the large worktables. "But I presume you meant to ask about what kinds of things we *attempt* to make."

After pulling out a stool, he waited for me to sit before he reached for a small rack of stoppered glass tubes. He removed one filled with a thick, dark substance. The fluid caught the light of an overhead lamp and glowed a deep, sanguine red. When he flipped the tube and righted it again, the contents adhered to the sides and oozed like syrup.

"What is it?" I'd seen enough stuff like it to have a pretty good guess, though. "It looks like blood."

Dr. Dwivedi's face brightened. "You are mostly correct."

"What are you doing with it?"

"What indeed..." Dr. Dwivedi's mustache twitched as he pressed his lips together. Beside me, Erik shifted, and his scowl deepened. Dr. Dwivedi's attention turned to him. "Cy, I shall defer the explanation of this particular experiment to you while I slip away to gather a few necessary implements."

I spun around on my stool until my knees aligned with Erik's thighs. His body faced me, but he kept his eyes trained on the ceiling, studying an iridescent stain on the tile above us.

"Just spit it out," I said. "Whatever it is, I can sense that you don't want to tell me."

Erik inhaled, and when he let the breath out, his shoulders sagged. He turned, hiding his scar, and peered at me from the corner of his dark-brown eye. It gave me the willies when he looked at me that way. I glared at him.

"Don't do that."

"Do what?"

"Hide your face like that. You probably don't even know you're doing it, but I don't like how you're always looking at me over your shoulder or out of the corner of your eye."

Throwing his shoulders back, he raised his chin and faced me boldly. He allowed me a moment to take it in again—the extent of the damage and the way it contrasted with the rest of his striking features. I nodded, indicating he should go ahead with whatever Dr. Dwivedi wanted him to tell me.

"It's my blood, mostly, in those vials." He pointed at the rack.

My eyes bugged, and my mouth fell open. Erik smirked as if he had anticipated my response. "Dr. Dwivedi knows about my immunity. I've been trading blood with him for years."

"Trading for what?" I asked, aghast.

"Whatever I want." He shrugged. "Supplies mostly. Food, fuel; a lot of the stuff at my place came from here."

That explained the foreign feeling of Erik's decor. "And what's Dr. Dwivedi doing with it?"

"Trying to find a cure."

"Or an immunization," Dr. Dwivedi said, returning to Erik's side. "We have concocted something that gives anyone who ingests it a limited resistance to the Dead Disease. And when I say limited, I mean it lasts for half an hour at the most." On the table, he set down several more glass vials, a length of rubber tubing, and another frightful-looking item: a silver cylinder with a sharp needle jutting from one end.

Dr Dwivedi presented the needle for my inspection. "It's a syringe for drawing blood or for injecting other things subcutaneously."

"Subcu-what?" I asked.

"Under the skin. The device comes from France, invented by a doctor named Pravaz. A marvelous invention with so many practical applications." Dr. Dwivedi held his hand out toward Erik and waited.

Erik snorted and shrugged off his long black coat. He unbuttoned the sleeve of his white lawn shirt and rolled the cuff past his elbow. Over the shirt, he wore a black waistcoat, and a shiny silver watch dangled from his breast pocket. He hadn't bothered with a neckcloth, and who could blame him? Formality went out along with the certainty of death. His shirt collar folded open far enough to reveal a glimmer of jet beads around his neck.

I widened my focus, discarding the details in favor of evaluating him as a whole. I had underestimated his size earlier. Long and lanky, yes, but his broad shoulders suggested strength and sturdiness. I had a feeling he could be a formidable force if the occasion called for it.

Dr. Dwivedi motioned for Erik and me to trade places, so I slid off the stool, and Erik took my place. Dr. Dwivedi tied the length of rubber tubing below Erik's left bicep. Then he thumped the thin skin at the inside bend of Erik's arm.

"Why'd you do that?" I asked.

Dwivedi smiled wolfishly, revealing broad white teeth. "Why, to bring up a vein, of course."

Erik grimaced as Dr. Dwivedi slid the syringe into his swollen vein. As soon as the tip broke the skin, I swooned. So much for thinking of myself as not much of a fainter. I put one hand to my forehead and clutched the table with the other.

"Sera?" Erik asked, noticing my distress. A drop of blood slid down his elbow, and my whole body shivered. How could I massacre hordes of undead on a regular basis and yet find this encounter so disturbing?

I put up one finger and warbled, "Don't mind me."

Dr. Dwivedi filled the little silver tube and removed the needle. Another fat red drop welled from Erik's arm and dribbled to the concrete floor. My stomach muscles tensed. "Dear Lord," I croaked.

Erik jumped to his feet and grabbed my elbow. "Sera? What's wrong"

Turning my head, I brushed him away and squeezed my eyes shut as I panted for air. "Done yet?" I asked.

Erik had the nerve to chuckle. "No, he's going to take a few more samples."

Somehow, I could smell it, the coppery odor of blood. The heavy metallic flavor settled onto the back of my tongue. I coughed and retched.

"*This* bothers you?" Erik snickered. "Really?"

"I guess I prefer blood spilled from the dead rather than the living." I clutched my stomach and stumbled toward the elevator. "I'm going to sit on the other side of the room. Come get me when you're done."

Erik hooted with laughter until Dr. Dwivedi censured him, telling him to settle down before he bled himself dry. I slid to the floor, stretched my legs before me, and leaned against one of the shelves. Closing my eyes, I inhaled deeply, trying to rid my sinuses of the stench of Erik's fresh blood. The chemical traces of concoctions brewed here over the years filled my nose: sulfur, ammonia, chlorine, and plenty of other noxious aromas for which I had no names.

With a clearer head, I considered what the world would be like if Dr. Dwivedi could create a cure. His temporary immunization potion must have been the thing giving him leverage over Moll Grimes. What kind of power could Dr. Dwivedi wield if he found a way to rid the world of the Dead Disease?

Years ago, before the world fell apart, I had seen a fox running down the sidewalk in the middle of the day. Thick saliva dripped from its jaws, and it growled and snapped at anyone who came near it, not out of fear but out of pure malice; hatred had filled its beady black eyes. A policeman shot the poor thing before it bit anyone, and Bloom had explained the meaning of rabies to me. Rabies would eventually kill an animal, but when it succumbed, it stayed dead.

With the contagion of the Dead Disease, the victims suffered something like a fast case of the worst influenza ever. The infected experienced fevers and chills within minutes after a bite, and he or she died shortly thereafter. Not a deep sleep, not a catatonic state: dead as in no heartbeat, no breath, no nothing. But, unlike the rabid fox, the death didn't stick.

I'd seen it happen multiple times, and it was always a terrible sight.

Terrible wasn't a big enough word for it. There was no word ugly enough to describe having to watch that transformation happen to someone you loved, someone you grew up your whole life thinking of as something akin to God Himself.

For Dr. Dwivedi's cure to work, it would not only have to clear out the disease, but it would have to start the heart back to beating and the lungs back to breathing. It would have to bring someone back from the grave. As I recalled from my Easter Sunday visits to church, only one man ever possessed the power to do such a thing, and I was pretty sure Dr. Dwivedi wasn't Him.

"Miss Blite." Dr. Dwivedi's voice broke into my thoughts. "It is quite safe for you now if you care to join us. I cleaned up your friend and hid away all evidence of the violence I committed on him."

I returned to Erik's side to find him pale and wearing a grim smile. "So, what's going on?" I asked. "What's the point in showing me all of this?"

Dr. Dwivedi smiled like a hungry tiger catching a whiff of its prey. It was a curious look for his unassuming face. "You want us to use our connections to verify the location of your sister?"

I bit my lip and nodded.

"Then I will need to make a deal with you. Reaching out to Moll Grimes is never something we take lightly or do on a whim."

I had hoped, though it was selfish of me, that Erik's blood sacrifice had rendered sufficient payment for Dr. Dwivedi's help. "What are the terms?" I asked.

"I require some particular assistance to carry out the next step of my experiment."

If his experiment involved trying to cure the Dead Disease, then how could he know it would work unless...

Dr. Dwivedi must have read the dread on my face. He frowned and said, "Yes, Miss Blite, I need you to administer a sample of the curative to a test subject, and I need that test subject brought here for observation."

So, not only did I have to stick a zombie with Dwivedi's medicine, but I had to make nice with it, pal around with it until I figured out a way to get it back to Dwivedi's college. Maybe it would come along nicely if I promised to feed it tea and cookies in the café upstairs first. Then Dwivedi could make a pet out of it—a giant undead guinea pig. *Ugh. Disgusting.*

I wanted to say no, but I wanted my sister back even more. "How do I go about administering this cure?" I asked.

Dr. Dwivedi flushed, his cheeks going red under his brown skin. "Oh, good girl, good girl." He clapped like an excited child. "Cy, I will be forever thankful to you for bringing this one to me. She is quite fearless."

"Yes," Erik agreed. "Or foolish."

Crossing my eyes, I stuck out my tongue. *I'll show you foolish...*

Dr. Dwivedi retrieved a small leather case from a drawer under the tabletop. He untied the clasp and opened it to reveal a smaller version of the syringe he used to draw Erik's blood. The case also contained small vials of a dark liquid substance. Individual leather straps secured each vial and the silver syringe in the case.

Dr. Dwivedi motioned to the syringe. "You will simply draw the solution from the vial into the syringe, and then you will inject it directly into the flesh of one of the creatures, preferably into a large muscle in the arm, leg, or buttocks. Bring the creature back to me, alive... or *animated,* if you will. I would prefer for you to choose a female subject, but beggars cannot be choosers, as they say."

They also said something about looking for trouble and finding it.

Dr. Dwivedi closed the leather pouch and held it out to me. "Do we have an agreement?"

Remember how I was the type who didn't like sitting around waiting for things to happen, and how I wasn't much of a planner? Yeah, well, nothing had changed. "Sure thing, Dr. Dwivedi." I took the proffered pouch. "You've got yourself a deal."

Chapter 19: Red Hot Chili Peppers

After we left Little Delhi and returned to his subway car, Erik concocted an early supper out of rice, beans, and a jar of hot peppers. We ate picnic style on top of his bed, me sitting with my legs tucked under myself, him half reclined beside me. The situation was more intimate than I was used to, but I wasn't complaining.

It was nice to be close to someone other than Bloom for a change, and though he was intense, Erik was proving to be a useful acquaintance. Maybe something even more, but it was way too soon to start putting labels on things. I liked him, but it would take a lot more than donating a couple of vials of blood to earn my trust.

The brazier's dim light reflected off his black hair in fiery streaks. How would he react if I touched those sparks in his hair? *Probably call me foolish again...*

"How did you learn to cook?" I dragged my fork across my plate, raking my dinner into a pile. Tiny flecks of indiscernible meat were scattered through the rice. The flavor and texture resembled chicken, but I didn't want my delusions ruined, so I ate without questioning its origins.

Erik drew a pepper from the jar between two long, graceful fingers. "I've been on my own a long time. Either learn how to cook or starve, right?"

An image of those same fingers trailing over my skin bloomed in my imagination. The unexpected vision startled me, and I choked on a mouthful of rice. Erik pounded on my back until I coughed it out. "All right?" he asked.

"Yeah," I croaked and gulped the remainder of my tea. I'd been reading too many sensational novels. Next time I went out foraging, I'd stick to dry philosophy books or historical texts. No more romances for me.

He peered at me, eyes narrowed, lips pressed into a thin line. "You should slow down."

"It's been a long time since Bloom and I had any rice. Guess I got carried away."

"You have a garden. That must be nice."

I paused, a forkful of navy beans halfway to my mouth. "How do you know so much about me?"

Erik shrugged but wouldn't meet my gaze. "I watched you sometimes."

"Why?" My heart fluttered, caught on a current of uncertainty. His confession both concerned and comforted me.

"I've never really had a family, and most people who did don't anymore. I wondered what it would be like."

I tilted my head to one side and studied him closely, watching for tells in his expression and posture. Mostly he looked uncomfortable, shoulders tense as he refused to look at me. "You've saved me a few times."

"Yeah."

I piled my remaining rice into a tall mountain and swung my fork into it like a wrecking ball, scattering grains across my plate. "Why?"

"Don't want to see another family split up, maybe. I'm not sure. I know it makes me weird."

"No, not really. There's nothing much left in the world I would call weird anymore." I dropped my fork onto the plate and rubbed my hands on my knees. "You didn't know your parents?"

Erik stared at the pepper still pinched between his fingers—it even *smelled* hot—and he seemed to be still making up his mind about whether or not to eat it. "My mom died giving birth to my little sister, and my sister only managed to live for a day."

My heart cringed painfully in my chest. Bloom was my whole world. I couldn't imagine never knowing her or vice versa. We'd only managed to survive this long because we'd done it together. Sure, I liked thinking of myself as an independent person, but that wasn't being completely honest. Erik, however, knew all about solitary self-reliance. How utterly lonely must he have been? "How old were you?"

"Five," he said.

He and his sister would have been the same number of years apart as Bloom and I were. My mother had survived my birth, but I'd lost her to consumption before I was old enough to really know her. Erik and I had a lot in common, it seemed.

"My dad was a Sandhog. Built a lot of the subway with my uncles and my grandfather."

That explained the engraving on the box of matches Erik gave me, and also, possibly, his knowledge of the underground. I was afraid to ask what happened to the rest of his family, and while I wondered if he would tell me if I sat quietly and waited, he tossed his head back, dropped the pepper into his mouth, and bit down. He turned to me and grinned.

"You shouldn't have done that." I bit my lip as I tried to gauge the severity of the pepper's burn. Erik's grin stretched into a grimace, and his face crumpled into a silent snarl as he battled the heat. "You want me to get you some more water?"

He waved me away and swallowed. I waited and watched, certain steam would soon be leaking from his ears. Or maybe his head would explode. After a moment, he opened his eyes and stuck out his tongue to prove he'd swallowed the whole thing. "Your turn," he said, grinning.

"Nuh-uh." I shook my head. "No way."

He pulled another pepper from the jar and dangled it before me the way one might dangle a dead rat by its tail. Covering my eyes and mouth, I rolled away from him, still objecting. Barking an enthusiastic laugh, he pounced, wrestling my arms to my sides and trapping them under his knees. In between bouts of laughter and curses, I screamed like a banshee. He ignored my pleas for mercy.

"If you eat it," he said in a softer tone, "I'll answer one question. Anything you want to know."

I stopped fighting. It was a pretty good offer, and there were things I wanted to know that he might never tell me otherwise. "Anything?"

His expression going grave, he nodded. "*Anything.*"

I closed my eyes and opened my mouth, ready to accept a pepper.

"Ready?" he asked, completely serious.

Reluctantly, I nodded. Instead of the pepper, though, his thumb swept over my bottom lip. My eyes popped open, and I gasped.

He shook his head, and bright color flushed his dusky cheeks. "I won't make you eat it. Just ask your question, and I'll answer it."

"Really?" My throat had gone dry, and my voice was a whisper.

"Go for it." He tossed the pepper back into the jar. Then he flopped over and stretched out beside me, propping his head up in his hand so he could peer down at me. Deep shadows hid most of his face. Unconsciously, my hand moved, reaching for his scars.

He pulled away.

"Don't." I reached for him again.

He paused and let my fingers sketch the tattered skin over his cheek and the jagged lines that scored his brow.

"It doesn't bother you?" he asked, his voice deep and husky.

"Not at all, and not nearly as much as it seems to bother you. Without the scar, I think you might be too perfect."

"Too perfect?" He grunted as if dismissing the possibility.

"You ever see any paintings done by the Renaissance masters? Da Vinci and those guys?"

"Actually, I have. The undead don't seem to like museums for some reason."

"You remind me of some of those paintings. Beautiful, but a little distant and a little cold. But the scars make you human. All the dashing heroes in my favorite adventure novels have scars, don't you know?"

Erik shook his head and harrumphed under his breath. "Ask your question, Sera, before I change my mind."

I didn't have to think about it. I had carried this question from the day Erik had first helped me escape the undead horde. "Why are you doing all of this for me? You barely know me, but you've risked your life, and you've given your blood."

Exhaling, he dropped onto his back and stared up at the train car's ceiling. "I can't think of any way to say it that doesn't sound ridiculous."

"I promise not to laugh."

He sucked in a huge breath as if preparing to tell a big story. "I saw you one day, a long time before the Dead Wars, you and your sister and your father, walking down the street together. I had moved into Saint Theresa's a few weeks before, and I was so angry and mad at the world for taking my family away, but then there you came, skipping along, oblivious to pain or loss. Your father held you by one hand, and Bloom had you by the other.

"One of the sisters was outside with us, letting us play in an open lot. She recognized your father and called out to him. Turns out he was a benefactor to the orphanage, made a lot of donations. You were standing there in this pristine white dress, not a speck of dirt on you anywhere, and I thought you looked like an angel. You didn't notice anyone at all. Your eyes were only for your father."

"I remember the orphanage," I said fondly. "And the nuns in their habits. I thought they looked like penguins. I used to play with a toy one made out of tin that would waddle across the floor when you wound a key in its back. I named it Sister Sophie after my favorite nun." Sitting up, I leaned over to peer into Erik's face. "I'm sorry I don't remember you, though."

"Like I said, you were so intent on your father. You'd think I would've been jealous, but I wasn't. I thought you were lucky, and very sweet and beautiful, and I swore if I could, I would let nothing hurt you the way I had been hurt. Of course, you were probably five or six then, and I wasn't a whole lot older, so it was a silly vow at the time."

My heart pinged, and I laid my hand on his arm. "Not silly. You kept your vow."

"I didn't. I couldn't save your father."

"He wasn't yours to save."

"I've tried to do my best for you and help you out whenever you've needed it."

"It's a pretty amazing story. I mean, I've done nothing to earn your regard. I could have turned out to be a royal brat or something."

Erik snorted. "Who says you didn't?"

I dug an elbow into his ribs until he grunted. Dropping his gaze, he toyed with a loose string on the quilt. "I've watched you long enough to know better," he said. "You work hard. You love your sister. You can shoot like hell, and you're not afraid of anything."

I cracked out a sharp laugh. "I'm afraid every God-given moment of the day. I'm even afraid in my sleep."

He brushed a tentative finger across my knuckles. His touch left behind a warm streak. "But you don't let it stop you."

"No." I watched him stroke my hand. "If you stop, you die."

"A lot of people gave up."

"And a lot of people died."

Erik pulled my knuckles to his lips, and my own lips tingled as he pressed a kiss to my fingers. At first, I thought my reaction had something to do with the way he was staring at me with dark, hooded eyes, but then the room spun, and my stomach lurched.

"You are fearless, Sera. You're smart too."

I tried to smile at the compliment, but my face had gone numb.

"You're smart not to trust me, even though you should. I promised myself to protect you, even if you didn't want me to."

What's he talking about? And why are weird little spots swirling around his head? And why is my body so heavy?

Erik helped me slide down in the bed then pulled a blanket over me.

This isn't right at all... I opened my mouth to tell him something had gone wrong, but my voice had disappeared.

"I'm sure you don't want me to leave you here while I go out and finish Dr. Dwivedi's experiments, but I can't bear to see you do anything that dangerous. You're probably going to hate me in the morning. I'm willing to risk it. What I'm not willing to risk is you, and as far as I know, only one of us is immune to the Dead Disease."

"Blabbidy blahgetiss," I said. I had really meant to say *I'll make you regret this*, but my tongue was refusing to cooperate. So were most of my other motor functions. My bones were turning to iron and my muscles to water. I sank into blackness.

I'll make him pay, tomorrow, after I sleep for a bit. I have to remember to ask him how he did it, where did he get the—

Zzzzzzzz...

Chapter 20: Easing Your Concerns

I woke up sucking on a stinky wool sock, a swarm of angry bees buzzing in my head and the Loch Ness Monster swimming laps in my stomach. I tried spitting out the sock but realized I had confused it with my tongue. When I sat up, the bees swarmed, stinging my brain *en masse*, and Nessie abandoned my stomach to try crawling up my throat. I rolled over and heaved, emptying my stomach on the floor of Erik's train car.

I snarled and spat. Erik thought he was protecting me, but I would've preferred mutilation by an Unholy Wonder, a Meat-Eating Monstrosity, an—*ooh, my stomach.* I retched again, heaving until nothing but spittle strung from my lips.

Erik didn't appear at my side, offering to hold back my hair or dab my face with a damp cloth, as he should have, considering he was the source of my suffering—him and whatever he'd put in my food—but the vomiting had eased the worst of my discomfort. Nessie settled into the darker recesses of my belly, the bee swarm retreated, and the wool sock thinned into a stale silk stocking.

I spied a stack of folded dishrags beside the brazier, near a pan of lukewarm water leftover from rinsing the supper dishes. As I stepped out of bed to grab one of the rags, I discovered I'd been stripped and left in nothing but my undershirt and cotton underdrawers. *Well, I'll add that to the top of my stack of reasons to murder Erik the next time*

I see him. I scrubbed my face and neck thoroughly then guzzled the few sips of clean water that remained in the pan.

Perhaps I should've left the cleaning up for Erik, but I couldn't bear the smell of my sickness. Besides, I had plenty more direct and aggressive ways of letting him know how I felt about what he had done. So I wiped up my mess and tossed the rags outside the train car. Erik could deal with those later—it was the least he deserved.

Before I had passed out, Erik had said something about carrying out Dwivedi's experiment on his own. To that, I thought: *Bloom was* my *sister, and finding her was* my *problem.* If completing Dwivedi's experiment was the price to pay for getting her back, I would do it. Erik had no right to go without me.

As soon as I'd finished that thought, an ungodly howl echoed through the cavernous subway outside Erik's train car. That singular cry turned into two then into a dozen. Those weren't animal howls, either, although I had seen the occasional wild dog in the city. It was unlikely a dog would find its way into the subway, though not impossible. No, those howls had definitely come from what used to be a human throat.

Another shriek slithered into Erik's cavern, closer, louder. *Had Erik locked me in before he left?* Rule number one: take nothing for granted. I leaped through the car's doorway and dashed for the big, heavy door at the head of the maintenance bay. As I reached for the handle, the door flew open, and I stumbled back, barely avoiding a face full of steel.

Erik lurched in and fell to his knees. "*Shut it,*" he said, panting. "Shut it quick."

I threw my weight against the door in time to stop an old woman with hair like steel wool from coming through. The door closed on her grasping arm, trapping it against the jamb, and she shrieked, her cries raising goose bumps across my neck and shoulders. Erik recovered his footing and helped me hold the door while I shoved the dead lady's hand through. When the door finally latched, he threw a massive bolt. Then he bent and grasped one end of a nearby railroad tie, a four- or five-foot-long block of heavy oak, still rich with the stench of creosote.

"Help me get this across the door," he said, hefting his end up and settling it into an iron holster on one side of the door. Together, we lifted my end into a matching holster on the other side of the door.

"Will it hold them?" I panted, still woozy from too much physical exertion and excitement after being so sick.

"Should," he said, brushing his hands together.

"'Should' doesn't instill a great deal of confidence in me."

The dead keened and wailed like mourners at an Irish wake, and they threw themselves against the door. Their protests made a terrible clatter, but the door held against their attack. With my immediate safety restored, I sighed and sank to the floor. "I'm gonna be so, so mad at you when I have the energy for it. Maybe tomorrow, after I've slept off the rest of whatever you gave me." I narrowed my eyes at him, which required minimal effort compared to punching him. "What *did* you give me anyway?"

"Something Dwivedi mixed up." He wouldn't meet my eyes, and he stared, unfocused, into the dark shadows behind his subway car. "Told him I was worried about your safety. He gave me something to help ease my concerns."

"If you needed your concerns eased, then you should have taken it yourself." I pushed myself off the floor and shuffled to the train car. Erik trudged behind me. "I hope to God it was worth it."

After we climbed aboard, he collapsed into his corner chair, where the shadows were thickest. I paced the short open space in front of the bed, too mad to sit. Erik watched me, wearing a strange look, almost hungry or predatory like the Living Dead. It gave me the willies.

"What?" I stamped my foot and folded my arms over my chest.

He shook himself, and his face blanked. "What do you mean, 'what'?"

"Why are you looking at me like you're one of them?" I pointed toward the groaning mob outside his door. "Like you're going to eat me."

One corner of Erik's mouth curled into a crooked smile. "Maybe I do want to eat you."

"Not funny!" I grabbed a pillow from the bed and flung it at him. He caught it, chuckling. His mirth made me want to punch him even more than I already did. Instead, I drew a coverlet from the bed and wrapped it around my shoulders. Erik's smile turned to a sulk. "So, did you stick one of them with Dwivedi's stuff or what?" I asked.

Sitting up straighter, he peeled off his coat and folded it over the arm of his chair. "Yes, I stuck one."

Leaning over, he unbuckled a boot. Black beads slipped from his collar, and the crucifix at the end of the long strand thumped onto the floor. I crossed the room, sank to my knees in front of him, and fingered the jet carving of Christ writhing on the cross. Going still, Erik watched me study his necklace.

My father had taken us to an Episcopal church occasionally, but I knew enough religion to recognize this set of beads. "A rosary?"

"It was my mother's."

"All I have left of my father are his guns."

"Those are more practical."

"I guess that depends on what you believe in." I met his gaze. "Do you say the prayers?"

His Adam's apple bobbed. "Every night."

"Do you believe they work?"

Smirking, he flicked his fingers toward his ruined eye: the proof of his immunity and of a miracle, perhaps. "Yes, I suppose I have to."

Dropping his necklace, I backed away and slumped on the bed. Erik tucked the rosary into his collar and finished removing his boots.

"Well, if you stuck one of those Rotters," I said, "where is it? Dwivedi said we had to bring it back to him for observation." I pulled my feet off the floor and crisscrossed them under me. "Tell me what happened."

Now barefooted, he slumped into his chair and rolled up his shirt sleeves. He looked vulnerable without his big boots and long black coat. Purple smudges darkened the skin under his eyes, evidence of his lack of sleep. "Don't be too mad at me for what I did to you, Sera. It looks like you're going to see some action after all. Unless I can convince you to stay behind again."

My heart thumped excitedly. "For what?"

"I found a girl, maybe about your age. I got Dwivedi's inoculation into her, but I couldn't get her back here and get away from the others at the same time. I had to dump her and run. I might be immune to bites, but I'm pretty sure an angry mob can still rip me to shreds."

I waved toward the doorway again. "So we have to go back out there and get her?"

Erik's head bobbed. "Yep."

"You think we can find her again?"

He raised one shoulder and dropped it. "Dunno."

"When are we going to look for her?"

"When they calm down and back off from the door. In a few hours, I guess."

"You're not leaving me behind," I said in an emphatic tone that left no room for argument. "And I'll be fixing my own meals from now on."

Flinching, he ducked his head. "I don't have any more sleep draught anyway."

"Still..." I narrowed my eyes. "It's going to be a long time before I accept any more of *your* hospitality."

His dark brows knitted together. "What do you mean?"

Spying my canvas pants folded up at the end of the bed, I reached for them. "I mean that we're going to go out and find this dead girl, and we're going to take her to Dr. Dwivedi like we agreed." Looking up, I met his gaze and held it so he would understand how serious I was. "Then our partnership is over."

He gasped. "Sera—"

"I don't want to hear it." I slashed a hand at him as I reached for my shirt. "When this is over, you go your way, and I go mine."

Chapter 21: Sweet Gum

Erik leaped to his feet. "No, Sera. Don't say that."

I threw up my hand, stopping him before he reached my side. "I can't be constantly worrying that you might stick something in my drink or my food whenever you don't want me to do something." I yanked on my shirt and buttoned it with trembling fingers. "I've done a pretty good job of protecting myself for the last five years. I acknowledge you've helped me, and I thank you for that, but that doesn't give you the right to control me or decide what I can and can't do." I knelt and rooted under the bed for my boots.

Erik crouched beside me. "I know you're mad, and I don't blame you. But please don't go."

I found one boot and rolled onto my rear so I could slide my foot into it. "You're right that I worshiped my father, loved him as if he hung the moon each night and set the sun afire each morning, but he's dead now, and I'm not looking for another man to take his place."

I had worked up a good head of steam, and if Erik knew what was good for him, he'd shut up and get the hell out of my way. But he didn't. He grabbed my other boot and held it behind his back, out of my reach.

"C'mon, Erik, give it to me." I shoved my hand out at him, palm up.

He scowled. "You can't leave yet. They're still ganged up outside the door."

"I know that," I said, full of piss and vinegar and steam. Goodgodalmighty, my head was about to burst open with anger. *Lord, give me just one minute away from him, just one minute... But where the hell was I supposed to go?* I could've used a good dramatic exit complete with a slamming door, but a swishing bit of curtain lacked the same emphasis. The only door I could slam had a brace of Ungodly Beings waiting for me on its other side.

"Argh!" I jerked my fingers through my knotted hair. Usually, I kept my unruly curls tamed in a tight braid, but it had mostly come loose. My hair surely looked a fright, like I'd stood on a rooftop during a windstorm, but what did it even matter right then? "God, what I wouldn't give for a hot bath..." I muttered as I stomped out to the maintenance tunnel, one boot on and one foot bare.

Whenever I needed to work off some anger, I would usually take out my rifle and take target practice on the undead, but opening Erik's front door would have been suicidal. With my one booted foot, I kicked a broken bit of brick. *Clank.* It nailed the side of Erik's train car. I looked around, searching for another loose piece of rubble, and found one. *Clank.* Then another piece. *Clank.* I had just pulled back my foot for another kick when Erik appeared in the train car's doorway.

"What are you doing?" he asked.

"Pretending this is your head." I aimed and kicked. My missile slammed into the side of the train. *Clank.*

Grinning, he dangled my other boot by its laces. "Diddle diddle dumpling, my son John."

Pausing in my search for another brick chunk, I cocked my head like a dog hearing a curious noise. "Diddle what?"

"One shoe off and the other shoe on." He swung the boot, teasing me.

"You've gone nuts, haven't you?" I stumped up to him, snatched my boot, and plopped to the ground to put it on. "Too much time on your own. You're no longer properly socialized."

He chuckled. "It was something my mother used to say to me when I was little. Diddle diddle dumpling, my son John. Went to bed with his trousers on; One shoe off, and the other shoe on."

"Do you have many memories of your mother?" The rock kicking had released some of my anger, so I managed to ask the question in a civil tone.

Crouching beside me, he picked up one of the bits of rubble I had used to assault his house. "Some. It's the silly things like that nursery rhyme that stick with me the most."

"I don't remember my mother. Bloom does, but she doesn't like to talk about her."

Erik chucked his rock at the maintenance bay door. *Clank*. Demonic shrieks and moans answered from the other side. "Humph. You're still not going anywhere for a while."

"Humph," I echoed, folding my arms over my chest.

"You said something about a hot bath, didn't you?"

I squinted at him. "Maybe."

"I have a pan of water heating on the brazier. Maybe in a few minutes, when it's warm, you'll let me wash your hair for you. It's the best I can offer." He fingered one of my curls, and my breath froze. Then he presented the piece of dried leaf he'd removed from my hair.

A blush lit my cheeks, and I turned to hide it from him, embarrassed by my dirtiness.

"Sometimes," he said, ignoring my discomfort, "when the light hits it right, your hair looks like a sweet gum tree in the fall."

"What color do sweet gums turn?"

"Deep red, like a Burgundy wine."

"Bloom says I get my hair from our mother. I can't really remember what she looks like."

"I bet she was lovely if she looked anything like you."

I swatted his knee. "Don't think a little sweet talk is going to soften me up. I'm still plenty mad at you."

"I expected you would be. You'll forgive me or you won't, but in the meantime, you should let me take care of you."

"I don't need anyone to take care of me." I had said it without much conviction because Erik had sunk his hands into my hair. He worked through some of the knots with gentle fingers, and his touch eased the remaining symptoms of my hangover and embarrassment.

"No, Serendipity Blite, you do not *need* me to take care of you, but you should let me anyway."

He must have been part snake charmer, because I couldn't help giving in. "Why?"

"Because it will make me feel better about drugging you, and it will make you feel better too."

He must have been part mind reader as well. "Maybe," I said.

Releasing my hair, he chuckled. Then he stood and held a hand toward me. "Come on, Sweet Gum."

Later, Erik and I sat on the floor before his blazing brazier, and he untangled my damp hair with an ivory comb. He had washed it in something laced with sandalwood, a scent I'd noticed on him before—something he received in trade from Dr. Dwivedi, no doubt. "How do you know how to do this?" My eyelids slipped closed, and I hovered on the edge of falling asleep.

"I don't know. I used to pickpocket some when I was little. I guess I have nimble fingers."

"Bloom has nimble fingers. She plays music with them. Do you?" Unlike our vault filled with Bloom's collection of stringed instruments, Erik kept nothing musical around his place.

"I mess around with a piano sometimes, but not much. Can't get one down here on my own."

I imagined him towing a baby grand on his back, and the vision made me chuckle.

"How about you?" he asked. "Do you sing or play anything?"

I shrugged. "I can make mean music with most anything filled with gunpowder, but that's about it."

"Well, that's a more important skill anyway."

"I don't think so," I said as his fingers slipped from my hair to work on the knots in my neck and shoulders. I suppressed a moan. "I think it's important to hold on to what makes us human. Sometimes it worries me that the only thing I'm really good at is killing things that are already dead."

He dug a thumb into a stubborn muscle near the top of my spine. "You read a lot, too, don't you?"

I groaned, unable to contain it.

"What was that?" He snickered.

I ignored him. "Reading is just taking up something someone else has made. Playing music is creating something, making something. That's an important thing these days."

"You grow a garden every year. That's making something."

"Something that I just gobble up again and again. Nothing lasts. Not even death."

"You're being too hard on yourself. Besides, music only lasts until the last note is played."

Erik's touch had eased, and he trailed soft circles over my neck and shoulders. Sleep crept in around the edges of my consciousness, and my chin sank to my chest. In a display of chivalry, he hefted my dead weight—excuse the pun—from the floor and carried me to the bed, where he tucked me under the covers.

"Did you drug me again?" I asked, only half joking.

"No. But maybe that dose hasn't entirely worn off."

"Don't go anywhere without me." I yawned. "Don't leave me behind this time."

"I won't." He bent and dotted my forehead with his lips. "I promise."

Chapter 22: Ride of the Valkyries

I dreamed of toast.

That might've seemed strange, but when you hadn't eaten toast in four or five years—the kind made from bread leavened with yeast and white flour—you'd be surprised how much you missed it. As much as Bloom and I joked about eating fine foods like lamb chops and chocolate cake, I missed the simple, everyday things most of all.

Not only had I dreamed of toast, but I also smelled it—the ghost of baking bread had come to haunt me. *What wouldn't I have killed for a crock of fresh-churned butter and a thick slice of sourdough like our housekeeper used to bake?* The smell intensified until I could no longer ignore it, and when I rooted out from beneath the pile of covers and sinkhole of a feather mattress, I found Erik stacking a plate with flat, crispy squares.

"Is that... *toast?*" I croaked with a sleep-roughened voice.

"It is." Turning, he smiled at me over his shoulder. "My peace offering to you."

I rubbed my hands together, eager to snatch a slice from the pile. "You've made a good start down the path toward earning my forgiveness."

"I've got butter too. From goat's milk."

"Where'd you get it?" I scooted to the edge of the bed, closer to the toast.

He passed me several slices on a delicate china plate trimmed in pink roses. "The same place I get most everything."

I put my nose close and inhaled. "Dwivedi."

Erik built a pile of toast for himself, brought out a little ceramic crock of butter, and let me have the first scoop. I raised the delicacy to my lips with graveness, as if taking Communion. After slipping a corner between my lips, I eased my teeth into the grainy texture, savoring every moment of this rare experience. The butter pooled onto my tongue. Tears sprang to my eyes as I chewed and swallowed. *Bliss.*

Sucking butter from my fingertips, I sighed. "Mmmm."

Erik swallowed, licked his lips, and gave me a curiously dark look. "When was the last time you ate toast?" He tried to keep his lips closed around a mouthful of bread and butter as he spoke, but he was as hungry as me and not doing a good job of hiding it.

"Dunno. But if I knew it was going to be the last time, I would have tried harder to remember it." I nodded toward the door between us and the Not-So-Dead. "Are they gone yet?"

"Yes. I checked a little while ago." He polished off the last of his first piece and sank his teeth into a second. "We'll head out to look for our test subject as soon as we finish breakfast."

"Did you sleep?" I asked.

He paused, bread still locked between his teeth. He tore off the chunk in his mouth, chewed, swallowed, and cleared his throat. "Don't sleep." He averted his gaze. "Not much. A couple hours, maybe."

"Why's that?" My interest in food paled next to this fascinating tidbit.

"Ever since this bite," he swept his fingers along his scarred browbone. "I don't really have the urge anymore."

"Huh," I said, returning to my breakfast. How wearying that must be, being awake all the time. "Do the undead never sleep?"

"Not as far as I know."

"I guess it makes sense. Why sleep when you're already mostly dead?" Erik wasn't undead, I was confident. Well... fairly confident. He'd had a dozen opportunities to infect me already if he'd had a hankering for raw flesh, but I didn't quite know what surviving a bite really meant. I wasn't sure what truths he might still have been hiding.

He wiped his plate clean and set it in the dishpan on his brazier. Then he gathered his guns and ammunition. The last half of my toast went into my mouth in a cheek-bulging bite before I slid to the floor and laced up my boots. *When did I take them off again?* Erik must have removed them, but at least he had left me in the rest of my clothes this time, even if I did sleep more comfortably out of the heavy canvas pants.

I tied on my apron, cocked and checked the chambers in each of my pistols, and stuffed them both in my apron pocket. After examining the contents of my duffel bag and estimating the amount of ammunition I had left, I threaded my arm through the handles and swung it onto my back. Then I slung my rifle over my other shoulder. "Ready to go?" I asked.

Erik rolled his eyes and shook his head but stood and held aside the tapestry door over the entrance to his train car. He waved toward the opening. "After you, my lady."

Thick clouds, the kind not just threatening rain but guaranteeing it, greeted us on the surface.

"They might be active today without the sun," Erik said. "She might be on the move."

I studied the ominous clouds. "Where was she when you found her?"

"In an offshoot of the main subway tunnel."

"So what are we doing up here?"

"I already looked there, right before you woke up. She was gone. All of them were."

"How many was she with?"

"Maybe twenty."

"Where do you think they went?"

"I think I stirred them up, kind of like stomping on an anthill. If we wait long enough, they might come back, but I think for your sister's sake, the sooner we find our girl and get her to Dwivedi, the better."

Nodding, I agreed. "So, where do we start?"

"Well, I have an idea, but it could be dangerous."

I pulled my revolver from my apron pocket, drew back the hammer until it clicked, and blinked my lashes at him.

"Right." He scowled. "Look, you see the balcony in that building over there?" He pointed to an apartment several rows up and on the other side of the street. "Get to it and cover me."

"What does she look like? I don't want to shoot her by accident."

"Brown hair, most of it pinned up, light-blue dress. She's pretty fresh, not so damaged as the others. Your age, like I said."

"What are you going to do?" I asked.

Deep sigh. "I'm going to make a lot of noise."

As soon as I reached the balcony, I laid out cartridges and bullets for easy access and reloading. Then I searched for a steady place from which to sight my rifle. Erik had disappeared into another nearby apartment building, so I checked over my things to make sure all was clean and ready to go while I waited for him to return.

A few minutes later, he trundled out to the street carrying a heavy burden, a big box with a horn-shaped speaker attached at one corner. *A Victrola?* Erik settled the record player on the ground and wound it up with several hard cranks. I lined him up in my sights and watched while he fiddled with the record needle.

"Ready?" he asked, glancing up at me.

"Ready." Anticipation coursed through me like a discharge of static electricity. What song had he chosen to play?

He dropped the needle, and Wagner stomped out from the ornate speaker: *Ride of the Valkyries*. Should have known. The opera gained popularity when the government adopted it as a fight song to reenergize the troops near the end of the Dead Wars. Instead of making them shake in their boots like the war commanders had hoped, the Living Dead came to equate the music with the sound of a dinner bell. It had the same effect these many years later.

"Ready or not..." I pointed to the convening, undead mass shambling in our direction. "Here they come."

Chapter 23: Hell in a Handbasket

Erik removed his pistols from their holsters, dashed up the steps at the front of an apartment building opposite my position, and waited on the stoop. To my left, a big man in the tatters of a merchant marine's uniform led the way, and a woman in a lopsided white wig shuffled forward on my right. Behind those two came the widest variety of citizens to ever assemble in one place at the same time. The Dead Disease had been the world's greatest social equalizer, and neither money, class, nor education had saved anyone.

A ridiculous undead parade shambled down the street: skinny men, fat women, a few gangling adolescents whose lack of grace had grown more pronounced in quasi-death. Children, corseted society women—one wearing a sash supporting women's suffrage—and a ballerina in pointe shoes and a long tulle skirt. She got my first bullet for the simple absurdity of her existence. Who had ever heard of a dancing monster?

My philosophy might have seemed pitiless, but I had long since given up feeling sorry for those creatures. The people they had been in life were gone, and the thing left behind was nothing but a cruel reminder, a mockery. After the dancer, I put down a tightly laced lady, meticulously buttoned and corseted in heavy skirts. Her undeath had cursed her to an eternity as a slave to fashion. Hell on earth, if you asked me.

I would have already stopped looking at them as individuals if I hadn't needed to spot our test subject. Shooting her by accident would have ruined our experiment and rendered everything Erik and I had done so far pointless.

Target. Squeeze the trigger. *Boom.* Eject the shell.

Target. Squeeze the trigger. *Boom.* Eject the shell.

It was rote. Mechanical. I was a gun-firing automaton. Reload, target, squeeze the—Hold on...

"Erik, is that her?" Raising my voice, I pointed toward a creature matching his earlier description. She stood at the edge of the rabble, seemingly disinterested in the fracas.

He fired off three quick rounds, dropping a large woman in an old-fashioned lace dress, what might have been a middle-aged man in a worn suit and spectacles, and another man in a smoking jacket. Then he glanced up at me and followed the direction of my pointing finger. A newsboy in knickerbockers and braces lurched up the stairs toward Erik, showing more athleticism than his cohorts. Distracted by trying to locate our target, Erik had failed to see him coming.

Boom! The newsboy slumped to the ground. *Like a sack of potatoes.*

Startled, Erik jumped back. He glanced at the body lying still at his feet and threw a wave of acknowledgment in my direction. Immune didn't mean impervious, and a bite could have slowed Erik, weakened him, made him more vulnerable to the encroaching mob. He hopped onto the railing over the brick balusters lining the steps and skidded down it toward the sidewalk.

I cleared the way for him, taking down any Devouring Damned in his path. Erik reached the girl, the one who might've been our test subject. She strained toward him, licking her lips and gnashing her teeth. Grabbing her grasping hand, he whipped her arm behind her back, bending her elbow and bringing her wrist high up between her shoulder blades. She rose to her tiptoes, seeking relief from his grip.

He dragged her away from the crowd that seemed more interested in the Victrola.

But then the record screeched to a halt when one of the Rotters ripped the needle from its hinge. Another bent down, gathered the whole shebang in a bear hug, and dashed the Victrola into the street, where the wooden case housing the gears shattered into splinters.

Erik whipped a length of rope from one of his coat pockets and bound the girl's hands behind her back. He lashed her arms, pinning them to her sides. If she'd been alive, I might've worried about him dislocating her shoulder. The girl gnashed her teeth, seeking purchase in his skin, but he avoided her bite and cinched her up as tightly as a Christmas goose.

Having silenced Wagner and his Valkyries, the mob returned their attention to hunting breakfast. I dropped two more ambling corpses before stopping to reload my guns. The majority of the crowd had arrived at the same time, but more were trickling in, attracted by the excitement and noise. Erik ignored his surroundings while he fitted a scarf gag around our prisoner and secured another rope around her ankles. He had left his defenses entirely up to me.

"Get a move on, Erik! My ammo's running low!"

Blam! Blam! Blam! I cleared out three more Rotters who had lurched close to Erik, but as fast as they went down, five more took their places. The undead were adding up faster than I could subtract them, and the bitter taste of panic rose in my throat.

"Erik, hurry!" I switched to my Colt and emptied round after round into the crowd. From my height and distance, my aim with the pistols was shoddy at best. Sure, bodies fell, but not enough of them. Not nearly enough. Erik tossed the struggling undead girl over his shoulder and rose to his feet, pistol in hand, firing with each step. But it made little difference. I took out five more before I ran out of bullets.

"I'm out," I yelled, my voice high and sharp.

He pushed forward, shooting with calm determination, but my point of view showed the futility of his actions. The Rotters would overwhelm him shortly—as soon as he had to stop and reload. This plan had gone to hell in a handbasket.

What plan?

We never had a plan.

That was probably a bad idea, in hindsight.

"Erik!" I screamed, just as a bald fellow with no lips or chin to speak of reached for Erik's shoulder. Erik spun, pressed the barrel of his pistol in the bald man's face, and pulled the trigger. Even from several stories above, I could hear the click of the hammer striking an empty chamber.

The bald man buried his face into Erik's neck, and everything in my vision turned blurry. My peripheral sight faded to black, and my hearing dimmed. As if on their own, my lungs expanded, drawing in air before squeezing it out along my vocal cords, forcing a scream from my throat. Then nothing, silence, except for the thump of my pulse pounding against my eardrums.

Chapter 24: Whose Side Are You On?

Falling to my knees, I scrabbled through my bag, searching for anything I might've missed. My fingers bumped against something hard, metallic. A shell. One lone shell. Hell of a lot of good it would do, but I jammed it into my rifle. Rising to my feet, I searched for Erik, but he wasn't where he'd been before, and neither was the bald man who had been preparing to make Erik his next meal. I scanned the crowd and...

There! Erik was slumped on his knees, hand clasped to the bleeding wound in his neck. Our captive revenant writhed on the ground next to him, and the bald Rotter that had chewed out Erik's neck lay motionless beside them with most of his head torn away.

How...? I blinked and rubbed my eyes, trying to make sense of the scene before me.

CRRRAKAW!

Flinching, I raised my head, scoping the street for an explanation. That had been no mere pistol pop. Finally, I spotted the source of the explosive sound. Marching down the street was one of Grimes's soldiers, wearing the bowl helmet and weird armor. He carried a long, bulky weapon that looked like the bastard brother of a shotgun, but with four barrels instead of two. *What the hell is that thing?*

The soldier stopped, aimed, and fired again. An ear-shattering blast echoed down the street, bouncing off buildings until it sounded as though a hundred thunderstorms had rolled in. He marched several yards closer to our position before stopping again, but not to fire his weapon. Instead, he lobbed something not much bigger than a baseball into the crowd. The sphere hit the ground in a flash of blinding light and a concussive blast that shrieked in my eardrums. Falling to the balcony floor, I mashed my palms over my ears and clenched my eyes shut. Three more explosions rocked the street before everything fell still.

My eardrums rang like church bells, but over the jangling and buzzing in my head came the sound of someone yelling. I lowered my hands, and the roaring voice sounded more familiar. "Sera!" It was Erik, calling for me.

Relief swept through me so swift and sweet that I nearly cried. Instead, I rolled to my knees and peered through the balcony railing. Except for the ones taken down by our bullets, the undead had disappeared. Erik stood on the street below me on his own, unsteady and swaying. A deep-red splotch stained the white collar of his shirt, and blood glistened on the shoulder of his black coat. He pressed a hand over his neck at the site of the wound, and blood seeped between his fingers.

"This might be a dumb question," I said, "but are you okay?"

He nodded. "I will be."

I started to say something else, but Grimes's soldier stepped into my field of vision with the stock of his strange gun pointed at Erik's temple. My heart clenched, and my breath froze. "Hold it right there," he said. "You're not going anywhere, Corpse Bait."

After a moment of dazzling panic, a memory clicked in my head. I recognized the voice and the wide-legged stance. Breathing a heavy sigh, I called to him. "Shep! Corporal Baumgartner!"

The soldier looked up at me, first in confusion and then in recognition. "Hey, Blite girl, is that you?"

"Sera Blite, yes." Inanely, I waggled my fingers at him. "You remember?"

"You're not easy to forget." Shep motioned toward Erik. "Your friend there has been bitten."

"No," Erik rasped. "Just a scratch."

Shep stepped closer and pressed the shotgun barrel against Erik's skull. "A scratch, a bite, it's all the same to me."

Oh God. Oh no. "Just a second, Shep," I said, talking to him as though we were old buddies, trying to keep him calm, trying to keep *me* calm. "It's not what you think."

"It's not? He's infected. He'll turn. Grimes's policy is to shoot all infected."

"He's not infected," I said.

"The hell you say." A red flush crept into Shep's face. "His neck is torn to shreds. That ain't no scratch, and what are you planning to do with this other one you got all tied up over here?" He pressed the barrel harder against Erik's temple. Erik grimaced, and my heart strained as if it were tearing apart.

"Wait, Shep." I eased my rifle up so he could see it. "Don't do it."

"Sera," he said like an amused parent addressing a petulant child. "Are you threatening me?"

"Oh, no." Derision coated my words. "I'm not that kind of girl. I just want to talk."

"Nothing to talk about." Shep's grin was big, broad, and completely fake.

"He's immune to the Dead Disease."

Shep belched an ugly laugh. "Nice try."

Maybe he hadn't understood me. Perhaps I needed to make my point clearer. Raising my rifle butt to my shoulder in a swift motion, I sighted on Shep's red, angry face. "Step away from him. *Now.*"

Erik's countenance had gone sickly pale. He swayed on his feet again.

"You're gonna kill me to save your corpse-bait boyfriend?" Shep asked.

"If I have to."

"You don't want to do this, Sera."

"No, *you* don't want to do this. He's immune. He won't turn. Look at his face, his scar. It's an old wound. He was bitten before, and he survived it." Even as I said it, I realized I had doubts. Erik claimed the scar was a bite from the undead, but how could I know for sure? Because Dr. Dwivedi had said so? It was a fantastic claim. Still, I preferred not to let Shep be the one to make the decision about its veracity. If there was any possibility Erik's immunity was real, then he would need the chance to prove it. I meant to give him that chance.

Erik looked ready to pass out, and he struggled to stay upright. A gust of wind blew his hair out of his eyes, and it brought along the scent of rain. Shep studied Erik's blind eye, and the wheels of thought seemed to turn slowly in his head as he warred with what decision he should make.

Thunder cracked overhead, and the heavens dumped buckets of rain over the street. Erik slumped to the cobblestones and lay in a lifeless heap.

"Erik!" I screamed.

Shep dropped the rifle to his side and crouched. He cupped his hand over Erik's mouth and checked for breath.

After shoving things into my bag as fast as I could, I left the balcony and hurried through the building, heading for the street. At the main entrance, I paused and peered through the murky glass door. The thick rainclouds had dimmed the late-morning light to a gloomy glow, and the Rotters had scattered, but for how long?

Nothing unseemly appeared on the street except for the undead girl, still gagged and rolling around on the cobbles, drenched and muddy. When I opened the door, it squeaked, and Shep glanced at me.

"Shep," I said, easing my way to his side. He still stooped over Erik with his weapon held ready. "Help us, would you?"

"What do you want me to do?" His voice was pitched high, and it warbled a little.

"We need to get him to Dr. Dwivedi."

"What about her?" Shep pointed to the bound and gagged girl.

I went to her and knelt. "She's got to come too."

Shep's blue eyes bugged. He rested the butt of his strange long gun on the ground, holding it up it by its barrel. The weapon was nearly as tall as he was. "What the hell for?" he asked. "This is some messed-up stuff. I never would've took you for crazy."

"I'm not crazy. I got a deal worked out to get my sister back." I pointed at the undead girl "This Rotter's part of it."

"Get your sister back? Bloom's gone missing?" Shep rolled back on his heels and stood fully erect, but he kept his gaze trained on Erik as if waiting for a sudden transformation. It said something about Shep that he hadn't put a bullet through Erik's brain yet. Exactly what it said, I wasn't sure. Something good, I hoped.

"Didn't you know?" I asked. "I'm pretty sure it's Moll Grimes that's got her."

Shep shook his head, and wet locks of his blond hair flopped against his forehead. "I don't know anything about your sister."

The dead girl beside me groaned, and a desperate hunger burned in her foggy eyes. I pushed saturated strands of brown hair out of her face and studied her features. She seemed familiar... I searched my memory until the face matched up with a name. A cold shiver rolled over me. "Amity?" I said. "Amity McCall, is that you?"

"You know her?" Shep asked.

"If she's who I think she is." I bobbed my head. "We went to school together. I haven't seen her in years, though."

"And Grimes is going to trade this dead girl for your sister?" Shep snorted. "Sounds like a bum deal to me."

"No. Grimes knows nothing about this. This girl is payment for someone who's going to help me get Bloom back."

Shep's lips thinned. "You aren't making any sense, you know."

"Look." I rolled Amity over, preparing to lift her. "You don't have to help me. You just have to get out of my way and pretend you never saw me."

Heaving with all of my strength, I managed to heft Amity over my shoulder. She struggled and grunted all manner of animal noises. It would take me most of the day to get to Dwivedi's college like this, and I had no idea what to do with the unconscious Erik. *Can't leave him here like a piece of cheese for the rats, though.*

Shep snorted and scuffed a heel over the cobblestones. "You're a pitiful thing, Sera Blite. How far do you think you're going to get like that?"

Amity grunted and wiggled until she almost rolled off my shoulder. "Damn it," I cursed and jimmied her back in place. Her drenched dress and petticoats weighed a ton. Tears prickled at the back of my eyes. I must have looked hopeless and ridiculous, but Shep could grow wings and fly before I'd admit defeat to him. "I'll figure something out. There's got to be a wheelbarrow or a cart or something around here."

Shaking his head, Shep dug into his pants pocket. He pulled out a tin of cigarettes and selected one. Then he struck a match and lit his smoke by cupping his hands around the flame to keep the rain away. He held in a deep lungful of smoke for several heartbeats before releasing it through his nose. The routine must have given him the time he needed to make his decision, because he inclined his head toward the muttering corpse on my shoulder. "If you can manage that carcass, I reckon I can bring along your boyfriend."

I paused and squinted at him. "Why would you help me, Corporal?"

Shep returned my narrow glare with one of his own. "Whatever it is that you're up to, I'm sure Moll Grimes would be interested to know about it. Just might turn beneficial for me to find out what I can and give her a report."

Blatant honesty? I hadn't expected that. "Well, just so we know what side everyone's on."

Shep crouched and pulled Erik's limp arm across his neck. He heaved and grunted until Erik's long, lanky body draped over his shoulders like some exotic trophy animal. "I'm always on the same side," he said. "Always on *my* side."

Chapter 25: A Hot Bath
and Real Chicken

D r. Dwivedi's niece, Parvati, answered my pounding at the College of Kimiyagari's alley door. She ushered us in as soon as she recognized Erik's limp form and realized the bound and gagged figure stealing all my wind and breaking my back was the crucial element in her uncle's latest alchemical experiment.

"What has happened to our dashing young hero?" Dwivedi said as he greeted us in the lobby. His eyes narrowed on the growing puddle at our feet as we dripped on his pristine floors. "Is it raining? I had not noticed."

"I've got what you asked for." Turning, I brought Amity's head closer to the aged scientist. She gnashed her teeth and snarled.

Dwivedi's face wrinkled into a sour countenance full of distaste, and his eyebrows and mustache bristled.

Shep dumped Erik's carcass into the waiting arms of one of Dwivedi's assistants. With less care, I dropped the thing that had been Amity McCall to the floor at the elder scientist's feet. "He was bitten," I said, sighing with relief.

"Oh dear." The corners of Dwivedi's lips turned down as he inspected Erik with a studious glower. "He seems to have taken a terrible turn."

"Are you sure he's not about to *turn* into one of the undead?" Shep asked as he watched Dwivedi's men shuffle Erik into the elevator car. "Sera claims he's immune."

"Oh, yes, yes." Dwivedi clapped his hands together. "She is quite right—nothing to fear. Our young friend should recover soon enough. He will be back to his old self in no time."

"Where are you taking him?" I inclined my head toward the closing elevator doors.

Dwivedi turned his attention to the mumbling, struggling creature on the floor and knelt beside her. "Cy will be taken to my suite. Parvati will watch over him."

"Parvati?" I asked, trying not to growl. I wasn't jealous or anything. Swear I wasn't.

Humor lit Dwivedi's gaze. "My niece is well-versed in the healing arts. He will recover quickly under her care."

For Erik's sake, I hoped Dwivedi was right. I had no medical knowledge nor any claims on Erik to support any protests I might've made otherwise. "So, here's your little experiment like you asked." I shoved the toe of my boot into Amity's side, and she squealed in outrage. It was a funny noise coming from a partially decomposed throat—sort of like an opera singer gargling glass. "Erik stuck her with your serum."

"I was hoping that was the reason you brought her here." With a groan and some creaking and popping from his joints, Dwivedi stood. "How delightful."

"Nothing about this should be described as delightful," Shep said. "I think I've got myself mixed up in something bizarre and uncanny, and I sure would appreciate an explanation."

The way Shep said it sounded as though he didn't appreciate anything at all.

Dwivedi let his crooked grin turn into a forthright smile. "Of course you would. And you will not be disappointed. First, though, I must ask for your assistance once more. I would like to get this test subject"—he looked pointedly at the undead girl on the floor between us—"into my laboratory for immediate observation. Sera, when did you inject her with the treatment?"

"Erik stuck it in her late last night."

"Oh, dear." He frowned, thick brows crawling closer together, and tapped a finger against his bottom lip. "That long ago?"

"She wasn't alone. He had to leave her until he could get her away from the crowd."

"Didn't seem like he was having much luck with that," Shep muttered under his breath before saying louder, "What exactly are you expecting your, um, *serum* to do?"

Dwivedi fiddled with the elevator controls, calling the car back to our floor. "Put her in here, Sera." Dr. Dwivedi pointed at the waiting elevator. "If you will help us, Mister..." He paused and waited for someone to supply him with a name.

Remembering my manners, I gestured between the two men. "Dr. Dwivedi, meet Corporal Shepherd Baumgartner. Shep, this is Dr. Dwivedi of the College of Kimiyagari."

"I take it by your armor and by your rank," Dwivedi said, "that you belong to Ms. Grimes's personal guard?" He and Shep both seemed happy to ignore me as I heaved and groaned while hoisting Amity's unwieldy body into the elevator.

"Yep." Shep shrugged. "That's the gist of it."

"Well, Corporal," Dwivedi said, "you are under no obligation to assist us, but the only way you will find any answers is if you do."

Shep narrowed his eyes as he contemplated Dwivedi's proviso. He must've decided he wanted answers more than he wanted to get back to Mini City, because he squatted and heaved Amity's legs through the elevator doors. I hadn't noticed her overripe-garbage stench so much while lugging her in the open air and rain. Here in the elevator, though, her putrescence was concentrated.

Dr. Dwivedi pinched his fingers over his nostrils as the elevator slowly descended. "Oh dear," he said in a nasally voice, "that is *quite* unpleasant."

Shep gagged as he tugged a handkerchief from his pocket and pressed it over his nose and mouth. "That's putting it mildly."

With a bit of grunting and retching, the three of us managed to reach Dwivedi's laboratory and convey Amity's body into a steel cage in the corner. She curled into a lifeless ball on the floor after we shut the door. A tiny shard of pity pricked my heart, but I reminded myself she'd rip apart my flesh without hesitation or remorse if given the chance. The knowledge of that fact kept me from looking back when Dr. Dwivedi led us up to the library, where another of his nieces greeted us with another pot of fragrant tea.

Dr. Dwivedi poured while I helped myself to jam and bread—soft, chewy, white bread. It took a great deal of effort to keep from moaning out loud.

"My dear Miss Blite," Dwivedi said as he liberally buttered another slice for himself. "Let me provide you with a private room for the night. I am certain you must be *quite* exhausted."

Contrary to how I'd behaved in regard to Erik's hospitality, I actually hated accepting other people's generosity and kindness. Five years of living in survival mode had made it hard to let down my guard and allow other people to do the providing.

Dwivedi raised his hand, obviously sensing my imminent rejection. "Every room in this place has been outfitted with hot-water pipes. You can have a hot bath with the turn of a handle."

My mouth fell open. *A hot bath, did he say?* I found myself suddenly reevaluating my accept-no-kindness-from-strangers policy.

"Miss Blite." Dr. Dwivedi gestured to my face. "Is your look of astonishment an indication that you accept my invitation?"

"She accepts," Shep said, chuckling. "She definitely accepts."

I said nothing to contradict either man because a hot bath *would* be welcome. As much as I needed to get back home to check on my garden and make sure Bloom hadn't tried getting a message to me, I didn't want to leave before finding out how Erik was faring.

Apparently humored by my reaction, Dwivedi also chuckled. "And you as well, Corporal. You are welcome to stay."

Shep winked at me and grinned. "I think that's an offer I'd be an idiot to refuse."

Dr. Dwivedi clapped his hands. "Delightful. Let us all retire, and I will have someone bring dinner trays to your rooms." A bit unsteadily, as if his internal gears were slow to warm up, he rose from the table and gestured for us to follow.

"We haven't talked about my sister though," I said, trailing the scientist.

Beyond the library, Dwivedi turned through an opening and led us along a hallway lined with doors on each side. "I have not forgotten your sister, Miss Blite, but I assure you that if what you have told me about her talents is true, then she is in no immediate danger. If Moll Grimes has her, then she will expect your sister's cooperation, and so long as Ms. Grimes receives it, your sister will come to no harm."

I suspected Bloom would do her best to appease Moll Grimes, even though part of me wished my sister would do whatever she could to throw a wrench into Grimes's operations, if only for pure spite. Bloom was not too big on pure spite though. That was probably more my area of expertise.

Dr. Dwivedi stopped before one of the doors and fished a key ring from a pocket in his loose-fitting pants. He rifled through the keys, selected one, and unlocked the door, pushing it open to reveal a small, plain room with simple furnishings.

"You must remember your sister is a survivor." He gestured for me to cross the threshold, but he didn't follow me into the room.

"You both are, to have made it on your own for so long. I would have faith in her if I were you."

It wasn't my sister in whom I was lacking faith. If Moll Grimes could kill her own boyfriend, there was no guaranteeing she'd treat my sister any better. *Hang on, Bloom. I'm coming for you as soon as I can.*

After Dwivedi's and Shep's departure, I made short work of filling the bathtub and shedding my clothes. As I lowered myself into the pool of steaming water, my eyes rolled back in my head, and I groaned. Leaning against the high, sloped back, I let the water rise almost to my neck before twisting the waterspouts closed. Remembering the sensation of Erik's fingers on my scalp, I added this bath to my small repertoire of feel-good moments.

I should stop thinking about Erik so much.

And I definitely shouldn't have been fretting about the various ways Parvati might've been applying her "healing arts" to him.

After I'd lathered, rinsed, and lathered again, the water developed a gray, murky haze. Had I really been *that* nasty? If so, then I couldn't have smelled much better than Amity. But hygiene had become something of a luxury in this strange new world. Few could afford to be always fresh as a daisy.

Several fluffy white towels had been folded and stacked on a shelf over the sink. I drained the tub and wrapped a bath sheet around my dripping hair and another around my chest. Beside the towels, I found several jars of fragrant substances, probably lotions and skin tonics, with unfamiliar labels. I dropped my towel and went to work on my bedraggled skin, smoothing crème onto my battered cuticles and parched knees and elbows.

And that was exactly how Parvati found me, buck naked and singing "Sweet Betsey Pike—hoodle dang, fol-de day" at the top of my lungs while rubbing lotion into the dry spots between my toes.

"I've brought you something," she said with a giggle, cutting her gaze to the ceiling.

"*Oh*," I squeaked and whipped my towel into place as a blush rushed all the way from the tips of my toenails to the roots of my hair.

"I also brought you a robe." Humor still glittered in her eyes, though she was doing her best to avoid looking at me. "My uncle said you might need it." Holding up a sheet of shimmering, moss-green silk, she helped me shrug it on, then she ushered me to a small table set in the corner of the living area, where food had been set out. She removed a cloth napkin covering a bowl of white rice and plates of chicken and vegetables swimming in pungent, colorful sauces. My stomach rumbled with excitement—it didn't care that nothing on the table looked or smelled familiar.

"What is it?" I asked.

"That big dish is chicken tikka masala." She smiled. "Uncle asked me to go light on the spices to suit your foreign tongue."

"Real chicken?"

She turned laughing eyes the color of smoky quartz upon me. "What else?"

I imagined her lovely eyes staring into Erik's as she hovered over him, soothing him, healing him, and I had to swallow past a sudden dryness in my throat. "Pigeon."

Parvati giggled. "What?"

"Pigeon. The hungry girl's substitute for chicken."

Her perky nose crinkled in disgust. *Oh, to have never eaten something out of starvation or desperation. What a privilege.* "You do what you have to in order to survive," I said with a shrug.

She offered a limp smile. "I'm sure everyone has to make sacrifices from time to time."

Parvati looked as though the only sacrifice she ever made was the time it took to pick out which magnificent sari she would wear every day, but I caught myself and remembered not to make harsh assumptions or judgments. The Dead Disease affected everyone, and no one had survived this long without knowing loss and grief.

"Put your tray in the hallway when you finish." She turned for the door. "Someone will come by to collect it."

"Wait," I said as Parvati opened the apartment door. "Tell me about Erik. How is he?"

She paused. "He is sleeping. He has a bit of fever, but it should pass soon enough."

"Is that normal?"

"What is normal for him?" She shrugged a single shoulder. "If he was going to turn, he would have done it by now. His body needs time to chase away the sickness."

"But he'll be all right?"

"I think so." She stepped into the hallway. "He says your name in his sleep."

I gaped at her, blinking dumbly. "He does?"

"'Sera,' he says. Does he know any other by that name?"

"I don't think so."

A sad smile lifted the corners of her lips. "Then it must be you."

"Thank you, Parvati," I said as she pulled the door closed.

Her only reply was the soft click of the door against the jamb.

I crawled to bed with a warm simmer in my belly that had nothing to do with the spicy food I'd eaten alone at the table in my room. *So... he says my name in his sleep.*

Chapter 26:
Scientifically Virginal
Audience

After smothering a gob of sweet orange marmalade—*How did they make this stuff? Alchemy?*—onto the last piece of toast on my breakfast tray, I stuffed it between my teeth and finished tying my bootlaces. I had to find Dr. Dwivedi as soon as possible, settle the balance on our deal for information about my sister, and get on the road. I'd enjoyed the vacation, but it was time to return to the real world.

I began my search for the inscrutable scientist in the most logical place: his laboratory. Unsurprisingly, I found him there, drawing, umm, blood? from the body of Amity McCall.

"What are you doing?" Stopping behind him, I peered over his shoulder.

Maybe he'd been so engrossed in his work he hadn't heard the clank of the elevator's arrival or the clomp of my boots across the cavernous room. When I spoke, he yelped and jumped nearly out of his seat, jerking the syringe from Amity's arm.

"Oh, Sera, I didn't hear you come in," he said in a high, excited voice.

"Obviously." I motioned to the test subject gagged and belted to the examination table. "I've never seen one bleed like that."

The dark stuff oozing from the puncture wound in Amity's skin didn't resemble blood, but I didn't know what else to call it. Maybe that explained why I didn't go all swoony like I did when Dwivedi had taken Erik's blood.

"Of course you haven't." Dwivedi nodded. "The heart doesn't beat any longer, so it cannot circulate the blood. Without the pressure created by the pumping of the heart, the blood usually sinks to the lowest point in the body and sort of coagulates there. But it seems as though my concoction has some effect on this poor creature. I have managed to take a sample from her."

Urp! A yes or no would've sufficed, but I supposed brevity was too much to expect from a scientist talking about his particular field of study. "Dr. Dwivedi, this is all very interesting, but I actually came to talk to you about my sister."

While explaining his scientific observations, Dr. Dwivedi had reinserted the syringe into Amity's arm and finished taking his sample. Now, he withdrew it and turned to a worktable beside us where he'd spread out five thin strips of glass, each not much wider or longer than my thumb. With meticulous care, he applied a tiny droplet of Amity's blood to the center of each strip. "Yes, yes." His attention remained focused on his work. "A subject that can no longer be delayed, am I correct?"

"Well, it's been three days since I left home. I've got to get back to my garden before it dries up." John Brown, chief of security, be damned. Fear of his retribution wouldn't keep me away from home any longer. "I want to be sure I've found out everything I can about my sister before I leave."

Dwivedi paused and looked up at me in surprise. "Leave?"

I nodded. "I can't stay here forever."

"Well, of course not, but you must stay for dinner at least. I have arranged for a grand affair with all the residents of the college, and Parvati assures me Cy will be quite well enough to attend."

My throat went dry at that, and I had to swallow before I could speak clearly. I had purposely put Erik out of my mind. My feelings for him, whatever they were, couldn't get in the way of my mission to find and save Bloom. "He will?"

"I told you he would recover." Dr. Dwivedi turned back to his work. Having applied blood to each strip, he proceeded to cover each droplet with another thin strip of glass.

"But I've got stuff to do at home," I said, trying not to sound petulant. "I can't afford to take off and leave for so long. I have a garden to water and vegetables to pick and preserve if Bloom and I are going to make it through the winter. I've got all sorts of stuff to do, and before I get to it, I need to know what you're going to do about helping me find my sister. I've upheld my part of the bargain."

Dr. Dwivedi seemed unmoved by my impassioned speech. He slipped one of the glass strips into a gadget on the table that had a set of protruding tubes and a little mirror at the bottom to reflect light. A microscope. I'd seen them illustrated in encyclopedias, and the corner apothecary near our townhouse kept one on a work desk.

"Have you ever seen a microscope?" he asked.

I puffed a breath of exasperation that stirred the curls on my forehead. "I have, but I've never looked into one."

"It is a wonderful piece of scientific equipment. With it, I can see things undetectable by the naked eye. It works rather like a magnifying glass but much stronger. You see, the blood is not a simple liquid as it appears."

"It's not?" I said in the blandest voice possible, but Dwivedi wouldn't be discouraged. On any other day, I probably would've been interested in what he wanted to tell me. But for today, my thoughts were only for my sister and my frustrations with Dwivedi's constant need to change the subject.

"No, no, no," he said with delight, obviously excited to have a scientifically virginal audience on whom he could expound. "You see, for the longest time, mankind thought all substances were nothing more than exactly how they looked when observed by his own eye.

Only in the last two hundred years have we come to understand almost every object is composed of infinitely smaller particles." His bushy eyebrows danced above his shining eyes. "A scientist who was looking at a sample of cork named those particles cells because he thought they looked like the cells in a honeycomb."

My frustration with him made me want to shriek. Taking a deep breath, and with the steadiest voice possible, I tried again to raise the subject of Bloom. "Dr. Dwivedi, I appreciate you explaining all of this to me. It's really interesting, but right now, I have to find out about my sister."

"Yes, of course." Returning his attention to the microscope, he peered through the eyepiece again. "Your sister, daughter of Cardinal James Blite. Your father, one of the brightest engineering minds of his time, went missing five years ago, right before the first outbreak of the Dead Disease became public knowledge, and is now presumed dead, though never confirmed. Bloomington Cardinal Blite, his firstborn daughter, now twenty-four years of age, groomed to follow in her father's footsteps at the Bloomington Arms Corporation." He pulled away from his instrument and looked at me, eyes narrow, gaze intense. "Did you know... guns were not the only weapons they were devising at the time of your father's death?"

I opened my mouth to ask what Bloomington Arms Corporation had to do with Bloom, but Dr. Dwivedi must have read my mind. "But you do not want to know about that, do you?" he asked. "You want to know what has happened to your sister."

"Yes, Dr. Dwivedi, *please*." I clasped my hands together over my heart. Better than clasping them around his neck and squeezing.

"No need to worry, dear. She is perfectly fine. Moll Grimes keeps all of her valuables tucked safely away. And that brain of your sister's is certainly valuable to her."

"Moll Grimes?" I said in dismay. "You're sure? How do you know?"

He tapped his temple. "I know everything that happens in this city, or rather, the College of Kimiyagari knows everything that happens in this city, and so, therefore, do its inhabitants."

"But the college is just an apartment building."

Dr. Dwivedi's laughter echoed ominously around the room, making the fine hairs rise up on the back of my neck. "Kimiyagari cannot be confined between four walls. It cannot be contained in brick and mortar. I told you when you first came here it is the knowledge of the making that is at the heart of all things."

That's it. Dr. Dwivedi has officially fallen off his rocker. I turned to flee for the elevator, but he stopped me with a single word.

"Bloom!" he cried.

He continued after I turned around.

"Cardinal," he said. "Erik. The burdens of your heart—all of them out of your grasp. You are a small vessel lost in such a vast ocean, my dear Miss Blite. What will you do without them?"

"I don't intend to do without Bloom." I failed to keep the anger growling inside my head out of my voice. "I have every intention of getting my sister back and then maybe getting out of this crazy city. She wanted to leave, and now I think maybe she had a good idea."

"But how will you get her back? And do you mean to leave Cy behind?"

"Erik's not family." It was a cold thing to say, but my sister would remain my highest priority. I owed Erik, perhaps, but not as much as I owed Bloom.

Dwivedi shook his head. "Family is what you make it, Miss Blite. Cy has watched over you and protected you for years."

I didn't want to think about Erik that way, so instead, I said, "Dr. Dwivedi, has anyone ever told you that talking to you gives them a headache?" I squinched my eyes closed and pressed my fingertips to my temple for emphasis.

"Of course they have." He chuckled. "All of the time."

Even while shaking my head with incredulity, I couldn't help liking the peculiar alchemist. "You've been kind to share your home and your knowledge with me. I thank you."

"Oh, no. If I were kind, I would have told you about your sister, told you that she was safely and most assuredly ensconced within the walls of Moll Grimes's compound, without making you carry out this perilous scientific experiment."

"So why did you?" Annoyance bubbled through me, but I lacked the energy for true outrage. Dwivedi might have manipulated me for his own gain, but I probably would have done the same in his position. That was the kind of world we lived in now. Maybe it was the kind of world we'd always lived in, and the Dead Disease had only accentuated it.

Dr. Dwivedi sank to his stool and rubbed the bridge of his nose. "Knowledge is my only currency, the only thing I have of any value to trade. I truly needed your and Cy's help, and the only thing I had to offer in return was my knowledge." He turned to his microscope and inserted another slide. "Now that we have gotten all of that nonsense out of the way, you will most certainly be able to stay for dinner."

I didn't get the impression he was making a request, but before I could answer, he said, "How about we make another deal? You stay for dinner, and afterward, we shall discuss a plan for retrieving your sister from Ms. Grimes."

Surprise rooted me in place. "You'd do that? Help me rescue Bloom?" *But how many hoops will he make me jump through in order to earn that help?*

Dr. Dwivedi looked up at me with a queer smile. "The real question, my dear, is whether or not your sister wants to be rescued."

"Of course she does." Bloom was the one who'd always said, "Moll will pay you in beans, and in return, she'll have you by your frank." Wink-wink, nudge-nudge. But then, there was our argument a few weeks back when Bloom sounded like she was starting to sing a different song...

Dwivedi left his work, coming to put a hand on my shoulder. "Never mind, Miss Blite. I think I have put enough jam in your gear works for one day. We shall talk more after dinner. Go find Parvati. I have told her to help you find something more..." He looked me over from head to boots and back up again. "Suitable to wear."

"What's wrong with canvas and leather?" A smile tugged at my lips.

He chuckled. "It is perfectly respectable for when a man-eater asks you to dinner, but I assure you, everyone in attendance tonight will only be craving good curry and better company."

"Is Parvati with Erik?" I asked, trying to keep my voice free of any tones of jealousy.

Dr. Dwivedi tapped his forehead again. "I believe you will find her in the library."

Taking my hand, he led me toward the elevator, but I had one more question for him before I left. "What about the experiment?" I nodded toward the bound and gagged creature in the corner of the workroom. "Did you say you saw signs that the treatment was working?"

Dr. Dwivedi's expression froze, giving nothing away. "'Science, my girl, is made up of mistakes, but they are mistakes which it is useful to make because they lead, little by little, to the truth.'"

Earlier, I had called Erik my Professor Lidenbrock, leading me on a journey to the center of the earth, but clearly, Dr. Dwivedi was a more comparable reference. He could even quote straight from the novel.

"Patience, Miss Blite." He winked. "Everything in its own time."

Chapter 27: Square Pegs and Round Holes

Parvati was not alone in the library. Along with several older patrons making use of the resources, she also had the company of one particular young patrolman from Mini City. I'd mostly forgotten about Shep after he and I parted ways the previous evening. Perhaps I should've shown more gratitude after all he'd done to help me. Parvati, however, seemed to be enjoying his companionship. She and the corporal huddled over a stack of white tiles, a teapot, and a pile of little cookies dusted in powdered sugar.

Should I repeat myself in case you missed it? Powdered. Sugar.

"Care for tea?" Parvati asked after I took a seat on a cushion beside her.

"This one isn't big on tea," Shep answered for me. "But if you've got any fruit mash wine, she'll be your best friend."

"Don't you have somewhere you're supposed to be?" I wrinkled my nose. "Grimes ought to be missing you by now."

Shep sat back in his chair, laced his fingers together over his stomach, and chuckled. "Ready to be done with me? Just when I thought you and I were starting to develop a rapport."

I snagged a cookie from the tea tray and stuffed it into my mouth—*mmm, dates and almonds*—before responding. "How is it you have all this freedom to do as you please? I always thought Grimes kept her Forces on a short leash." I'd been too distracted by

138

more urgent matters to question his appearance in the street the day before, but things were less perilous now.

Shep waggled his eyebrows. "Woof woof."

An older lady sitting at a nearby desk glanced up from her book and gave Shep a curious look.

"What were you even doing on that side of the city?" I asked. "Erik and I were a dozen or more blocks away from Moll's territory."

"I was out for a stroll." He shrugged a shoulder. "Heard a commotion... decided to investigate."

Skeptical, I narrowed my eyes at him. "So it was just a coincidence?"

He turned serious, sitting up straighter. "Not coincidence. Just a little ambition and luck. You don't get ahead in Moll's world without taking some initiative, without going out and looking for opportunities." He sneered. "Sometimes, if you're in the right place at the right time, those opportunities might just fall in your lap. Moll won't mind so much about my absence when she hears about your boyfriend. I'm planning to stick around long enough to verify his miraculous recovery. Once I'm satisfied he's all you say he is, I'll be on my way."

"And when do you think that will happen?" I turned to Parvati, who seemingly hadn't paid attention to our conversation. She'd been focusing, instead, on the tiles stacked between her and Shep. "When do you think we might lay eyes on Erik again?" Perhaps I should've attempted to see him sooner, but his presence complicated my emotions and made me lose sight of my goals. It was easier to remain focused on Bloom if I kept my distance from Erik.

Parvati selected a tile from a row facing her and laid it on the game board beside two others with similar patterns. Without taking her attention from the game, she said, "He's sleeping now. I gave him a draught to help him rest, but he'll be well enough to join us for dinner this evening."

"A sleeping draught?" I asked with delight, wondering if she'd given him the same concoction he had slipped to me. The irony of it would be too sweet.

"He has terrible dreams."

"Oh?" I said, feigning only mild interest.

She shrugged and laid down another tile. "He won't speak of them, but he hasn't been staying lucid long enough to explain anyway. But the last time he was awake, he said he felt well enough to attend dinner tonight."

"About that..." I motioned to my current attire. "Your uncle sent me to you to ask for some help with my, uhh, wardrobe."

"I suspected as much." Her tone was dry. "Corporal, it's your turn."

"What are you playing?" I asked, trying to make sense of the game.

"A variation of mahjong," she said. "The real game requires four people."

"Is it hard?"

"Not really. It just takes patience and strategy. I'll teach you sometime if you like."

"Did you have to teach the corporal?"

Shep rested a studious finger on his lip but had not yet moved any of his tiles. If he could figure it out, then I could too.

Parvati shook her head. "Oh, no. He already knew the game."

"He did?" I blinked wide-eyed at the corporal.

Shep flashed me an arrogant grin. "Don't underestimate me, Miss Blite. There's much more to me than meets the eye."

"That's what I'm afraid of."

He laughed.

I pursed my lips and frowned. I didn't know what to make of him. Corporal Baumgartner was a square peg, and all I had was a bunch of round holes.

"Sera," Parvati said, "you and I will worry about dressing for dinner in a little while. Why don't you choose a book from the library? It would be much better than staring over my shoulder for the rest of the morning."

Taking her not-so-subtle hint, I went to the bookshelves lining the room and selected several volumes at random, reading the first few lines of each until one caught my interest. And that was how Parvati came to find me much later, stretched out on a sofa, a third of the way into *Great Expectations*. Part of me felt guilty for indulging in such luxury. I should've been tending my garden or hunting, doing something productive. But Dwivedi had promised his help in retrieving Bloom, and I aimed to take him up on his offer, even if it meant exercising patience, a virtue of which I was normally in short supply.

I rubbed my eyes. The long period of reading had left me bleary. "Are you done with your game?"

"A while ago," Parvati said. "I've cleared away our tea things, put up our game pieces, walked the corporal to his room, and even stopped to check on Erik. You, however, have not moved from this space for the whole of the morning."

I gasped. "It's been that long?"

Smiling, she nodded.

"Books are how I escape reality." I waggled the book at her. "The fastest way to get back to the Time Before."

She patted my shoulder. "I wished they worked that way for me. I guess that is why I smoke opium instead." She turned away and motioned for me to follow her. "Usually only when I can't sleep, or when my memories become too heavy a burden."

I understood the weight of memories. They were the only things I had in abundance. "How is Erik?" I asked, changing the subject.

"Still sleeping," she said. "But his color has returned. By tonight, he will be quite ready to look at something other than the backside of his eyelids."

Parvati led me to my room but stopped short of following me in. "I'll be back with some help in just a bit."

"Help?" I crooked an eyebrow at her. "For what?"

Parvati looked me over, similar to the way her uncle had appraised me earlier—foot to head and back down again. "Oh, dear," she said. "You have no clue."

"A clue about what?" I crossed my arms over my chest and tried giving her one of her own petulant looks, but she only laughed, rolled her eyes, and scooted away without an answer.

If I had known what was coming for me, I would have barricaded the door or escaped out my window. I never could have suspected the torture Parvati had in mind. But by the time she returned with reinforcements, it was already too late for me to run.

Chapter 28: A Storybook Prince

When I naively let Parvati into my apartment, her two cousins were trailing behind her, arms loaded with stacks of fabric, yard upon yard of brilliantly colored silk. For the next several hours, the three harbingers of feminine torment subjected me to the horrors of their regular beauty regimens, packed into one long, painful afternoon. At the end of their ministrations, I was relieved that they hadn't forced me into a corset. It was the only nice thing I could say about the hairpulling, tweezing, curling, scrubbing, creaming, and painting.

I was ready to curse Parvati and her harpies to hell, but before I could open my mouth to say the words, they brought me to stand before the image of a remarkable stranger. Not Freya or Aphrodite but maybe some other, lesser spirit I'd never read about.

I stood before the mirror so long in stunned silence that eventually, one of Parvati's cousins giggled. "She doesn't recognize herself," she said, and all three girls fell into fits of hilarity.

The face in the reflecting glass changed to pink, then red. Turning away, I searched for my pants and boots. *Forget Dr. Dwivedi's stupid dinner. I'll have to try talking to him afterward. It's not worth the ridicule.*

Parvati grabbed my arm and yanked me into place before the mirror again, though she never stopped laughing. "Sera, look at yourself." She heaved a few breaths, trying to reestablish her composure. "I mean, really look at yourself. Don't you recognize that girl?"

Truth be known, I avoided mirrors. Vanity was a luxury, a waste of time, and that whole afternoon had only gone to reinforce my belief. Did a shambling corpse care if I put on lipstick or brushed my hair before it tried to eat me? Would the undead have felt better if I put on a dress before I went out to shoot them?

Any remaining levity drained from Parvati, and she looked at me with something akin to disbelief. "You truly do not know how lovely you are, do you?"

I sniffed and rolled my eyes. "Maybe *she* is." I pointed at the reflection. "But she isn't me. Not the real me." The real me had no trouble blowing apart a Rotter's skull or skewering a rat and roasting it over a flame. The real me rejoiced in violence and thrived on subsistence living. The real me often went days without a bath or brushing my hair. But none of what had happened since arriving at Dwivedi's college had seemed very real.

"There is no illusion here." Parvati gestured at the mirror. "It is merely a few cosmetics and a curling iron."

"And a gorgeous sari," said one of the cousins. Sweetie, if I remembered correctly.

The sari *was* gorgeous, the shade of a deep-pink rose. Somehow, it brought out the red in my hair and the green in my eyes. Maybe Parvati's talents wouldn't help her in an attack of the Living Dead, but she was very good at what she did with fabrics and face paints.

Instead of my bulky boots, the girls presented me with a pair of embroidered silk slippers. Once I'd accepted that it was truly me in the mirror and not some alchemical illusion, I wondered if I didn't look a little absurd.

Parvati reassured me when I voiced my doubts. "In this place, you will look like another flower among a bouquet of lovely blooms. It may feel ostentatious to you, but I assure you, this is—how do the

French say it?—*de rigueur* for one of my uncle's special suppers. It helps us remember our humanity."

When she kissed my cheek, I regretted my earlier unkind thoughts about her.

"I must leave and get myself dressed now." She gestured to herself as though her lovely sari were a rag. "My uncle will be here shortly to escort you to the dining pavilion. You are to be his guest of honor, you know."

I didn't know, and I would've preferred remaining ignorant.

"Erik will be speechless." Parvati waggled her eyebrows and nudged me with her elbow. "I hope I get there first. I cannot *wait* to see the look on his face."

"Really?" My cheeks heated. "You think he'll like it?"

She clucked an exasperated noise as she left the room. "Tonight, even the dead would stop in their tracks for you."

I scoffed. "If that were true, I'd wear this getup every day. It would make my job *so* much easier."

I must've stood there inspecting my reflection a lot longer than I'd realized, because Dr. Dwivedi arrived in what seemed like an instant, wearing a beautiful silver brocade kurta and pajama set.

"You look very handsome, Dr. Dwivedi." I tried for a curtsey. "Silver suits you."

A wide smile split his face. "And that sari suits you. Our residents will be honored to meet you." He took my hand and planted a dry kiss on my knuckles. "You look most divine, indeed."

My nerves gnawed at me as he led me out of my room and into the elevator. I suspected it was the closest I would ever come to riding a carriage, and boy, did I feel like Cinderella. Parvati had been my fairy godmother, transforming me with her peculiar potions and magic.

As Dwivedi held my hand in the crook of his elbow, I wondered if he felt it shaking. When the doors parted, he escorted me down a hall, through a doorway, up a short flight of stairs, and…

Onto the roof.

But it was nothing like the roof of the Savings and Loan. The college's residents had converted the outdoor space into a world of colors and textures that surely existed only in dreams. Candle-filled crystal lamps glowed warmly all about. A white-tiled floor felt like cool water through my thin slippers except in the places where someone had laid plush carpets. Guests strolled around potted gardens of blooming jasmine, bougainvillea, hibiscus, and other warm-weather-loving plants that could have only survived in hothouses during the city's harsh winters.

"What do you think?" Dwivedi asked.

I hoped my stunned speechlessness was a sufficient reply.

Young men in starched white jackets and loose black pants passed trays of drinks and food. Dwivedi stopped one of the waiters and selected a glass of golden liquid. Then he handed it to me.

"What is it?" Tentatively, I sipped and realized it was some variety of grape wine, though I was no expert. Bloom and I had found wine in our foraging expeditions from time to time, but I'd never developed a taste for it.

"It is wine made from the Anab-e-Shahi cellar, imported from southern India before the world fell apart. Not much remains in our stocks, but we all enjoy it on special occasions, such as tonight. Now come, let me introduce you to the other residents."

I kept an eye out for Erik but had no luck spotting him among the crowd. The faces and names of Dwivedi's guests ran together, but everyone treated me kindly, and by the time he finished showing me around the rooftop, I was ready to find a seat on one of the pretty couches. The slippers Parvati had lent me pinched my little toes.

Before I could make my excuses to leave his side, though, Dr. Dwivedi was introducing me to yet another person. "Miss Blite, I believe you already know my friend."

A young man with dark glossy hair, wearing a midnight-blue kurta, turned from his conversation with another young man. He reached to take my offered hand, but we both froze when we saw each other's faces.

Dwivedi inclined his head toward both of us. "Mr. Erik LeRoux, it is my honor to introduce you to my special guest, Miss Serendipity Blite."

LeRoux? I searched my memory but couldn't recall knowing his last name before now. We stared at each other like buffoons, our mouths hanging open like broken gates. With his hair brushed off his forehead, the deep-blue highlights matching the blue of his suit, I barely recognized him. Without the formidable black coat and his usual scowl, he looked like a storybook prince—one from *One Thousand and One Nights*, perhaps.

Hot-cha-cha.

Chapter 29: Something Wrong

"Aren't you going to say anything, Erik?" Parvati appeared at my side, wearing a knowing grin. She motioned toward me. "I know you've been concerned for Sera's safety during your... erm... *ordeal*, but she is looking rather well cared for, don't you think?"

Erik closed his mouth, swallowed, and licked his lips. "Yes, very much."

I hadn't realized what a relief it would be to hear his voice again—to see him safe and whole. Hot tears sprang to my eyes. *Make me look like a silly girl, and the next thing you know, I start acting like one.* I blinked until the tears disappeared.

"Erik," I said hoarsely. Clearing my throat, I tried again. "I'm glad you've recovered."

Dr. Dwivedi slipped my hand from the crook of his elbow and offered it to Erik with a slight bow. Erik took my fingers, his eyes never leaving mine. Dwivedi snorted with obvious mirth. "I'll leave you two young people to catch up with each other before dinner, which starts"—he checked the watch in his jacket pocket—"in just a few minutes."

Turning on his heel, Dwivedi gestured for Parvati and the young man who'd been talking with Erik to follow him. Erik and I stood for several more heartbeats in silence, but when we finally spoke, we began at the same time.

"Sera, I never—"

"Erik, I thought—"

We stopped and laughed.

"You go first," Erik said, folding my hand into the bend of his arm as he led me toward an empty corner of the roof.

A blush warmed my cheeks. "Parvati said you would be here, but knowing it didn't prepare me for actually seeing you. You look as though the last two days never happened."

"It's nice to hear you say that." His thick black lashes lowered as he peered at his feet. "But I feel like I've been run over by a wagon and a team of horses." He tugged his jacket collar, revealing a thick bandage. "It'll take a while for this to fully heal, and I think it'll leave me with more scars."

"I don't mind your scars," I said without thinking. To my dismay, another flush of heat erupted across my cheeks. I'd never believed I was the blushing type, but something about Erik and this place brought out another side to me, a side I wasn't sure I liked. I felt vulnerable here... with him. Vulnerability was a strategic blunder to be avoided at all costs. "So, no sudden cravings for a bite of human flesh?"

Erik didn't laugh as I'd hoped. Instead, his eyes roamed over me in slow perusal. "Not until you showed up."

I swallowed. It was the only response I could manage.

"Good God, Sera." Slowly, he shook his head. "I thought you were something before, but now...?" He took my other hand and pulled me closer, his warmth enveloping me. There it was—that scent of sandalwood and whatever bits of him were mixed in with it. Against my own self-interests, I closed my eyes and inhaled. "Now..." Erik's voice turned rough. "I feel like I should kneel and worship you."

I had just opened my mouth to say something about how ridiculous that sounded when the roof door flew open with a bang and Corporal Baumgartner strode out, heading straight for Erik and me as if he had known exactly where to find us. He cocked a finger at Erik as though he were aiming a gun. "Ah, just the Corpse Bait I was looking for."

Erik threw back his shoulders, preparing for confrontation.

"Come to see the miraculous recovery for yourself?" I said, hoping to diffuse the tension that erupted the moment Shep had stepped onto the roof. "You can see he's recovered."

Shep glanced at me, obviously noticing me for the first time, and for the second time that evening, a mouth fell open in my presence. I rolled my eyes and snorted.

Shep looked pretty impressive himself in a starched olive-green jacket. It looked like something an officer in the Army would've worn in the Time Before. It smelled vaguely of cedar and camphor. For the first time, I wondered about Shep's life before the Dead Wars. Pretty brass buttons gleamed on his chest and lapels. He'd brushed his blond hair back, and from the slight scent of pomade wafting from him, I figured he'd used some kind of hair treatment to hold it in place.

Because he was already itching for a fight, I decided it would be a bad time to call him a dandy.

"Damn—I mean, my my, Miss Blite. You do clean up well." Shep's eyes lingered a little too long on my bare parts for my taste.

Erik snugged his arm around my waist, clearly a possessive gesture. That moment was not the time to call him out on it, but I would later. I didn't mind his appreciation, but I'd never let anyone think they could own me. "I understand I have you to thank for helping Sera bring me here while I was... *incapacitated.*"

Shep gave me a greedy look. "I'm happy to help Sera *any* time she likes."

Erik stiffened, but I put my hand over his and raised my voice before he said or did something regrettable. "So, now you've seen him,

Shep. You can run back and tell Moll all about the miracle you observed."

Shep grinned, baring his teeth. "I'm not in any big hurry to leave just yet."

"Moll knows all about me," Erik said. "You'll only waste her time if you bring up my name."

"She does?" I asked. At the same time, Shep said, "Is that so?"

Erik smirked and gestured at Shep's hip. "Where do you think that bit of temporary immunity medicine you keep in your pocket for emergencies comes from?"

"Moll has been getting regular shipments from this place," Shep said, "even though I didn't know where it was or what it was called before Sera brought me here. But we all knew Moll had connections to some fancy scientists doing stuff that looked like magic. Whaddaya call 'em?" He snapped his fingers while trying to find the word. "Alchemists, right? They whip up something, magic-like."

"Magic?" Erik spat the word as though it were bitter.

"Well, what else do you call something that can bring the dead to their feet? Something unnatural."

Erik snorted. "You've thought hard about this, haven't you?"

"I'll tell you what I've thought about." Shep ground his teeth, jaw muscles bulging. "There's something wrong about this place." He leaned forward, pointing his finger at Erik like a sword. "There's something wrong about *you*."

"I'll say." Erik sniggered. "It's *my* blood they make the immunity serum from." He hadn't let go of me. In fact, he pulled me closer, holding me uncomfortably tight. "Think about that the next time you toss that stuff down your gullet."

Fed up, I pulled away from Erik and slipped between the growling men, blocking their view of each other. "I don't know about you two, but I'm so hungry my belly button's near to touching my backbone. Let's go see what kind of spread these folks lay down."

At first, neither acted as though they had heard me. "Erik?" I put my hand to his shoulder. If that didn't work, I'd have happily given them both a good stiff punch in the gut.

He blinked and shook himself. "Sure, Sera, let's get something to eat. Parvati's fed me nothing but tea and broth."

Shep, still watching Erik closely, nodded and motioned for me to lead the way, but the devious look on his face made me uneasy about putting my back to him. Then my stomach growled, and I decided my hunger was more urgent than my worry over Shep. I could deal with him later.

Chapter 30: A Fighter
Not a Dancer

"Parvati was a good nurse?" I asked, trying to distract Erik from Shep.

Erik nodded. "I can't say I was very aware for much of her treatments, but here I am, alive and well."

"I hope it was okay that I brought you here. I didn't know where else to go. I was afraid to show Shep where you lived, and I wanted to make sure we got Amity back here as soon as possible."

"Who?" Erik asked, black brows knitting.

Dr. Dwivedi's voice reached us at that moment, calling everyone to dinner. Erik and I followed the crowd to a corner of the roof, where a long banquet table waited for us, covered in candles and crystal. Dwivedi caught my attention and motioned for me to take a place next to him at the head of the table. I latched onto Erik's arm and dragged him with me.

"What are you afraid of?" He chuckled. "I thought you were fearless."

"I don't like too much attention."

"Then you should've worn a veil and a robe to cover everything else. Looking like that..." His gaze swept over me again. "What did you expect?"

"I wasn't expecting anything. Parvati snowed me over."

Speaking of Parvati seemed to summon her. She appeared at Shep's side wearing gold and looking ethereal, as though she'd descended from some heavenly realm to walk among the mortals for the night. After nudging Shep's arm to get his attention, Parvati motioned him toward a seat near hers. Convenient for me that she stepped in because I wasn't looking forward to spending an entire dinner sitting between Shep and Erik and playing peacekeeper.

"Sera," Dr. Dwivedi said as we took our seats. Waiters appeared, bearing plates of food for each of us. "Have you had time to tell Cy everything that occurred while he was feeling under the weather?"

"No, sir." I shook my head and glanced at Erik. Thanks to Shep's tumultuous arrival, Erik and I hadn't had time to say much to each other. "I haven't."

"Cy, has she told you we verified the location of her sister?"

Erik raised an eyebrow. "Is she with Grimes like you suspected?"

"Yes." I stabbed my fork into a piece of roasted eggplant on my plate. It was like butter in my mouth, a pleasant contrast to the toughness forming in my heart. "They used to say money was the root of all evil, but now I think you can blame all the bad in the world on Moll."

A woman on Erik's right side laughed. "Do you think we can blame her for our problem with the dead-who-won't-stay-that-way?"

I shrugged. "Why not? I wouldn't be surprised to find out she had something to do with it."

"How is your research going?" Erik asked Dwivedi. "Did Sera bring you what you wanted?"

The elder alchemist held up a finger, asking for a moment to finish chewing before he answered. He swallowed and said, "Yes, she did, and we have had some interesting developments in that area."

I paused with a forkful of eggplant halfway to my mouth. "You have?"

"If you will both come down to my laboratory after dinner, I would be most happy to share it with you."

The waiters removed our small plates and replaced them with bowls of red lentil soup. Dr. Dwivedi described everything as it was placed before us, and I devoured it all with gusto. Even if I hadn't spent the last five years eating scraps and crumbs, the food in this place would've tasted divine. In this otherworldly domain, this rooftop oasis, it felt a bit like I had joined the gods and goddesses dining on ambrosia at Mt. Olympus.

The waiters whisked away our soup bowls and returned with plates of chickpea dumplings, green curry prawns, okra seasoned with cumin—that particular dish took a little getting used to—and spicy cauliflower fritters. I drank more wine and demolished everything on my plate, including the okra. The meal ended with strong, syrupy cups of coffee.

"What did you think of the meal, Miss Blite?" asked a tipsy Dwivedi.

I patted a napkin to my lips. "It will be hard to go back to eating the stuff I usually survive on when I have to leave this place."

"Any time the pigeon becomes too gamy for your taste, you are most welcome to come and share a meal here with me." Dr. Dwivedi winked, or tried to, but the wine had stolen his coordination, so instead, he blinked both eyes like an owl.

After the last dishes were cleared away, many of the older people retired for the evening, but some of the younger crowd brought out musical instruments. The wine and food made me sluggish, but I didn't object when Erik dragged me to my feet.

"Dance?" he asked.

"Nope." I popped the "p" sound a few extra times, enjoying the way it tingled against my wine-numbed lips. "Don't dance."

With a chuckle, he tugged me into his arms, and the earth's gravity shifted with us, swirling and whirling like a top. My head was spinning as he started us on a gentle sway in time with the music. "Are you sure?"

"Nope-p-p-p." Yup, I was definitely tipsy, if not completely sloshed. I wondered how bad the hangover would be in the morning then decided I didn't care.

"Why not?"

"Dunno how."

"I thought they taught ladies that sort of thing at the fancy school you went to."

"Nuh-uh." I shook my head. The world spun again, and I closed my eyes until it stopped. "Wasn't old enough."

"Your father didn't teach you?"

I stopped mid-sway. "Father didn't dance." I tried making a serious face, wrinkling my brow and pursing my lips. My lips were still numb, though, so I pursed them again to make sure I was doing it right. Erik snickered, so I stopped and focused on trying to keep still. "Or if he did, he didn't do it with me."

"How about Bloom? She didn't dance either?"

I scoffed. "She would rather build a machine that did the dancing for her."

Erik started us swaying again. One boy played something like a flute or a clarinet. Another tapped on a set of small drums, and a young woman strummed an unfamiliar instrument that looked like a distant cousin to Bloom's guitar but with a much longer neck.

"There's not much to it," Erik whispered in my ear. "No fancy waltzes, no complicated steps. Move however the music tells you to."

His breath smelled like the rose syrup from our dessert, and his hands blazed against the small of my back. I leaned into him and whispered, "I'm not a dancer. I'm a fighter."

He choked down a laugh. "Dancing and fighting have a lot in common."

"Dancing doesn't hurt, though."

"So long as you don't step on my feet."

I pulled away to give him a glare, but he tightened his arms to keep me close. Parvati and Shep, I noticed, had taken a seat near the edge of the roof and bowed their heads close to whisper to each other. *Hmmm, wonder what that's about.*

"What are you going to do?" Erik asked in a low voice, his breath tickling the hairs at my temple.

"Dance?"

Chuckling, he shook his head. "No, I mean now that you know about your sister, what are you going to do?"

"Not sure." The wine went from making me warm and fizzy to tired and dizzy. I pulled away and stumbled to a nearby sofa. Erik caught me before I tripped over the hem of my gown and helped me take a seat.

"You okay?" he asked, still holding my arm.

I put my head in my hands. "Drank too much."

"Put your feet up and lay your head in my lap." Gently, he tugged me, and I fell against him. With a bit of wiggling, I managed to do as he suggested. His fingers rubbed circles at my temples. "How's that?"

"Mmm," I moaned.

Laughter rumbled in his chest.

"How is it that you always end up tending to me like this? I'm not sure I care for it."

"Sounds to me like you care for it very much. What was that noise you just made?" He dug his fingers into the base of my skull, and a little knot of tension gave way.

I groaned again, more emphatically this time. "*Mmm.*"

"Yup, that's the one."

"I have to take care of myself. I can't rely on other people to provide for me or protect me."

"Who says?" His fingers crept down my neck, kneading, rubbing.

"That's just how the world works now." I stabbed a finger into the air. "Every girl for herself. You can't rely on anyone, because at any moment, they could develop a sudden desire to eat you. You start needing them, and then poof—" I snapped my fingers "—they're gone. If you can't take care of yourself, who else is going to do it?"

His hands disappeared from my neck, and I swallowed my disappointment. Leaning against the back of the sofa, he braced his arms along the top and looked up at the stars. "Things were like that in the Time Before, too, Sera. People got sick, died, accidents happened. I understand not wanting to feel helpless, but there's nothing wrong with working together. Community is as important as it was before—even more so.

"Look at these people." He waved his arm, gesturing at the rooftop gathering. "They work together and have made a good life in spite of everything."

"But I don't belong here," I said. "And I have my own place."

"That you share with Bloom. Even you have your sister. You're not totally alone."

"Bloom is family. That's different. Besides, she's gone now, which is my point. If I don't get her back, it will be just me. Alone."

Peering down at me, he cupped my jaw. His thumb traced across my cheekbone. "It doesn't have to be that way."

"What do you mean?"

"You're not as alone as you insist."

"No?" Exhaustion and intoxication tugged at me, making my body heavy. I could barely keep my eyes open.

He gulped audibly. "You've got *me*."

"I'm not sure what you mean."

Grunting, he jerked a hand through his hair, mussing it so it looked like it usually did, hiding his scarred eye. He even went so far as to turn his shoulders until I could only see him in profile on his unscarred side. I knew him well enough by now to recognize his classic defense posture.

I'd offended him. *Who knew boys could be so sensitive?* Dropping my feet to the floor, I sat up with a groan, and Erik didn't stop me. Some sobriety had returned, and my thoughts were forming more clearly. "Dr. Dwivedi said he would help me rescue my sister. He wants me to come talk to him after dinner."

Refusing to look at me, Erik gazed at something distant.

"And he wants us to come see his progress with Amity." Standing, I held out my hand. "C'mon. Come with me."

He finally turned his face to me. "You said that name before. Who is she?"

I forgot he'd been unconscious when I'd recognized her on the street. "Oh, she's a girl I went to school with. Amity McCall. Funny I happened to recognize the girl you chose to make Dr. Dwivedi's lab rat." The world that was left after the Dead Wars was turning out to be a small one filled with many uncanny coincidences.

"You know her?" Erik took my hand.

I pulled him to his feet. "She looks a bit more, well... *dead* than I remember." I nodded. "But, yes, I think it's her."

Chapter 31: The Beat of Life

Dr. Dwivedi had bound Amity to an examination table, and she noted our arrival with dark, flat eyes, but she didn't moan or gnash her teeth in response to the scent of live, fresh human.

"Sera," Dwivedi said as he looked up from his perch over his microscope. "Come over here and take a look. Tell me what you see."

After crossing the room, I put my eye to the scope, not knowing what to expect. "What is this?"

"What do you think it is?"

"Well," I said, still peering through the lens. "It looks a little like the blood cells you showed me before, but these are redder and fatter."

A wide smile cracked the scientist's wizened face. He pumped his fist into the air. "Exactly, exactly. Cy, would you care to look?"

Scooting away, I let Erik take my place at the microscope. He peered into the lens and then looked up at Dwivedi with both eyebrows raised. "What am I supposed to be seeing? It looks like any regular blood to me."

"Exactly my point," Dwivedi said. "Regular blood. Only, I extracted it from our test subject moments before you arrived."

"But..." Erik's mouth fell open. I was similarly stunned. "How?" he asked.

Dwivedi's voice squeaked with excitement. "Her cells appear to be regenerating."

"How is that possible?" A sick look washed over Erik's face. Shock, perhaps, because that was exactly how I felt. The contents of my stomach turned over.

"I think..." Dwivedi paused, putting a finger to his lip. "I think the curative is working." He bustled over to the microscope, removed the slide, and replaced it with another. "Look again."

Erik motioned for me to go first. "This is what you showed me before," I said. "From the first blood sample."

"Right." Dwivedi hiccupped then giggled. Clearly, he'd overindulged in the wine. "You notice how much darker and more flaccid they are? Like the belly of a fat man who lost weight too quickly?"

"Well, I haven't seen that many men's bellies," I said.

Erik snickered before looking into the microscope himself. "This was her blood? From when?"

"Yesterday morning," Dwivedi said.

"Whoa."

Dwivedi agreed with a sloshy nod. "Whoa indeed."

"So, she's cured?" I asked doubtfully. When I looked at Amity, lying as motionless as the corpse she is... was... whatever, she still looked dead. She didn't make tiny, unconscious movements like a live person. Her chest didn't rise and fall with the rhythm of breathing. Maybe some pallor had left her cheeks, but her skin still hung slack over her bones like dustcloths over old furniture.

Dr. Dwivedi waved both of his hands before him as if brushing away my words. "No, no, no. I said nothing about her being cured. There has been no real response to stimuli other than hunger, and there has been only a slight increase in her body temperature." He paused, taking a long breath. "But that is not all."

We waited for his revelation, but he said nothing. Before I could lose the rest of my patience and implore him to spit it out, Amity opened her mouth and gasped. Erik and I both flinched. She let out the gasp with a long, low groan that prickled over my skin like the touch of a phantom.

"She's breathing again." Dwivedi grinned like a delighted cherub.

Erik stepped back, shaking his head. "No. They have to take in air to vocalize. It doesn't mean she's breathing."

Dwivedi held up a finger. "No, this is different. Our young lady began sucking in a lungful of breath every quarter of an hour or so since early this morning. She's up to twice that many now, whether she's making sounds or not."

Oh, well, that gives me the creeps.

"Come here, Miss Blite." Dr. Dwivedi shuffled closer to Amity's body and picked up an instrument that looked a lot like a trumpet. He didn't put it up to his lips and toot out a *reveille*, though. Instead, he pressed the horn to Amity's chest and lowered his ear to the piece where I would've placed my mouth if it were a musical instrument.

When I approached the dead girl, her flat stare followed me.

Dr. Dwivedi gestured to the trumpet. "Put your ear here and listen."

I swallowed the acid rising in my throat. Fear, disgust, or something else entirely? "What am I supposed to hear?"

"You tell me," he said.

At first, I heard only the muted roar of my blood drumming in my ears, but then...

Da dum...

Da dum...

Have you ever had a moment when panic hits you so hard it feels like a fist in your gut? Your chest cramps, your pupils dilate until everything blurs, and a maddening buzz fills your ears. It used to happen to me as a child whenever Father caught me doing something I wasn't supposed to do, such as touching one of his guns. More recently, it happened whenever one of the undead got the drop on me, and for the briefest moment, I would go numb, unable to think or react.

The same thing happened when I realized the slow thrum at the other end of Dr. Dwivedi's ear trumpet was the pulse of Amity McCall's heart.

Dropping the listening instrument, I stumbled back. Everything in my vision turned gray and hazy. I couldn't get air into my lungs.

"*Sera!*" Erik shouted, rushing to my side. "What is it? What's wrong?"

The panic subsided long enough for me to choke down a breath. Shoving Erik aside, I reeled away from Amity and Dr. Dwivedi. "Her heart," I croaked. "I heard it. It's... it's *beating*."

I had no time for modesty or apologies. Bile rose in my throat so fast I had no choice but to lean over and let it out. Perhaps I should've done with one less glass of wine and fewer gulab jamun.

"Not possible!" Erik's protest fell between my bouts of retching.

"The Dead Disease should not be possible," Dwivedi said. "Your immunity to it should not be possible. This creature's biological response comes from the same source as your immunity. Why should it not work?"

I stopped retching long enough to glance over my shoulder and see Erik filling with outrage. "Because *I'm not dead*!"

Guess what.

Neither was Amity McCall.

Chapter 32: Never Been Kissed

After freshening up in Dwivedi's bathroom and gargling several glasses of a minty concoction he'd provided, I joined Erik on the scientist's balcony, taking a seat next to him on a rattan settee. Cooling on a side table beside him was a pot of tea. Dwivedi seemed certain most of life's ills could be remedied with tea, and it wouldn't have surprised me if Amity's treatment included an infusion of Darjeeling or oolong.

It was not oolong in the pot Dwivedi had left for us but ginger. He'd claimed it would calm my stomach and cleanse my palate. The latter half of his claim was proving true—my mouth no longer tasted like acid, but my stomach remained stubbornly tied in knots. "What do you think this means?" I asked.

"I'm not sure." The shock of our recent discovery flattened Erik's voice. "But Dwivedi said he wouldn't let her out of her cage. She still has the same monstrous urges. Unless that changes, having a heartbeat doesn't mean much."

"But what if she *is* cured? What if there comes a time when she doesn't want to eat us anymore? Will that make her human again instead of whatever it was she was before?"

Erik rubbed his hands over his face and slid off the seat. He crossed to the balcony railing and leaned over the edge. A stiff breeze stirred his hair. "I don't know, Sera."

"I never thought they had souls." I tried ignoring the unease in the pit of my belly that had nothing to do with overindulging at dinner or the failure of Dwivedi's ginger tea. "I don't really know if I have one either, but I know I have something that makes me different from them. At least, I thought I did. That's why I never minded killing them the way I did. I thought whatever spark it was that made us who we are had left the undead in the time between their deaths and their resurrections.

"I thought they were just hollow carcasses with a need to taste human flesh—they don't care or hurt or feel scared." I took a deep breath and hugged my arms around my waist. "They don't feel love."

Erik turned around, facing me. The light inside Dr. Dwivedi's apartment anointed the high spots on his face, and he looked like an illustration, a two-dimensional drawing. His expression was impossible to read.

"Have I been killing a bunch of potentially innocent people?" I swallowed a sob.

Erik flinched briefly before sliding to the ground before me. He put his head in my lap, and reflexively, I stroked his hair.

"We couldn't have known," he said.

"But does that excuse me? Does that make it okay, the things I've done?"

"I've done them too."

"Then we'll go to Hell together?"

"If we must."

"I killed my father." Tonight was a night for unexpected outbursts, it seemed. I hadn't known I was going to confess. The words had tumbled from my mouth on their own, as if my conscience could no longer bear the poison of my guilt.

Erik lifted his head and met my gaze, but he said nothing. His expression was blank.

The story poured from my tongue like grains of sand from a broken hourglass. "I knew nothing about the Dead Disease then. I think no one did. Father was rarely home; some special project at work kept him away. Bloom was home from school."

Erik remained still, crouched at my knees, but he gripped my fingers, holding them vise tight.

"One night I had a strange dream about two dogs fighting, but then I woke up, and the growling didn't stop. I followed the noise into Bloom's room. They were both there—my father and my sister. I couldn't tell what they were doing at first. Even though he designed guns, my father was never a violent man—stern, strict, but never vicious. It made no sense that he and Bloom would fight, wrestling like two wild animals.

"Then, I guess he caught my scent or something because he paused and turned to look at me. It was night, so I couldn't see much, but something about the way he held his body, the way he moved—" I shivered, remembering the horror of it. Remembering that nothing in the whole world was ever the same again after that moment. "It was the most frightening thing I ever saw. I screamed and ran for my room. My body knew what to do even though my brain was trying to convince me it was my father, so there was no reason to fear.

"I didn't make it far. I tripped when he lunged for me, and he knocked me to the floor right in the middle of our... our living room..." I didn't know if I could finish the story because my throat closed as if a pair of strong hands had encircled my neck and was squeezing. *Squeezing.*

Erik's long fingers cupped my face. He peered into my eyes. At least I thought that was what he was doing. It was hard to tell out here in the dark.

"You don't have to tell me," he said.

Talking like that had been compulsive. I'd never been hypnotized, but the way I was feeling must've been similar to a mesmeric trance. I swallowed and continued. "H-he trapped me underneath him. He and Bloom were much bigger than me, so I didn't stand a chance of fighting him off, especially if *she* hadn't been able to. When Father went after me, Bloom told me she grabbed a gun from the drawer in her nightstand and took off after us. She didn't shoot because she was afraid she might hit me. She managed to pull Father away before he could bite, but then he attacked her again. Bloom dropped the gun.

"I didn't even hesitate. I picked up the gun and... and..." My whole body seized like a piston in an overheated engine. I'd said everything except the part that mattered most, but the effort to get out the final words had become a Sisyphean feat.

Sensing my distress, Erik stood and hauled me against him like we were two characters in a tragic play. Normally, I didn't go in for dramatic stuff, but it felt so good to be held. Especially by him. When the tears took over, he rocked me and rubbed my back. He let me cry until the wave of emotion waned and receded. Eventually, I calmed down enough to hear him. He'd been humming a soft, soothing tune in my ear.

I wiped my nose on the loose end of my gown and blotted my eyes, hoping Parvati would forgive me for soiling her sari. I'd also ruined all the makeup she'd taken so long to perfect, but none of that mattered anymore.

"It's not your fault, Sera." Erik stroked my hair as though I were a timid kitten.

If I hadn't felt so wretched, I might've purred for him.

I hiccupped. "Bloom and I've had that discussion a million times. But knowing it in your head and knowing it in your heart are two different things. I killed my father. I can't take that back."

"He would've killed you."

"We could've run. If it turns out Dwivedi has a cure, then maybe we could've saved him."

Erik harrumphed "Every single one of us is haunted by the ghosts of what might have been, but we can't live in the past. There is no life in the past. Only death."

"It's been five years, and there's not a day goes by that I don't think of him."

Resting his cheek against my temple, Erik sighed in a deep way that made me tingle all over. "Then he's not really gone. Maybe that's what afterlife is. People's memories of us, keeping us alive somewhere."

"I'm sorry about crying all over your suit." I sniffled and rubbed my eyes.

"It wasn't really my style anyway."

"I think it looks good on you."

He stilled. "Really? It's not too... flashy?"

"Not any more than this getup." I flicked my fingers at my gown.

"I meant what I said earlier."

"'Bout what?"

"About you looking like something to be worshiped."

I was glad for the darkness that kept him from seeing me turn red. "It's just smoke and mirrors. A magic show. Tomorrow, I'll be the girl I've always been, and this night will have been a dream."

"A very good dream." His voice was low and gruff. "I'm not sure I want it to end."

Suddenly self-conscious, I tried pulling away, but he wouldn't let me go.

"Why do you do that?" The light from Dr. Dwivedi's apartment caught in his seeing eye, and silver flecks shimmered in it like the stars in the sky behind him.

"Do what?" I asked.

"Pull away from me."

"I- I just thought to give you some space."

He grunted a sound of protest in the back of his throat. "I've been trying to tell you all night that I don't want space."

"You don't?"

Impossibly, he drew me closer. My breath thinned as his face inched nearer to mine. "No, Sera. I don't."

"What... what *do* you want?"

He inhaled, and I thought he would say something, but no. Instead, he lowered his head and brushed his lips over mine like a question. A request.

Oh, dear me. Was that what I think it was?

I had no chance to formulate a response before he did it again, but this time, he lingered so there was no question. No uncertainty. His lips covered mine, soft at first and then firmer as I pressed against him, wanting more.

I had a feeling, when it came to Erik, I would always be wanting more.

His mouth opened, his tongue seeking and finding mine. The intoxicated feeling from earlier in the night returned, spinning my head, warming my body, spiking bubbles in my bloodstream. He was heat and life and excitement and hope. His touch felt like the opposite of being alone.

I would've had more to say about his mouth on mine and the carnal feelings his touch elicited, but my brain had melted into a useless puddle along with the rest of my body.

Sometime later, he broke away and drew in another deep breath. He put those wonderful lips to my ear and said, "You don't have to be alone. I won't go anywhere, I promise."

With every element of my being, I wanted to believe him, but... "That's not a promise anyone can make."

"I'm not just anyone," he said, stepping aside as the sliding door opened to admit Dr. Dwivedi onto the balcony.

"Hello, my friends. I have come to see if you are feeling any better?"

Uncomfortable with public displays of affection, I pulled away from Erik, smoothed my dress, and patted my hair into place. Awkwardly, Erik fidgeted with the collar of his jacket.

Dr. Dwivedi's eyebrows performed a little dance of excitement. "I suspect that you are feeling much better. It was my ginger tea, of course. See? I told you it would help."

Snorting, I rolled my eyes.

Dwivedi's gaze slid to Erik. "The evening is so late, and after everything that has occurred today, I find myself exhausted. I know we said we would discuss plans for your sister's liberation, but I must ask for a pardon. Our thinking will be much clearer in the morning after a night of good rest. Do you not agree?"

I glanced at Erik, who lifted his chin in a subtle nod.

"Sure thing, Dr. Dwivedi," I said. "If you don't mind putting me up for another evening, then I guess I don't mind staying. The streets aren't the safest place to be this hour."

Apparent relief washed over Dwivedi. The concern on his pinched face eased, and he smiled. "Thank you. You have been very tolerant of my idiosyncrasies."

"I guess if I want your help, then I don't have any other choice."

He shook his head. "Maybe not, but your patience is most appreciated."

Dwivedi led me through his apartment to his front door and bade me goodnight.

Erik watched from the balcony with his brows drawn tight together, a contemplative look on his face.

"I will meet you for breakfast in the library, then?" Dwivedi asked.

"Will there be marmalade?"

He lit up with laughter. "I'm sure that can be arranged."

Chapter 33: Journey to the Center of the Soul

"I have an idea." Dr. Dwivedi shoved a plate of English muffins toward me. He had also asked Parvati to bring us a pot of coffee and an assortment of jams and jellies, including marmalade.

After plopping two cubes of sugar into my cup, I drizzled in a little cream. "Well, I'm glad somebody does, because I have nothing."

Erik remained silent, which was the agreement we'd made when he'd met me at my room and escorted me to breakfast. I'd told him if he wanted to participate, then he had to agree to keep his—marvelously talented—mouth shut unless any of the plan directly involved him. And I sincerely hoped my plan wouldn't have to involve him. Bloom was not his problem. At the end of the day, I was still a Solo Practitioner, and rescuing Bloom was one hundred percent my responsibility alone.

"Yes, well, designing a plan is my specialty." Dwivedi pushed the marmalade jar closer to my hand. "It is in the execution that I often have trouble. But you and Cy seem quite capable, so let me explain my scheme, and then you tell me if you are willing to do it."

While I slathered jam onto a muffin, Dwivedi launched into his proposal, explaining that Moll Grimes had sent word that she required a new shipment of Dwivedi's temporary immunity serum. Normally, he made a few sparing doses at a time because only Erik's blood provided the basis of the serum. But if Erik agreed, then Dr. Dwivedi proposed to extract an extra donation, enough to make

171

at least double the standard number of dosages. It was sounding as though my intentions of keeping Erik out of my plans were quickly fading.

"With this bargaining chip," Dwivedi said, "I believe Ms. Grimes might agree to allow Bloom and you to meet. As I said before, my dear, we must first determine if your sister desires her freedom."

Even though Bloom had said some things to make me doubt, I still functioned on the belief that Moll took Bloom against her will. Otherwise, it would mean Bloom had abandoned me without a word, and it hurt too much to believe she would've ever done that to me.

"Since we're talking about *my* blood," Erik said as he dusted crumbs from his fingers, "I figure I have a right to offer an opinion." He cut his gaze to me and raised his eyebrows, waiting for me to object. I huffed but nodded in agreement. "Why should I give Moll anything? What if I told her to release Bloom or else I won't give any more of my blood?"

Dwivedi's dusky complexion paled. "No, no, Cy." He waggled a finger. "I have no desire to aggrieve Moll Grimes. The people in the college depend on good relations to keep our trade routes open."

"It'll be temporary." Erik swirled his coffee cup as he gazed at its contents. "An embargo."

Dwivedi waved Erik's words away. "You underestimate Ms. Grimes. She will not bow to pressure. She does not give in to demands. She takes what she wants, and she will take you, Cy, by force if necessary."

Erik set down his coffee and stiffened his back. "But if I refuse to give you my blood, then you won't have any choice."

Dwivedi narrowed his eyes, obviously not cowed by Erik's threat. "Then the consequences will be your responsibility alone. Your blood is most valuable, but it is not everything. So long as I do nothing to damage the trade relationship with Ms. Grimes, then this community will survive. I cannot say the same for you."

I'd had enough of watching the two bulls circle each other, snorting and pawing the dirt. This whole plan came down to me getting my sister back, and Erik could grow a tail and swing from trees before I'd let him jeopardize any plan to retrieve Bloom The same went for Dwivedi.

"Dr. Dwivedi." I waited until he turned his attention away from Erik and back to me. "I like your plan. I support it. But we can't force Erik to give his blood against his will. If he doesn't want to do things your way, then we'll have to find another way."

Erik's shoulders slumped. His gaze dropped to his lap. "I don't like the idea of giving in to Moll, but I'll do whatever you want, Sera. If you like Dr. Dwivedi's plan, then I'll give my blood until my veins run dry."

Dwivedi chirped with delight. "Oh, that will not be necessary. We will not take enough to hurt you, but you may feel quite unlike yourself for some time."

WHILE DR. DWIVEDI PREPARED his implements for drawing Erik's blood, I went to Amity's cage, peeled back the cloth covering her, and immediately noticed she didn't stink nearly so much as usual. She was resting peacefully, and I hated to see her caged, but I believed Dwivedi when he said she couldn't be trusted with her freedom.

"Hello, Amity," I said. "Do you remember me? We went to school together." I pointed to myself. "Serendipity Blite, but everyone calls me Sera."

She didn't respond, but she didn't try to eat me either. She didn't really look at me at all but lay listlessly on the floor of her crate. Along with the loss of her death smell, her chest rose and fell with regularity, and her skin had plumped and pinkened. Her recovery astounded me and made my heart heavy with the familiar regret of all the things that could never have been.

Erik suffered Dr. Dwivedi's ministrations in silence, and before long, they had filled several glass vials. The blood drawing didn't bother me the way it had before, and once I gave up trying to get a response from Amity, I took a seat on a stool beside Erik.

He scowled, bottom lip poking out in a petulant frown. "Not feeling sick this time? Is it because you've got such a big stake in the outcome?"

His comment hit a little too close to home, and defensively, I snapped back at him. "I said you didn't have to do this." I slid off the stool and returned to Amity's cage, preferring her silent company. One of her inhalations caught in her chest, and she coughed.

How interesting.

Erik heaved a sigh I could hear all the way across the room. "I'm sorry, Sera. I really do want to help."

His apology only made me feel worse.

Dwivedi filled his last vial full of blood.

Erik caught my eye as he rolled down his sleeve. He tilted his head and raised a brow. I gave him an apologetic smile. He offered his own soft smile in return.

Just then, Dwivedi dropped one of the full vials, and it crashed to the floor, glass shattering. Blood splattered everywhere.

"Oh, dear—" Dwivedi said, but a vicious snarl from Amity interrupted him.

She launched to her feet, fingers curling around the bars of her cage, knuckles straining white against her skin. She licked her lips, and a thin string of spittle dripped from her chin.

"Amity?" I eased back several steps.

Grinding her teeth, eyes rolling, she ignored me. She flung herself against the cage's bars, and the whole contraption rattled. She howled, obviously outraged. Dr. Dwivedi shook himself, recovering his composure, and hurried to clean the blood spill.

Erik scurried to help him.

Clang! Amity threw herself against the cage again.

"I thought her kind didn't like your blood," I said to Erik.

He looked at me with a stunned expression, eyes wide. "I said they're more inclined to ignore me than compared to other people. But blood is blood. I don't think they're all that picky when it comes down to it."

"Sera, put the cover over her," Dwivedi said, pointing at the cage. "It will calm her."

I yanked the canvas sheet over the top of the cage, but before I let it drop between us, Amity's eyes turned on me. I searched for a sign, a glint of something human. Instead, she growled and lunged, her teeth chomping with a ghastly crack.

I dropped the cloth, and moments later, she went silent. "She looked like she was doing better," I said sadly.

"She *is* doing better, physically." Dwivedi rose from his knees, clutching a bloody rag. Erik took it from him and deposited it in a metal bin marked for the incinerator. "But I've seen no improvement in her mind. I fear that part of her is not regenerating like her body. In that sense, I'm afraid the cure may have failed."

"Are you going to keep treating her?"

Dwivedi nodded. "'As long as the heart beats, as long as the body and soul keep together, I cannot admit that any creature endowed with a will has need to despair of life.'"

More Jules Verne quotes. How apropos and unsurprising. Whether Amity was endowed with a will was still very much in question. Perhaps it would take a journey not to the center of the earth but to the center of her soul to find out. But who knew if she had one of those anymore?

Chapter 34: Life Is Pain

In the lobby, Parvati waited for us in the company of Corporal Baumgartner, who had buckled himself into his armor. They stood close together, obviously comfortable with each other's proximity. I would've speculated about the nature of their relationship, but Dr. Dwivedi arrived and gave us our departing directions. "Corporal, I have one favor to ask you."

Shep nodded and clicked his heels together. "I'd be happy to assist, Doctor. Anything to repay you and your niece for your hospitality."

Dr. Dwivedi arched one white eyebrow. "You can repay my niece on her own terms. But for myself, I am asking you to speak to Ms. Grimes and make her aware I have received word of her request for a new shipment of immunity serum. Tell her I will happily oblige. In addition, I will supply her with double quantity *if* she allows Miss Blite to meet with her sister for a short family reunion, and with no further obligations from anyone else beyond that."

Shep's darted his eyes to me then to Erik before returning his gaze to Dwivedi. "I will tell her, but I have a feeling she's not going to like it." Under his breath, he said, "I just hope she's not in a shoot-the-messenger mood."

Dwivedi pressed his hands together in a prayer gesture. Briefly, he bent from the neck and then straightened, squaring his shoulders. "I bid you all a fond farewell."

We made our goodbyes with promises to meet again soon. Shep and Parvati parted in silence, but it seemed a lot passed between them in a meaningful look.

Erik, Shep, and I traveled through Little Delhi together, but our paths diverged after several blocks. Shep settled his funny helmet into place before heading out on his own.

"Good luck, Sera Blite," he said. "I hope you know what you're doing."

"Same to you, Corporal. If you see Bloom, tell her I say hello."

Shep saluted and turned on his heel, armor clacking as he strode away.

"Where to?" Erik asked. He looked a little pale and tired from the bloodletting. I studied him, trying to determine what he was thinking. No luck. It was like trying to read a blank wall.

"I need to check on my garden," I said. "It's probably dried up and nearly ruined by now. I want to go home."

"Are you sure that's safe?"

I squinted at him. "The world hasn't been safe in five years, or did you not notice?"

"You know that isn't what I meant." He shook his head. "What about John Brown?"

"Forget John Brown." I marched in the general direction of the Savings and Loan.

"*Sera.*" Erik hurried to catch up. "You're on your way to getting your sister back. There's no need to be reckless."

"If you don't like it, then go home."

He grabbed my shoulder, swirling me around. "You're not going to treat me like this."

Stomping my foot, I set my hands on my hips. "And you're not going to tell me what to do."

His nostrils flared, revealing a hint of his irritation. "We're going to have this argument again?"

Snorting, I pulled away and started forward again. "No. We're not. I'm going. You do what you want."

"What I want is to be with you. And I think you want to be with me. You're more afraid of needing someone than you are of fighting an army of undead."

I spun around, preparing to tell him where he could stick his opinion, but he stumbled and fell to one knee. The extra blood donation had obviously fatigued him. A bolt of concern cracked the shell around my heart. Crouching at his side, I offered to help him stand, but he brushed my hands away and took a couple of deep breaths.

"See." I set my hands on my hips. "You need to go home. Get some rest."

"I will after I know you're safe."

This time, when I peered into his face, he revealed everything, his longing, his open heart. He should've known better than to do that. People who left themselves unprotected got hurt. That lesson had been pounded into my head since the day I woke up to find my father undead. It was reinforced the morning Bloom disappeared. Keeping myself guarded was the reason I was still alive, but Erik's persistence was wearing me down. And, yeah, okay, that terrified me.

"*You're* the one who needs protecting," I muttered under my breath.

"What?"

"Never mind." I tugged his arm, taking some of his weight as he stood. "Come on. It's going to be a long trip if we have to go at your pace."

"You're not the only one who knows the pain of loss," he said after we'd walked most of the way in silence. "I lost everyone I used to love and couldn't even blame it on some freakish, end-of-the-world disease. Not all of it anyway."

"You mean your family?" When Erik offered a personal tidbit, it was like gold to me. Better than gold. It was like a four-course meal with ice cream for dessert. He had said his mother died in childbirth, but he never spoke of what had happened to his father, and I'd never asked. Don't think I wasn't curious, but I figured it wasn't my place to pry.

"Dad and his brothers worked underground in the subway. It was dangerous as hell, but it paid well. Kept us living in reasonable comfort, as much as I can remember."

We walked another half a block in silence before he said the part I wanted to know most of all. "A cave-in got them. It wiped out my whole family. My aunts couldn't take me in; they had trouble enough feeding their own kids afterward."

"So, you went to St. Theresa's?" I tried to picture a young, unscarred Erik but couldn't quite do it. I couldn't imagine him existing before that day he rescued me from the undead horde.

He shook his head. "Not at first. I stayed with my grandmother for almost a year, but my grandfather had died the year before—from consumption—and then on top of that, to lose all her sons... I think the grief broke her."

"So, do you suppose she would have said it was worth it, going through all that suffering?"

He laid a soft hand on my shoulder. "Yes, I think she would have. She told me in her last days how she looked forward to seeing them. She said death couldn't put an end to real love, and she knew they'd be together again."

"In Heaven? I don't think I believe in it."

He blew out an exasperated breath. "Of course you don't."

We had maybe two blocks left, and I was looking forward to going home more than I'd expected. I wanted to feel close to my sister, to smell her scent and touch her things. "It sounds nice. But I've only found that hope winds up turning into disappointment."

"You have hope for getting Bloom back."

I huffed. "Yeah, I guess so."

"I once said you didn't let fear hold you back, but I was only partially right. Life is pain, Sera. But that's not all it is."

I wasn't willing to say he didn't have a point. If he thought I didn't trust him, he was wrong. But he was right about me being afraid. Not *of* him but *for* him. He wanted to risk himself for *my* personal mission, but if something happened to him, it would be my fault. Something horrible already had happened to him because he had insisted on being an accomplice to my shenanigans. I already carried enough guilt and blame and wasn't eager to shoulder any more.

He exhaled loudly. "You might miss the hurt if you never reach out to another person, but you'll miss all the good stuff too."

I started to ask if he planned to take up an offering after he finished his sermon, but we rounded a corner, and my gaze fell on the Savings and Loan building. Who would have ever thought a commercial building could look like home? I quickened my pace, skipping forward, but as I closed in, I noticed the fire-escape ladder was hanging down. I remembered shoving it hard enough to set it back in place when I'd left days before.

My stomach turned cold and sank to my feet. My heart jittered nervously in my chest. Erik brushed past me, but I grabbed his hand and tugged him back. "Wait a second, Erik. Someone's been here."

That someone was likely a vengeful John Brown, and I had a feeling I wouldn't like whatever was waiting for us inside.

Chapter 35: Girl-Shaped Pile of Ash

E rik pushed me behind him and reached for the dangling fire-escape ladder.

"Maybe it fell on its own," I said, although I didn't believe my own weak explanation. "I didn't lock it."

"I'm going first, just in case."

I rolled my eyes at his back but let him go without argument. At the first landing, we found Bloom's metal window shutters wrenched from their bolts. "Maybe you should wait here," he said with a pleading look.

I threw back my shoulders and gritted my teeth. "Like hell."

I shoved past him and ducked through the window into the dusty bank office.

"Sera, wait."

"*You* wait." I scurried up the interior stairs. After making my way up the access ladder, I strode onto the rooftop and found...

Devastation.

Using that word might've sounded like overkill, but I would have rated this assault on my home as one step past overkill. Over-massacre, maybe. Here was another word: vanquished. It described the state of my garden, my stove, my chance at winter survival.

Huffing and puffing, Erik appeared at my side. He tried to pull me into his arms, but I shoved him away.

"No!" Tears of scalding rage burned my eyes as I crossed the roof and fell to my knees. I buried my hands in the remnants of my garden, the scattered compost, the withered vines, the shards of broken planters. The tatters filtered through my fingers and splattered to the ground.

"No!" I shrieked, but before I lost myself to anguish, I pitched to my feet and dashed to the stairs descending to the bank vault and the little bits of home Bloom and I had stored there.

But our vault looked like a funeral pyre, a pile of black ashes and nothing more. Our cots, clothes, books, Bloom's instruments, photographs—nothing had survived, and nothing from that life would ever resurrect again in any shape or form.

I didn't realize I'd broken down until I registered Erik's scent over the smell of smoke. As always, he was there, holding me up. And there I was again, letting him. I freed myself from his arms and climbed back to the roof. He arrived several moments later but lingered in the doorway. For the first time, he was hesitant to approach.

"It's all gone." I gestured to the destruction. "Everything. Bloom, the things she loved and made, our garden, our survival. Nothing's left."

Erik leaned against the roof access door and folded his arms over his chest. "Bloom's not gone."

"She might as well be," I said, full of self-pity. I'd never felt more alone in my life, as if I stood not on the roof of the Savings and Loan but in the center of Antarctica with not even a penguin to keep me company.

"*I'm* not gone," he whispered, barely loud enough for me to hear.

But I did hear him, heard his anguish and dismissed it before allowing myself to acknowledge his hurt. I had too much of my own pain to digest at that moment. If that made me selfish and callous, I couldn't work up the will to care. "Don't take this the wrong way, but what good does that do me? I can't expect you to make up for all of this." I waved my hands at the remnants of my life, meager though they were. "This isn't your problem. *I* am not your problem."

"Oh, shut up." He said it in such a casual way, as if commenting on the weather. Still, I recoiled as though he had struck me. He strode across the roof and gripped my shoulders. "Just stop it. I'm tired of this act."

"What act? I'm not—"

He cut me off with one firm shake. Lowering his voice, he spoke each word with care. "It *is* an act, your I-don't-need-anybody routine. It's a thin suit of armor, a weak excuse for self-protection." His hands moved from my shoulders, stroking up my neck. He cupped my jaws, thumbs brushing my cheekbones. "I can poke holes in your armor all day long. All I have to do is wash your hair, rub the knots out of your neck. Dance with you." He leaned in closer and whispered, "*Kiss you.*"

My body reacted of its own accord, going hot and limp. My eyelashes fluttered closed as I leaned into him. Savored him. *How does he do this to me so easily?* It was his own personal kind of alchemy, impossible to resist.

"You're not as invincible as you want everyone to believe—or as much as you tell yourself you are. You need other people. You need *me*, Sera."

I opened my mouth to tell him what he could do with his need, but he cut me off with a kiss that dissolved my anger like a drop of salt in a glass of hot water.

Well, that's just fighting dirty.

His lips brushed over mine as he spoke, his arms sliding around me. "Yes. You definitely need me."

"Nuh-uh," I said feebly, my thoughts scattered to the wind by his touch.

He chuckled and kissed me again, and the last of my fight drained away in favor of warmer, lustier feelings. I didn't know about need, but I definitely knew about want. I wondered if it was possible to keep the two things separate when it came to him.

"Let's go home." Taking my hand, he pulled me toward the roof exit.

"How do you do that?" I asked as I followed him down the stairs.

"Do what?"

"You're like the Pied Piper. One kiss and I'm trailing after you, under your spell."

He chuckled suggestively. "I guess I'm a really good kisser."

I slugged him on the shoulder. He snickered and followed me down to the street. After landing on the sidewalk behind me, he caught my hand, laced his fingers through mine, and waited to see if I'd pull away. I didn't.

By the time we made it to his subway car, he was so tired he could barely put one foot in front of the other, and he required more than a little of my strength and support to barricade the garage doors behind us. "You're not as invincible as you think you are either," I said, leading him inside his snug little home.

Feebly, he shook his head. "Don't pick any more fights today, okay?"

After everything he'd put himself through, he needed to eat something and drink some sugar with a little tea in it, but he fell asleep before his head hit the pillow. Wrestling his limp form, I managed to remove his long black coat and heavy boots. He snuffled softly in his sleep. With his eyes closed and his face relaxed, he looked almost... vulnerable. Beautiful but completely normal. Not a hero, not an angel. Just a young man as defenseless as the rest of us. Well, mostly.

What must it have been like for him, finding sleep so easily when he usually had such a hard time with it? *Easily? Humph.* Walking I-didn't-know-how-many blocks after giving I-didn't-know-how-many pints of blood... no one should call that *easy*.

And he'd done it all for me.

I wanted to be mad at him for it, for putting himself out with no care for his own welfare. A loose strand of dark hair lay across his brow. I brushed it aside, and he smiled in his sleep. I wanted to resent him for refusing to protect himself, but I couldn't. I'd never admit it, but he was getting to me. I was starting to believe the things he said.

I stretched out beside his long, limp body, wanting to relax, maybe take a nap, but as soon as I went still, my outrage and anger returned. Memories of what I'd seen at the Savings and Loan shined vividly in my mind's eye, as if I were still there, seeing it all again for the first time.

John Brown's act hadn't been mere petty vandalism. It had been the destruction of my survival. There's a common saying you've probably heard before, the one that goes, "Revenge is a dish best served cold." I understood what it meant. I would've given anything to storm into Mini-City and pump John Brown full of lead. Wouldn't have felt sorry for it either. Unlike the undead, who acted only on impulse and instinct, John Brown had premeditated his attack. He had done it with terrific detail and purpose. Very thorough.

The living perpetrated at least as much viciousness as the undead. Maybe more.

I wanted my vengeance, but storming into Moll Grimes's compound hollering "John Brown!" at the top of my lungs would only get me dead. So I had to do something else with all my rage. Like the legend about people who died of spontaneous combustion, I needed to find release for my anger before I turned into a ball of fire and ended up a girl-shaped pile of ash.

Erik didn't budge when I rifled through his supplies and filled my duffel with ammo. Did Dwivedi's college provide Erik with his bullets too? Feeling a bit guilty about pinching his stuff, I left him a note. I planned to hit the street at the closest subway access and draw in the dead any way I could. The sun wouldn't be up much longer.

The dead would soon be coming out to prowl, and I would be there waiting for them.

Chapter 36: Lights Out

Things started out so well. Just by screaming and hopping around a bit, I attracted plenty of attention. You might call me foolish for going out on my own like that.

You might be right.

A dozen or so of the Decompositionally Challenged had fallen at my feet before one came along who had a boxer's build—a crooked nose from multiple breaks, scarred ear tissue from too many knuckles to the head. He wasn't John Brown, but I shot him in effigy, filling him with holes in John's place. If there was a chance for redemption for any of those poor suckers, I didn't care.

Not that night.

That night, I lived through my guns, and they were all I was.

I was Ready. Aim. Fire.

I was Force. Explosion. Penetration.

Some people drank to forget. Not me. I shot. And like an alcoholic, I didn't know I'd had enough until too late. Unless you've had an addiction, a vice of some sort, then you wouldn't understand what it was like to lose control. To let go of thought. To let fear, anger, and pain dissolve away, if only for a few minutes. If you hadn't experienced that, you couldn't understand how a perfectly rational girl could lose all common sense. You would judge me, call me reckless and stupid. So what if you had a valid point? It would change nothing. I still would've been out on that street, firing round after round, getting high on gun smoke and the sound of corpses dropping to the ground.

By the time the dead overwhelmed me, euphoria had filled me to the point that I didn't even care.

"C'mon, you rabid dogs," I said, taunting. They gawked at me with voided faces. "You've taken everything. What else do you want?"

They groaned and gnashed their teeth, those who had them. For a great number, their teeth had fallen out probably even before they died.

"Come on!"

Blam! Blam! Blam!

I pulled the trigger faster and faster, but fewer and fewer bodies fell, and eventually, my ammunition ran out. The bony fingers of one undead man slithered around my arm, pulling me close with remarkable force. Before he could bite, his head exploded into pulpy bits. I searched for the source of the shot as another putrid monster got a hand on my wrist and tugged me forward, its strength surprising me. Its slobbering mouth groped for my exposed wrist, aiming for the pulse point there.

"Sera!" Erik stood maybe twenty yards away, waving his rifle over his head like a banner.

The undead's moldering lips brushed over my wrist like a horrible parody of a lover's kiss. Contrary to how it appeared, I didn't actually want to die. So I fought, trying to free myself from its grasp, but its body tumbled into me, knocking me to the ground. Its rotten gums found purchase. One of the few remaining teeth in its festering mouth punctured the fat pad at the base of my thumb.

Aw, hell.

Screaming, I ripped my hand away, gouging my thumb against that undead tooth.

"*Erik,*" I shrieked as an explosion of sound and light rocked my world. The street's rough bricks dug into my back while everything else twirled round and round. Above me, the sky, the buildings, and the bodies of hungry corpses broke apart like the colored bits at the end of a kaleidoscope.

Then, Erik's face appeared over mine, and everything fell back into place.

"Quick," he said. "You've got to move. They've fallen back, but not for long."

I pitched my voice above the ringing in my ears. "What happened?"

He hauled me to my feet. "A shock bomb."

"A what?" My knees wouldn't hold, and I melted to the ground.

Erik caught me and tossed me over his shoulder. "A shock bomb. It creates a concussion that dazes anyone around it for a few seconds, but it wears off quick."

"Where'd you get it?" I wheezed from my upside-down position over Erik's back.

"Shep gave it to me before we left Dwivedi's place."

After a bit of uncomfortable jostling, Erik managed to get us both safely back to the tunnel near his rail car. "Can you walk?" he asked.

His shoulder in my gut had made for an uncomfortable perch. "I think so." He lowered me to my feet and held me steady until my bout of dizziness passed. "I think I left my guns back there."

He growled and turned on me with a black look. "If that's all they got from you, then count yourself lucky." Grabbing me by my shirt collar, he dragged me down the tunnel.

"Ow, Erik. You're hurting me."

His grip eased slightly. "Am I? Because I'd really like to tie you up and gag you right now. I figure this is a gentler alternative."

I thought better of making further complaints.

Back in his maintenance bay, Erik threw the locks and barred the door before turning on me with white-hot rage. His scars stood out in vivid contrast against his red face. I found no trace of beauty in him. His anger, however, was an awesome thing to behold, and I couldn't help cowering before it.

"What. In. The. *Hell.* Were you doing?" He gripped my shoulders. "Were you *trying* to kill yourself?"

"No," I whispered.

"*No?*" he mocked. "Because that's sure as hell what it looked like."

"Not on purpose." I hadn't intended to go looking for death, yet when it found me, I'd felt much less afraid than I probably should have.

He squeezed me tighter. "Everything you've done, all you've fought for... You want to throw it away?" Like a burst balloon, his fury suddenly dissipated, and he crumpled. He let go of me and sank to his knees. Sitting on his heels, he let his chin fall to his chest. "Is it me, then? Do you resent me so much?"

"Oh, God. No, Erik." My heart wrenched. I dropped to the floor in front of him and gathered his hands in mine. "No, no, no."

He glanced up at me, moisture glistening in his eyes. "I'm sorry, Sera. I only wanted to protect you. I never meant to force you. I didn't want to *make* you—"

"Now who's the one who needs to shut up?" I said, cutting into his attack of self-pity. Glad to know I wasn't the only one to suffer the occasional bouts of egotistical feebleness. "This has nothing to do with you. I was stupid and thoughtless, but I wasn't trying to kill myself."

He gave me a doubtful look.

"If I wanted to get away from you, I would've left. I wouldn't have started a fight right outside your front door."

His familiar scowl returned. "Then why did you go out there like that?"

I shook my head. "If I could give you a good reason, then that would mean I thought it over first. I didn't think. I just acted. I had all this rage inside me, and I needed to let it out."

Mouth falling open, he shook his head. "You foolish, ridiculous girl." He pulled me in for a bruising hug. "Next time you want to burn off some anger, take it out on me. I'll probably fight back, but at least I won't try to eat you."

I didn't resist his embrace. I wanted him—I knew I did. I needed him, too, and I opened my mouth to admit it, but a searing pain lit up the entire length of my arm, like my bone had suddenly turned into a bolt of lightning.

Color instantly drained from Erik's face. "What is it?"

My heart fluttered erratically, making it hard to catch my breath.

"Sera?" He searched my face then my neck and shoulders. "Are you hurt?"

I could manage a groan but nothing more. The pain climbed up my neck and across my chest. With icy tentacles, it lashed out, latching onto my heart and squeezing. Panicking, Erik tugged my shirt up, down, turning me around in his arms, touching, searching, and finally finding.

He sucked a sharp breath as he yanked my wounded hand up between us. "Were you *bitten*?" He ground out the words between teeth clenched with dread.

Dear me.

And then the lights went out.

Chapter 37: Kill Me First

"Sera. Sera, wake up!"

I came awake to Erik shaking me hard enough to make my teeth clack together. Instead of blood, fire now streamed through my veins, and the agony made me scream.

"I'm going to get Dwivedi. You're going to be okay."

"No," I rasped, my throat full of burning coals. "Don't leave me."

"I'll be back. Fast as I can. I want you to hang on."

I gritted my teeth, panting against the agony. "Hurts bad."

"Good. It means you're not dead yet." He stepped away and picked up a bag stuffed with guns and ammunition. "I'll go as fast as I can, but you've got to hold on until I get back."

My head felt like a perpetual explosion, as if one of Shep's shock bombs had detonated inside my skull then had frozen in time. It even hurt to think. "Be dead by then."

"Don't say that." Erik squeezed my arm, and his touch was that of a demon made of flame. I writhed and screamed. The sheets on his bed felt like puddles of acid against my skin. "Shit." He jerked away. "*Shit, shit shit*. I don't know how long it will take." Leaning over, he looked at me with a desperate face. "You have to still be here when I get back."

I shook my head. *Don't leave. Don't let me die alone. Not like this.*

"Wait for me, Sera."

"No good." My voice felt and sounded as though it had crawled across a bed of nails. "Won't work. Dwivedi's vaccine... no good."

Erik shook his head. "Look what it's done for Amity. It'll work better for you. You aren't going to die."

Jaw locked, I ground out a reply. "Won't die. Won't live either."

"Yes, you will. You never let anything beat you." Anger flushed through him, making his cheeks livid when I shook my head. "I don't have time to argue with you. I'll be back." He brushed his lips over my cheek, and I held back the scream his touch elicited. He must have seen it in my eyes, though, because he winced. "You hold on. Don't give up. Promise me you won't give up. Sera..."

"HOLD HER DOWN, CY."

"Look at how she's writhing. It obviously hurts her when I touch her."

"It will hurt very much more if she dies."

"*Get your hands off me*!" Shadows swirled above me, dark figures with infernal faces and hands of broken glass.

"Cy, please ignore her. Do as I say."

"*Leave me alone!*" Tongues of flame licked my brain, burrowing into the gray matter, burning everything to cinder and ash.

"Hold her arm. I will inject her now."

"*No. Arghhhh!*" Fangs of ice pierced my bones, sucking out my marrow.

"Quit fighting, Sera."

"*What are you doing to me, Erik?*" His fingers were razors, shredding my skin to ribbons.

"Dwivedi and I are trying to help you."

"*Then put a bullet in my head.*" Death was preferable to this agony.

"Don't say that."

Death would have been a release. Why wouldn't he give me that peace? "*Don't let me turn.*"

"That is exactly what we are trying to prevent, Miss Blite."

The devil himself stood over me, hoof planted on my chest, pitchfork buried in my throat. "*Erik, don't let me turn.*"

"I won't, I swear."

His breath was hellfire and brimstone. "*Kill me first.*"

"I—"

"*Kill me for real.*"

"Sera, don't ask me to—"

"I will not let you turn, Miss Blite."

I stood on the shore of a lake of fire, waves of flame lapping at my toes. "*Erik, please.*"

"What is it, Sera? What do you want?"

"*Don't let me fall in.*"

WHAT IS THAT SOUND? So much misery. Such pain, hurting my ears.

"In the name of the Father, and of the Son, and of the Holy Spirit. Amen."

What is that smell? Blood, meat, raw, hot. Flesh and bones.

"I believe in God, the Father almighty, Creator of Heaven and earth, and in Jesus Christ, His only Son, our Lord. He was conceived by the Holy Spirit..."

*Hunger. So much hunger. Hear it—*life—*so vital, with every beat, tha-thump, tha-thump.*

"Our Father, Who art in heaven, Hallowed be Thy name. Thy Kingdom come, Thy will be done, on earth as it is in Heaven..."

Blood. Smell it. Full of it. Coursing with it. Whoosh, whoosh, whoosh. Want it. Need *it.*

"Hail Mary, full of grace, The Lord is with thee. Blessed art thou among women, and blessed is the fruit of thy womb..."

Can't reach it. Come closer. Can smell you. Want to taste you.

"Glory be to the Father and to the Son and to the Holy Spirit. As it was in the beginning, is now, and ever shall be, world without end. Amen."

It's going away, leaving. No, come back. Dontgoaway.

So, so hungry.

Chapter 38: Eat Brains
and Be Merry

Finally! Blood in my mouth. But it's bad. So bad.

Sour. Bitter. Not the blood I want. Not his *blood. Smell his blood. Hear it inside him, in his veins, whoosh whoosh whoosh.*

Still hungry. Always hungry.

"Sera. It's Erik. You know me."

Blood in my mouth again. Want to spit it out. Horrible. Dead blood. Want his *blood. So alive and warm and* his.

"Sera, you're not dead yet. I don't know what it feels like to you, but it's not actually death. Not yet. I know you're suffering, but…"

His noise hurts my ears. Hurts my head. Shut it out. Shut it out.

"You've got to try harder. I can't ask you to do it for me—I know that's not reason enough. But fight for yourself. For your sister."

Bite him!

Missed.

"Sera."

Stop that sound, stop-that-sound, stopthatsound. Open my throat and howl. "Owoooooooh…!" *Scream until he goes away.* "Ahhhhhhhhhh-hh….!"

Scream until my lungs burn, my throat aches, my jaws creak.

"THERE IS ABSOLUTELY no reason why the treatment should not work, Cy. She has not technically died. Caught in some sort of *in-between*, I suspect."

Two bloods, two meats, two heartbeats. *Alive and warm. Want it so bad but cannot reach.*

Fury. Pain. Hunger. *Please... give me what I want.*

"Sera?"

"Eeeeee!" Scream at that word. Hate it.

"She does that whenever I say her name."

"How very interesting."

"She's still refusing regular food, but she doesn't like the goat blood, either."

Blech! Sour and old and dead. No life. No taste.

"I cannot say that I blame her. Regardless of her preferences, it is simply the best option at the moment. We must keep her strength up."

"There's nothing else you can try, Dr. Dwivedi?"

"Only time."

"It's been a whole week."

"Then wait one more. And another after that if you must. She still has not crossed. She still has not died. 'As long as the heart beats, as long as the body and soul keep together, I cannot admit that any creature endowed with a will has need to despair of life.'"

"WE'RE GOING TO TRY something new today. I'll feed you if you let me say your name without you going into hysterics."

He's here, he's here. It's him, it's him. His blood, whoosh whoosh whoosh. *His heart,* tha-thump tha-thump. *Want-to-taste, want-to-taste.*

"Serendipity Blight."

"Eeeyaaarrgh! Hate it. Those words."

"Try harder, Sera."

"Hungh..."

"Well, that's better I guess."

More old dead blood. Sour. Bitter. Blech.

"Yeah, this stuff is definitely disgusting."

Want his *blood. His flesh. His warmth. His life.*

"Sera."

"Argh." No names, only hunger. Only need.

"What's the matter? You need better enticement?"

Want his *blood. Smell it alive, smell it warm, red and flowing.*

"Sera."

"Humph..."

"Dr. Dwivedi said not to do this—that it would drive you closer to the monster inside, but I don't know what else to do. Please, you've got to try, Sera. For Bloom if for nobody else."

Bloom?

"Ah, your eyes lit up. You recognize that name, don't you."

Say it again. Again again again.

"Bloom is your sister. Remember her?"

Blond hair. Blue eyes.

"I've got something for you. Let me say *your* name without you getting angry, and I'll give it to you."

His blood. Gimme.

"Sera."

"Nuhh."

"Nope. You have to do better than that. Sera."

Hold it in. Hold in the anger. The pain. The rage.

"There. See? Not so bad, was it?"

Explosion in my mouth, so much taste. It's him. HIM. Give me more, please please please...

"No more today. You'll have to do better than that. Tomorrow, you're going to say it. You want to taste me, Sera? Then you have to ask for it. You'll have to say *my* name."

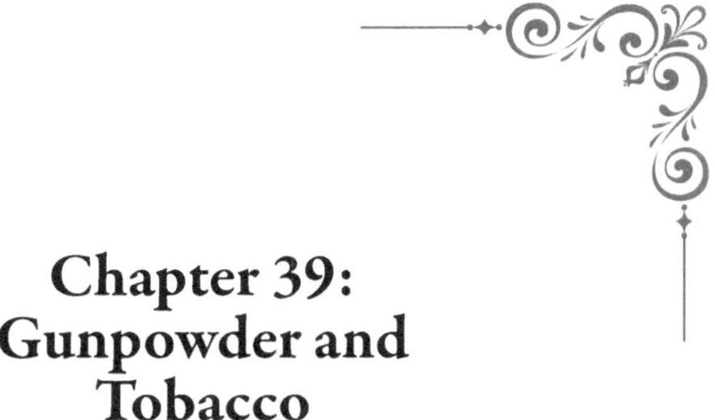

Chapter 39:
Gunpowder and
Tobacco

"Hello, darling." A tall man stood in the shadows of an empty room. His blond hair was long on top, brushed back off his brow, but silver at the temples.

"Father?" I asked.

"Who else?" He stepped closer and slipped his arms around my shoulders. He smelled like gunpowder and tobacco. I hugged him as hard as I could until I could barely breathe. He patted my hair and slid his hands down my sides, pushing me back to look at my face.

"What's this?" He ran a thumb across my cheek and smeared a tear.

I sniffled. "I'm just happy to see you."

"I'm happy to see you too."

"I've missed you."

He smiled softly. "And I've missed *you*. How is your sister?"

I sniffled again. "Lost."

Father tilted his head and narrowed his gaze. "What do you mean?"

"She's gone." I stepped out of his grasp so I didn't have to look him in the eyes anymore. "I've been looking for her, trying to get her back, but I've run into some trouble."

"I'll say." Father nodded as he led me to the table that had appeared nearby. It reminded me of the table from our old kitchen where we sometimes ate breakfast together. He looked as I remembered. Tall. Handsome. A little cold.

We sat, and he slid a cup of coffee across the table to me. "Tell me what happened."

I told him. Everything. Everything since the night he died. Everything, including my current precarious condition.

"Do you blame yourself for my death?" he asked.

I shrugged. "Who else?"

"Is it your fault I turned into that monster?"

I shrugged again.

"I would've made you like me. I would have turned you."

I barked a sharp laugh. "Apparently, it happens to us all sooner or later."

He shook his head and closed his hand over mine, squeezing so hard my bones ground together. "Not you. It doesn't have to happen to you."

"But it already has.

"What about the treatment? You said there was a treatment."

"It's an experiment. Who knows if it will work?"

He patted my hand and let it go. "You're still here."

"But for how long? I miss you, and I'm tired of being afraid all the time. I'm tired of being alone."

"What about this young man taking care of you? You don't seem so alone to me."

"Erik? I want to eat him up—literally. How is he going to take care of me when all I want is to have him for a snack? He's going to get tired of that pretty soon."

Father laughed and patted his jacket until he found his pocket watch. Flipping it open, he checked the time.

"Do you have to be somewhere?" I asked, miffed at his impatience. But it was so like him. Nothing could hold his attention for long. Nothing except his work.

"No, no." He waved away my question. "Old habits die hard."

I sipped my dream coffee. Cream and sugar, just the way I liked it. "I want things back like they used to be."

"That's not going to happen."

"Then what's the point? Why keep going?"

His brow crinkled, and the corners of his lips drew down. I dreaded his disappointment. I'd always needed his approval more than I'd needed air. "Despair is not your style, Sera."

I smoothed my hands over my face, trying to wipe away my exhaustion. How could I be exhausted in a dream? I didn't know, but it infected even the marrow of my bones. "If I stay here, I could be with you and Mother again."

Father shoved back from the table and stood. "What are you playing at, girl?" He ran a hand through his carefully slicked hair, mussing it so it fell over his eye like Erik's hair did. "You are not behaving in the way I raised you."

"How would you know?" I jumped to my feet on the opposite side of the table and glared at him boldly. "It's been five years. I've raised myself, fighting, surviving, struggling. I'm getting sick of it."

Father balled his fists, clenching and unclenching them, like he wanted to smash something. "That's part of life. Everyone has to fight and struggle for the things they need to survive. Nothing worth having comes easily."

"With all this free time on your hands, I'm disappointed you couldn't come up with something more original to say." I rolled my eyes. "Things were easier when I had you."

"That was *my* life, darling. You have to make your own way. Even had I been there, it would've been hard, but you would've done it. Growing up is hard on everyone."

Hot tears sprang to my eyes. "But you were supposed to be there to help me."

He laughed bitterly. "Says who? My father died before I became a man, and I did well for myself without him. Your young man has made his way with no family. Why should it be different for you? Why should you get to give up?"

"You didn't have to deal with an infestation of Man-Eating Corpses."

Father pursed his lips. "You obviously never attended a shareholder meeting at the Bloomington Arms Corporation."

I sighed a dramatic sigh and dropped my chin to my chest. "You have an answer for everything."

He rounded the table in two long strides and pulled me in for another hug. "That's what fathers do."

"Tell me everything will be all right."

He rested his cheek on top of my head. "It would be a lie."

"Say it anyway."

His body shook with a silent laugh. "Everything will be as good as you decide to make it."

"Do they teach situational philosophy in the afterlife or something? Where do you come up with these sayings?"

"You get your cynicism from your mother, you know."

"Forgive me. I've had a rough couple of weeks."

He cupped my chin in his hand and raised my face so he could peer into my eyes. "You'll make the best out of it. I have faith."

Unconvinced, I snorted. He pecked a dry kiss on the tip of my nose.

"Come see me again?" I asked.

Father nodded as his image started to fade.

"You don't have to wait until I'm in such a desperate spot, either," I said to his shadow.

And then he was gone.

Chapter 40: Who Wants to Eat Whom More?

Give it to me, give it to me, why won't he give it to me? No more crying, no more growling, no more whining.

"You're not trying hard enough. You don't want it badly enough, I guess."

I want. All I am *is want. I want him, his blood. What do I have to do?*

"Remember me, Sera. Remember yourself. Say my name."

No.

"Erik."

Blood.

"Say it, Sera."

Meat.

"My name. You have to say it."

Flesh and bone crunch crunch in my teeth.

"Say it, damn it. I see it in your eyes. You know who I am. I know you're still in there. I see you. Glimpses. Your sister needs you, and you're giving up! I thought you were a fighter. Bloom needs you. *I* need you. Don't leave us. You have to come back, Sera."

Anguish, pain, misery. Face is wet. Salt drips in my mouth. Want him so bad. Want his blood. Want him. Don't care which.

Go away go away. Let me die. This hurts. It hurts so bad.

"Say it, Sera, please."

On my tongue, a dab of him. A taste. I want more.

"You want it, don't you? How badly?"

It hurts. Remembering hurts. Blond hair, blue eyes, teeth, and fighting like two dogs growling in the night. Everything has to die. Why not me?

Bloom.

Father.

Mother.

They all go away. Why haven't I gone away too?

"Please, Sera. I love you. I'm not leaving you. I'm not giving up unless you do. And you'd better not give up."

Erik is here. Erik didn't leave. I don't go away because he keeps me here. He loves me? Why?

"*Please,*" he pleaded. "Say my name."

Streams poured from my eyes. Hurt flowed in those rivers, carrying pain out of my heart and down my cheeks into puddles on the floor. Such a big deal over a stupid little word. *Just spit it out already.* All this buildup for such a tiny moment. I didn't even want his blood anymore. I only wanted him. I wanted him to keep me and never go away. He said that one little word could make that happen if I believed him. *Do I believe?*

He stretched out, lying beside me on the cold ground outside his railcar, and closed his eyes. I shifted, and something rattled. Only then did I notice the cuffs and chains binding my hands. *That explains a lot.*

He took my fingers in his, trusting me. I didn't want to bite him anymore. He couldn't know that. He trusted me. He loved me.

Why?

"Erik?" My voice sounded as though it came from the bottom of a long, dry well. He didn't react. Maybe I had only said the word in my head.

"Erik?" I tried it again, putting more *oomph* into it. It burned my throat, but in a good way.

He sighed as his eyelids cracked open.

"Why would you love me?"

His eyes closed again, black lashes fanning over dusky cheeks. He had such a stunning face—a Michelangelo angel etched by the elements. His lips spread into a wide smile. "Because you're a fighter. And you never give up. You're smart and loyal and beautiful and courageous."

"*Wanted* to give up. Was very afraid."

"Everyone feels that way sometimes."

"Not you."

"Yes, I did. Every single day."

"But you didn't give up."

His eyes opened, and he gave me a look of tenderness. "Neither have you."

"How long?" I didn't have to clarify. He knew what I meant.

"Two weeks."

My head spun with the shock of it. From the day he'd saved me from Timber's attack at the river until the moment of the bite, barely a week had gone by. He had spent less than a week with me as a human but two with me as a monster. I shook my head, wondering how I could've merited that kind of devotion.

He sat up fast as a striking snake and caught my face in his hands. His eyes were dark and brutal. "Never do that again."

"Do what?"

"Try to leave me."

"I didn't try to leave, Erik. I just..."

"What?"

I glanced away, unable to hold his intense gaze. "I didn't know if it was worth staying."

"What changed your mind?"

"Hope."

"What are you hoping for?" He leaned close, his breath blowing over me.

"Bloom. I want to get Bloom back. And—" How could I lose my nerve now? After everything that had happened.

"And what?"

"And I want *you*."

His lips curled at the corners. His eyes slipped closed. "Say it again."

Lord, how I could've used a sip of water right then. Water, not blood. *What a relief.* "I want you."

"And I want more from you than that."

"Why am I not surprised?"

"You didn't come through all of that merely for want, Sera. Tell me the truth."

"You said I only had to say your name." I scowled. "Everything that's tumbled out since then has been gratuitous. I figure you owe me a big fat steak dinner by now."

He chuckled. "You want out of those chains?"

"That's not funny."

"I'm *dead* serious." Erik rolled away, coming to a crouch on the balls of his feet. He pulled something from his pocket and dangled it in front of me.

The key. "Bastard."

"You love me, Serendipity Blite. You want your freedom? Then all you have to do is say it."

"I'd say anything to get these cuffs off." I rattled my iron bracelets for emphasis.

"Then what's the holdup?"

Raising my chin, I howled his name like a wolf. "*Erik LaRoooux.*"

"We have moved past saying my name. Now you have to tell me you love me."

"I hate you." I didn't, actually. But I felt utterly exposed, and denial was the only self-defense mechanism left in my arsenal. If he wanted to torture me, then it was only fair I return the favor.

Throwing back his head, he laughed and slithered over to me, holding the key out of my reach. "You smell terrible. I'll unlock you *and* give you a bath if you tell me you love me."

I refused to look at him. "You're desperate."

"At least I'm not the one who smells like a two-week-old corpse."

"You're mean too."

He shrugged and waggled his head. "Just telling you the truth."

"Where's Dwivedi?" I glanced around the room as if I might find the wizened scientist hiding in a corner. "He'll let me go."

"Not due till tomorrow. You wanna spend another night out here—alone?"

I glared at him.

He laughed again before turning serious and leaning close. "You love me."

"If you're so damned sure of it, why do I have to say it?" I huffed, folding my arms over my chest. My cuffs rattled again. "Should I tell you the grass is green and the sky is blue too?"

"Pretend like I'm dumb and you have to explain it to me. You love me."

"Maybe." Baby steps. "But I don't like you very much right now."

He grinned. "You *love* me."

"You brought me back from the abyss. I feel very grateful."

"You looove me," he said with a silly, romantic look on his face.

I couldn't help but giggle. "I do." I loved him desperately. Vulnerably. But knowing it and admitting it out loud were two different things.

"What?" He leaned in, putting his ear near my lips.

"I do. I love you." And then I bit his ear. Not hard, mind you, but enough of a nip to make him yelp. Waggling my eyebrows, I gave him a hungry grin. "Maybe I'm not fully cured."

He unlocked my bindings. "Bath first. Then we'll see who wants to eat whom more."

Chapter 41: Open My Veins for You

Erik didn't own a giant porcelain bathtub with hot running water. He did, however, provide me with a galvanized washtub large enough to sit in and plenty of warmish water from a pot boiling on his brazier. He mixed it with a barrel of filtered rainwater collected from a broken drainpipe in one of the nearby subway tunnels. With his bar of sandalwood soap, I scrubbed away two weeks of accumulated grime, sluicing away spots and stains of which I never wanted to know the source. After setting up my bath in a dark corner of the maintenance bay, he had left me with a towel and a silk robe similar to the one Parvati had lent me when I stayed at Moksha.

I had vague memories of the days before. I remembered leaving the College of Kimiyagari and finding the Savings and Loan ransacked and vandalized. I remembered helping Erik into bed after he'd passed out from exhaustion. Everything after that...

When I tried thinking about it, flashes of smells, images, and urges assaulted me, none of them pleasant. As long as I stayed awake, I could keep it all from jumping out of the shadows and yelling "Boo!" I feared sleeping, though. *Oh, how I loathed those little slices of death.* I dreaded the nightmares that must've been lurking in the dark depths of my brain, waiting for the moment I let down my guard. Most of all, I feared that if I closed my eyes, I might wake up to find my cure was the dream and my near-death nightmare was reality.

While I bathed, Erik called to me from inside his railcar. "Need me to wash your back?"

A grin split my face. "No, but I hope you'll wash my hair in a minute."

His dim silhouette peeked from the train's doorway. "I'll get more water ready."

"A bath wouldn't hurt you either."

"I'll take care of myself after I'm done with you. Maybe you'll wash *my* back."

Tell a guy you love him, and he gets delusions of grandeur. It wasn't that I didn't want to put my hands all over him. He was gorgeous, flaws and all—especially because of the flaws. My knees trembled and my hands shook at the thought of touching him, but I'd only just returned from my journey down the River Styx. *Let's take one thing at a time.*

Later, after he'd finished washing my hair, Erik sat on the edge of his overstuffed chair, and I sprawled on the floor between his feet. "I don't ever want to go through that again." He gently raked a comb through my damp curls. "I thought I would die if you turned. I thought I would ask Dwivedi to put a bullet in my head after he put one in you." He set aside his comb, took my hand, and squeezed until my knuckles creaked. "You can't risk it. Never again."

The look on his face, the desperation and horror, the pain... it broke me a little. There was no way I could guarantee him that I'd never take another risk. Our world didn't work like that, and he knew it. But after all I'd been through, after all I'd put *him* through, I wasn't anxious to face the Preternaturally Dead anytime soon. So there was no point in arguing. Yet.

"What's for dinner?" I asked, changing the subject. My stomach gave a convincing rumble.

He exhaled, obviously relieved to have avoided a fight. "What do you want?"

"Roasted marrow, beef carpaccio, blood aspic." I named all the goriest dishes I could think of.

He studied me, eyes narrowed, probably trying to determine if I was joking or not.

"What did you feed me anyway?" I asked. "I only remember that whatever it was, it tasted horrible."

He winced. "You don't want to know."

I searched for a clue on his face. He'd pressed his lips into a thin line and picked at a loose thread on his cuff.

"Okay," I said. "I won't ask."

Eclectic best described the average Solo Practitioner's diet. With a plate of steaming rice, lentils, and scrambled quail eggs, Erik and I settled onto the floor for a picnic. We ate in silence for a while before I asked my next question.

"Is there news of my sister?" Had my temporary vacation from sanity interfered with the plans we had begun to put in place with Moll Grimes?

He sat up straighter. "I forgot all about it. Moll agreed to let you see Bloom. We told her you came down with a fever and needed time to recuperate. She agreed to set up a meeting when you felt better."

"Just like that? That easily?"

Erik's face flushed, and his gaze dropped to somewhere around my shoulders.

"What is it?"

"She raised the asking price."

"Meaning..."

"Dwivedi had to make an extra batch of the immunity serum."

I tilted my head and quirked an eyebrow. "You gave more blood?"

He fiddled with the pile of rice on his plate, still avoiding my gaze. "I'd open every one of my veins for you."

I dropped my fork and snatched his hand, stretching out his arm. He'd rolled up his shirtsleeves, and the pale remnant of a bruise lingered in the bend of his elbow—evidence of where Dwivedi had stuck the needle. For an instant, I had the urge to put my teeth there and taste him, but I shook it off. "Don't say things like that. It makes me uncomfortable."

He glanced up at me and blinked. "Why?"

"I want you to take care of yourself, too, is all. It does neither of us any good if you wind up sick or worse because you were trying to help me."

He leaned over and kissed my cheek. "We'll have to take care of each other then."

RECLINING BESIDE ME in bed, Erik's elbow was bent, his head resting in his hand as he gazed at me. A suggestive smile played on his lips. "Hello, beautiful."

Unable to form a reply, I smiled back. Overwhelmed by need, I couldn't shape coherent words. Instead, I pulled him in for a kiss. At first, he was an enthusiastic participant, but as I pressed against him, harder, more demanding, he pushed me away.

"Sera, wait. Slow down a little." He wiped a finger across his lip, and it came away smeared with blood.

Before he could protest, I grabbed his finger and popped it into my mouth, licking it clean.

"Sera, stop."

I didn't want to stop. He tasted so good. Catching his face in my hands, I drew him close and licked the blood from the wound on his lip. He fought me, struggling, squirming, but I didn't let go.

"*No, Sera.*"

His strength couldn't overcome mine, though he fought hard. I pushed him down, putting my weight on him so he couldn't get away. I wanted to taste him. Wanted to eat him alive. My teeth latched on to his lip, and he screamed as I tore into the tender flesh...

"Sera." Erik shook me until I came to. "You're having a bad dream. *Wake up.*"

The fire in the brazier cast a dim orange light, and shadows danced around the train car like hellish fiends. Heart racing, pulse pounding, hands shaking, I put my fingers to Erik's face, exploring every feature, verifying he was no more damaged than he had been when I'd fallen asleep next to him.

"I was afraid of this." He hugged me hard to his chest.

"You?" I sniffed. "You didn't have to see it. Didn't have to *feel* it." Sitting up, I pushed him away, shame and horror falling over me like a moldering blanket.

"Oh, I felt it." He tugged me back into his embrace and kneaded my neck, rubbing away the strain. "Your panic was shaking the whole room."

Surrendering to the magic of his touch, I burrowed my face into the crook of his neck. "I'm not sure it was panic."

"What was it then?"

"You don't want to know."

"Tell me about it?"

I shook my head. "No. Too horrible."

"Sometimes talking helps exorcise the demons."

I nuzzled his throat, kissing him, hoping to distract him. He reacted as I intended, scooting down so he could put his lips to mine. But that reminded me too much of my nightmare, so I pulled away.

His brows knitted. "What's the matter?"

"Can you just hold me for a little bit, until I fall back asleep?"

Turning me in his arms, he pressed close so that his body molded against mine. He folded his arms around me and buried his face in my hair. His warm breath puffed on my neck. "All night if you'll let me."

Chapter 42: A Scientific Breakthrough

"A miraculous recovery. A scientific breakthrough of epic pro-portions. How I wish I had a medical journal to publish the results like we used to in the Time Before."

Inside the confines of Erik's train car, Dr. Dwivedi had given me a full physical exam and granted me a clean bill of health. He had taken blood samples, listened to my heartbeat, and peered into my eyes and down my throat. He'd checked for a fever with a mercury thermometer and even went so far as to snip a sample of my hair, saying he wanted to look at it under his microscope. His glee was obvious in the tone of his voice and the sparkle in his eyes.

"There's so much more I want to ask you about the mental reper-cussions of your sickness. I could spend hours asking you questions."

I waved him off. "Oh, no, you couldn't. I remember almost noth-ing, and that's the way I want to keep it."

The alchemist's smile dimmed. "Erik tells me you had a night-mare."

I rolled my eyes. "Some people have big mouths."

"I would like you to write it down, at least, if you will not speak of it. There may be a time when you feel more comfortable about ex-amining your experience. It would help if you took notes."

"Maybe," I said, unwilling to make a promise.

"Please." He pressed his hands together. "For posterity's sake."

"Posterity?"

"Think of how many others can be saved, future generations. I think a new era is about to begin, Miss Blite. You can help with that."

Erik had been pacing outside the train car, giving me privacy while Dr. Dwivedi had looked me over, top to bottom. Now that the exam was concluded, I flipped aside the door curtain and waved Erik in. He settled beside me on the bed, taking my hand in his.

"What about Amity? How is she doing?" I asked.

Dwivedi had been packing up his medical implements, but he paused. "She is lingering."

"Explain, please."

He closed his medical case and took a seat in the chair in the corner across from us. "It is as though she has reached a plateau. She made massive improvements in the beginning, but now she has simply stopped. She will eat prepared food if offered nothing else, but she still prefers blood, and human is best. She sits quietly most of the time, but she does not respond to conversation or any other stimuli such as changes in sound or lighting or temperature."

"Her soul is gone," I said.

He waggled his head side to side. "It would appear that is true."

"And your cure can't bring that back."

His head wagged again. "That also would appear to be true."

"But it worked on me because you gave it to me before I officially kicked the bucket?"

"Kicked the bucket?" His fuzzy white eyebrows sprang up in question.

"I didn't actually die, right?"

He nodded. "Correct."

"So my soul, or whatever you want to call it, never left my body."

"Something like that."

"So maybe we can't cure the already dead, but we can cure the ones on their way to being turned?"

Dwivedi's head dropped against the back of his chair as he closed his eyes. "That is my hope."

I glanced at Erik, who was watching me with a guarded look. "So maybe there was nothing I could've done for my father after all."

"You gave him peace," Erik said. "You wouldn't have wanted him to live that way. I didn't really know him, but I suspect he wouldn't have wanted to live that way."

Chills slithered from the bottom of my spine to the top of my skull. Maybe I didn't remember particulars, but the aftereffects of my sickness had left me with a hangover. The hangover from hell. The hangover Lucifer felt the morning after he fell from Heaven. I didn't have to remember specifics to know that whatever had made me feel that way had been tortuous and agonizing.

Worse than that, even, but my vocabulary wasn't big enough to provide the words for it. Now, more than ever, I wanted to continue killing the undead. Not for vengeance but to stop their suffering. Maybe they had no awareness of their pain—the death they experienced before unnatural resurrection may have provided them that one small mercy. But I was aware of their agony now, and on their behalf, I couldn't bear it.

"What are you going to do with Amity?" I asked.

"I have incrementally lowered her doses. At the end of the week, she will be completely off the treatment."

"What will happen then?"

Dr. Dwivedi's whole body seemed to slump, and he looked older and much more tired than usual. "I do not know, Miss Blite. This is science no one has ever dealt with before. Even with her reduced dosing, she has not regressed or degenerated. My hope is she simply remains as she is. She seems comfortable, at least. Less anguished."

"That's something, I guess."

We sat in silence for a bit, thinking of Amity. Dr. Dwivedi eventually scooted to the edge of his seat and rubbed his face as if clearing away his dejection. "I have sent word through my niece to Ms. Grimes about your recovery. I hope to hear something from her about your meeting with your sister."

"Parvati?" Erik asked. "How does she know Moll?"

"She does not." Dwivedi rose from his seat with a glint of amusement on his face. He collected his black medical bag and shuffled toward the doorway curtain. "But she has become quite fond of your friend, the corporal."

"Shep?" I thought I'd noticed something between them when we'd left the college weeks before. Apparently, life hadn't paused for everyone else just because it had taken a break from me.

"Yes, Shep. Like a name for a dog, do you think?" Dwivedi huffed. "Anyway, they have been spending time together. He is due to visit us this afternoon, I believe, and I asked Parvati to pass the message to him."

"Can we come visit you soon?" I followed him through the doorway. A few young people from the college were waiting at the head of the garage to escort him home. "I'd also like to see Amity."

Dwivedi bowed and straightened with his hands pressed together. "Anytime, my dear. You are always welcome."

"Parvati and Shep?" I said to Erik once Dwivedi had departed. "Who would have seen that coming?"

Erik's nose wrinkled. "There's no accounting for taste."

"He's handsome enough, but he's lacking something in the charm department."

He slid his arms around me. "I'm sure people would say you're absurd for shacking up with a one-eyed recluse."

"You're not reclusive. You have friends, and you have me." I leaned into his embrace. "Are we shacking up?"

"What else would you call it?"

I glanced about his elegantly appointed quarters, the big bed, the lush fabrics and tapestries, the thick carpets, the stained-glass lamps. "This is certainly no shack. Maybe we're training up. Or rail car squatting."

"You can call it whatever you want as long as you share it with me."

I pretended to gag, but he silenced me with a kiss.

Chapter 43: Family Un-reunion

I knew doodly-squat about mechanics or electricity, but Moll's big piece of equipment at the river had grown. Even to my ignorant eyes, it looked more complete. Moll had chosen the construction site for my meeting with Bloom, and after discussing it with Erik, we could think of no reason to disagree. Sure, there were better places, somewhere more protected and secure from predators, but in the bright light of high noon, and with some of Dwivedi's finest young men and women accompanying us, we decided taking chances with the undead seemed like the lesser of two evils. The greater evil was instigating a disagreement with Moll Grimes.

Erik insisted I chug down as much immunity serum as I could stomach, just in case. All the way to the meeting place, we argued about his tendency toward overprotection and mine toward impetuousness. We hadn't stopped arguing by the time we arrived at the generator site and found Bloom, accompanied by Shep, waiting for us.

Bloom's presence hit me like a shotgun slug. I didn't think. I only reacted, running for her, tears already flooding my eyes.

"*Bloom.*" I launched myself at her.

She caught me and stumbled a few steps back. Saying nothing for a few heartbeats, she held me and snuffled in my ear. "Hello, darling," she finally said into the top of my head, pressing her words into my hair. "I've missed you.

Pulling away, I slugged her shoulder. "Where the hell have you been? Do you know what I've been through? How could you leave me like that? I ought to—"

"Sera." She gathered my hands between her own. "I know. I know what you've been through. Shep's told me everything. I never meant for any of this to happen."

I glanced at Shep, who had the decency to stare at his boots. "Everything?" I lowered my voice to a whisper. "But he couldn't have told you about the..." I could barely say it. "The bite." Turning my hands, I revealed the wound at the base of my thumb that had been stubborn to heal.

Bloom's voice cracked as she peered at the evidence of what I'd been through. "Yes. He told me."

"How'd he even know about it?"

"He's been spending a lot of time at the college, I gather."

I clicked my tongue and huffed. "Parvati."

"Is that her name?" Bloom chuckled. "He won't say much to anyone about her."

I waved my hand, swiping away those incidental matters. "What happened to you, Bloom? Where have you *been*? Dwivedi's going to help me get you out of Moll's place. We have a plan with—"

"Sera." She squeezed my hands, interrupting me again. "There are some things I need to tell you. Can you listen for a bit?" She leaned in and raised her eyebrows. "Listen with an open mind and try not to get mad?"

Cold foreboding drip-dripped down my spine. Stepping back, I pulled free from her and set my hands on my hips. "I don't know. Depends on what you're going to say."

Bloom's gaze shifted. Something behind me had caught her attention. "You're Erik?" She stepped forward, offering her hand for a shake.

Erik hesitated but then clasped Bloom's hand and returned a bold stare. "Erik LeRoux."

Shep had probably told her all about Erik in advance. Bloom's gaze briefly lingered on his scars before moving on. "You're the one I have to thank for saving my sister."

"I wish I wouldn't have had to," Erik said. "It never should've happened."

Sera squinted at him, wondering if Erik's statement was commentary on Bloom's failings as an older sister.

"Well, I owe you. Big time," Bloom said.

He shook his head. "I didn't do it for you."

Bloom snorted. "I heard it was like that. Wouldn't have believed it if I didn't see it for myself." She turned to me, both eyebrows arched. "He's the one, huh?"

"The one?" I asked.

"You love him?"

I rolled my eyes. "How's that any of your business?"

"I don't want to leave you alone, Sera."

"You're not leaving me. We're going to get you out."

"No." Bloom put her hands on my shoulders and leaned down so we met eye to eye. "You're not."

"You don't think I can? Because I'm not on my own. I've got Erik and Dwivedi's college to help me."

She gave me a crooked smile, half happy, half sad. "I'm so proud of how you've managed. I was worried for you, but I should've known better. You're a survivor. I'm a survivor, too, Sera. I don't need to be rescued."

"And why not?" I crossed my arms over my chest and glared.

She opened her mouth, but no words came out. She made a couple of false starts before Erik intervened. "She wants to stay with Moll," he said.

Ludicrous. Ridiculous. Preposterous. I chuckled at the absurdity of Erik's assumption. "No, she doesn't." Shaking my head, I frowned. "You don't want to stay with Moll, do you, Bloom? She'll own you. You know that."

My sister raised a hand to my cheek, stilling me. "I don't mind being owned. I'm full and safe, and I have a job doing something that matters. I don't have to struggle anymore."

"But—" I faltered, stung by her rebuff. "I've been struggling *for* you. Erik was bitten, and I almost died. For you. Everything I've done for over a month has been for you—to get you back." *Here comes those blasted tears again.* A mixture of salt and anger and hurt.

Color drained from Bloom's cheeks. She pulled me into her arms and let me pour my misery all over her nice white blouse. I heaved a breath, and it sounded horrible and broken. "You left me? How *could* you? You're my *sister*."

My fingers curled, forming a fist, but Bloom caught it before I could throw it. She'd taught me how to fight. She knew me too well. I kicked and spat and clawed, but she only held me and let me do my worst. "You just disappeared. No note, no warning." Tears streamed down my face and dripped from my chin as I railed against her. "I didn't know if you were dead or alive."

My bout with the Dead Disease had robbed me of my stamina, so I gave out quickly. I slumped against Bloom, and she rubbed my back while the last of my emotions drained away.

"I don't have the words," she said, "to explain my regret for what you've been through, but you have to believe I didn't want to leave you."

"But you *did*." I shoved her away. Suddenly, her touch was unbearable. I needed to stand on my own.

"Moll blackmailed me. She said she would take you, or worse, if I didn't come to her. I did it to protect you."

"You could've explained that to me. You didn't have to leave me like that, with no word."

"Would you have let me go?" Her gaze hardened. "If I'd left a note, would you have believed my words? Would you have just let me walk into Mini City without starting a fight, with me or with Moll?"

I shoved her hard, not wanting to hear what she was saying. Because what she was saying was too much. Too cruel. Too selfish.

"I could've tried telling you. But you wouldn't have wanted to hear it. Leaving was the only way I could convince you of my intentions and keep you safe from Moll at the same time."

"Keep me safe? *Safe?* What was safe about leaving me with no word? You had to know I'd come looking for you. That I would take every risk to find you. Safe would have been us leaving the city together instead." I stamped my foot and gestured vaguely to some place beyond the city. "You didn't have to make me let you go. Not like this."

"But you don't want to leave, Sera. And I didn't want to run from Moll and spend all our time looking over our shoulders. This was the best thing for both of us."

I didn't want to believe her, but I had always taken her word for granted. "You want to stay with Moll? You want to be with her more than me?"

Bloom's brow creased, her eyes shining with her own tears. "You're my sister. Nothing's going to change that. But the world still turns; people grow up, move on. The Dead Disease didn't stop time. I hoped you would find someone. Someone besides me. And now you have. I was never supposed to be your whole life or you mine."

I started to protest, but Bloom put her hand over my mouth and continued. "Moll might be a little overbearing, but she has plans to bring this city back to life, and I'm going to be a huge part of that. I've been designing infrastructure and foundations for a newer, modern world with things like electricity and engines for transportation. We're going to revolutionize this place."

"You're wrong." The truth of Bloom's confession was settling over me, and it brought me no peace. "You didn't leave for my sake. You left for your own selfish reasons, and I understand that, actually, but don't make this about me." My face crumpled into a snarl. "Own up to it at least. If you stay with Moll, you'll never see me. You're okay with that?"

Bloom's blue eyes smiled sadly into mine. Fine little crinkles filled in around the corners, reminding me so much of our father. "I'll see you. Maybe not as much as we'd like, but we'll work it out. Moll isn't sure of my loyalties yet, but when she trusts me, she'll give me more freedom to come and go as I please."

"How do you know? I didn't think you could trust her."

"I can't, but all that matters is she trusts *me*."

"I miss you, Bloom." My feelings of anger and betrayal didn't change that fact. "I'll always miss you."

She jutted her chin toward Erik. "You won't have a lot of time to miss me if you're keeping him company."

I glanced at Erik. He gave Bloom a stern look, eyes narrowed. "What's that supposed to mean?" I asked.

"If it's love..." She nodded toward Erik. "And, darling, it's written all over his face, then he's going to make sure the only thing you're thinking of is him."

Petulant, I folded my arms over my chest and arched an eyebrow. "How would *you* know?"

"Count yourself lucky to find that kind of thing in these times. It was rare before. Now it's even more so." Bloom took a deep breath and exhaled. "I had a girl when I was at university."

"You did?" My brows shot to my hairline. "You never said."

"Hurt too much to talk about her."

"What happened to her?"

I could have guessed Bloom's answer. "Same thing that happened to everyone, eventually."

"What was her name?"

"Natalie Anne. She was beautiful, and I wanted to be with her forever. I probably would have, but she disappeared like everyone else."

"Did you see her turn?"

"No. But I didn't have to. It's a pretty safe assumption." She nodded at Erik. "Take care of my sister, huh?"

Erik snorted. "Better than you would."

Bloom flinched.

"So... what now?" I asked, arms still folded across my chest, steam still leaking from my ears.

The generator construction site wasn't particularly picturesque, but we could've found a place close to the river to sit and talk a while longer, though I didn't really see the point. Bloom didn't need me. And maybe I didn't need her anymore, either. Maybe it was time to move on, let her go.

Before Bloom could reply, we were interrupted by the tromp of boots, the clank of armor, and a shout of "Oy! Bliters!"

My heart sank as, together, Bloom and I grimaced and said, "*John Brown.*"

Chapter 44: Scrap of Meat

"What's John Brown doing here?" Acid flooded my stomach. I glanced at the group Dwivedi had sent with me, wondering how far they'd be willing to go to protect me if this came down to a fight. I suspected it wouldn't be very far. They didn't owe me that much.

Bloom craned her neck, searching for John as her eyes filled with dismay. "I don't know, but it can't be good."

"My sentiments exactly."

Followed by a small troop of soldiers wearing the armor of Moll Grimes's Forces, John Brown strode from the shadows of a nearby warehouse. Several yards before us, he motioned for the soldiers to stop. Alone, he approached, closing in until he was close enough to reveal his arrogant smile. "The Bliter siblings reunited." He rested a hand high on his chest and curled his lips into a saccharine smile. "It warms the heart."

"What do you want, John?" Bloom set her hands on her hips and spread her feet. "The agreement was that I got to meet with Sera without Moll's interference."

"I ain't here to interfere with your meeting. In fact, Moll sent me to make sure you two stay together for a good while longer."

With his jaw clenched and fists curled, Erik lurched toward John. "Watch yourself, Brown. Moll Grimes has no say over Sera."

Brown's face lit up as though he'd won a prize. "Well, hullo there, LeRoux. Ain't seen you in a while. You got yourself fixed up with these two, have you?" His eyes flashed as a thought passed through his idle brain. "Awfully protective over Sera, ain'tcha? You got designs on her?" Brown clicked his tongue, expressing his disappointment. "What do you think a girl like her is going to do with a ragged scrap of meat like you?"

Erik growled and lunged to strike. I grabbed his shoulder and hauled him back. *Who's the impetuous one now?* "That's right, John. He's *my* scrap of meat, and I like him fine that way. So leave him out of this."

Moll's chief of security quirked a ginger eyebrow. "Desperate times, eh? I could have done you better, Sera. Ain't been all chewed up and spat out like that one."

Rolling my eyes, I sniffed. "Ever look in a mirror, John?"

Bloom stepped between me and John and glowered at him. "If you're here to take me back, then let's get going. There's no need to start trouble with Sera and her friends."

At that, the group from the College of Kimiyagari shifted forward, their postures menacing as if ready for a fight. John raised a hand, gesturing for them to remain in place. "No need for all that. Moll said to do this clean as possible, and that's what I intend to do." He pointed at Dwivedi's people. "You rabble will back down if you know what's good for you." He gestured toward his soldiers. "You ain't got nothing on twenty of Grimes's best fighters, and they came with a lot more bullets than you did, I guarantee."

Bloom bristled, baring her teeth. "What are you up to, John? Making threats like that. Why are you here?"

He executed a gentlemanly bow in my direction. "Ms. Grimes extends her cordial invitation to you, Serendipity Blite, to join your sister in her residence at Mini City."

I tried to keep my laughter contained, but a mocking snicker leaked out. "Are you serious?"

"Ain't a laughing matter, Sera. Moll says I'm to escort you back with your sister."

I folded my arms over my chest. "Well, tell her I regretfully decline her invitation."

Erik stepped closer and put a possessive arm around my waist. For once, I didn't mind.

"That ain't an option." John stepped toward me with an outstretched hand. Before he could clasp it around my arm, Erik drew his pistol and pressed it to the center of John's forehead. Moll's troops jumped to action, sliding bolts and shouldering their rifles.

"It looks as though we've found ourselves at an impasse," Erik said. "I'd gladly blow out your brains, John. Even if it means risking my own. My life is forfeit to Sera's. It always has been."

For a heartbeat, we all stood poised on the tip of violence. But then I decided to bite the bullet, metaphorically speaking. Curling a hand over the barrel of Erik's gun, I pushed it away. Moll's soldiers didn't relax, though, and I could tell they relished the advantage I'd just given them. Red in the face, jowls quivering, John Brown looked fit to explode.

"What does Moll want with me?" I asked.

John ground the answer between clenched teeth. "She knows about your brush with the unnatural death, and she knows about Dwivedi's cure."

"She does?" I glared at Shep, who had stood separate and silent through the entire encounter. "I wonder how she heard about that."

Shep wouldn't meet my eyes. *Coward.*

"Moll wants it," John said, "and she reckons your boyfriend will be willing to barter all of his magic blood to get you back. If that's what it takes."

"Take me, then." Erik shifted, raising his chin. "Leave Sera and take me. Moll can have all she wants."

"Huh-uh." Brown shook his head. "Sera's the insurance. You want her back? You gotta do like Moll says. You take yourself over to Dwivedi and make as much of that cure as you can. Moll will give your girl back when she's satisfied."

"And when is someone like Moll Grimes ever satisfied?" I asked. "What happens if I refuse to go?"

"Moll thought about that." Brown tapped his temple. "She's a real thinker, that one." He pulled his whistle from his waistcoat pocket and gave three short toots. From around the work area, several more men appeared, their rifles carefully trained on Erik, me, and the crew from the College of Kimiyagari. "Snipers," Brown said. "And these are just the ones you can see. The others put you in their sights the moment you arrived. You won't get a shot off before they blow Sera's head from between her ears." He sucked a tooth. "Now, play nice."

"Erik, listen to me." Realizing the futility of fighting, I tugged his arm until he gave me his attention, revealing his fear and resentment for John Brown in his gaze. I also saw his love and concern for me. "He's got the ace. He wins. For now."

"No, Sera." He shook his head. "I'm not letting you go."

"If you don't, one of us is going to wind up dead. Probably me, and I've already been there and done that. I don't want to do it again." Dead by bullet was a lot more permanent, and I was certain Dwivedi had no cure for it. "You almost lost me once—you won't let it happen again. I know it. Now that I'm resolved to loving you, I'm not willing to risk losing you either." Taking him by his jaw, I pulled his head close and whispered harshly in his ear. "Don't you dare do anything that's going to get you killed. You're right. I do need you, and I am not going to let it end this way. Please. Play along with this and buy us some time. We'll think of something."

Erik rested his forehead against mine, squeezing his eyes shut. "I can't lose you again."

"You won't. I promise." I pressed my lips to his, and he kissed me back. My heart fluttered into my throat, and all I could think was how I wished we could have more time. The sensation was so new, and I hadn't had nearly long enough to explore it before I had to let it go.

"Sera." Bloom's urgency broke us apart. "I'll talk to Moll. We'll work something out. I won't let her do anything to you."

I kept my eyes pinned on Erik, trying to memorize his face. "It isn't me I'm worried about."

Erik kissed me one last time before I gave myself over to John Brown's clutches.

Stoically, Erik watched as John Brown dragged me away. My last sight was of Dwivedi's men swarming around Erik, speaking to him with urgent gestures.

Then we turned a corner, and I could see him no more.

Chapter 45: Reckless

Surrounded by his small army, John Brown had escorted Bloom and me back to Mini City. With a greasy leer, he'd deposited me in Bloom's apartment and posted guards at the door with the promise to "give you what you got comin' should you try to escape." Whatever that meant.

Nearly a week had passed since then, and I had yet to lay eyes on that notorious villain, Moll Grimes. I halfway believed everyone made her up, like a bogeyman, or bogey*woman,* used to scare everyone into behaving. To have such an interest in my family, you'd think she would've had the decency to put in a personal appearance.

"Sera, you've got to believe I had no idea about this." Shep kept his voice lowered so the guards outside the door couldn't hear him. He sat on an upholstered chair in the living room of Bloom's little apartment on the tenth floor of Grimey Towers. Wringing his hands and biting his lip, he looked less like a pompous soldier and more like a puppy caught chewing his master's favorite slipper.

"You never tried to hide your ambitions with Moll from me." With a distrustful glare, I sat on an ottoman close to Shep's knee so we could hear each other's whispers. "Makes it hard to believe you feel sorry for me right now."

"That was before Parvati and Dwivedi's college."

Snorting, I rolled my eyes and tossed up my hands. "What is it about me that makes me look that dumb? I'm supposed to buy the fact you fell in love or something, and that makes you suddenly sympathetic?"

He scowled, and ire stained his neck and ears red. "I'm just saying, Parvati makes me question things, and I know when she finds out about this, she's going to kill me. If I ever want to step foot in her place again, then I've got to figure out a way to get you out of trouble."

"Who says I need *your* help?"

He laughed coldly. "Who else is going to help you? Dwivedi's people are not going to come riding up with guns blazing. Dwivedi won't put himself in jeopardy like that. Can't afford to lose trade with Moll."

I hated that he was right.

"And Erik doesn't stand a chance," Shep continued. "He might be dumb enough to come here with an idea of rescuing you, but he'd never make it. This place is locked up tighter than the gates at San Quentin, and Moll won't stand for any challenge to her authority."

I sank further into the ottoman. It all sounded so hopeless. "What do you think you can do? And are you seriously willing to give up this life?" I gestured to the apartment around us. "Because you know you'll have to run if you try to help me."

He grinned, and for the first time, I had to say it seemed genuine and born out of warmth rather than malice. "If Parvati will have me, then I say it will be worth it."

Cocking my head to the side, I gave him a questioning look.

"What?" he said, flinching back.

"So it's like that, huh?" It was what Bloom had said to me about my feelings for Erik.

"Like what?"

I had only recently discovered the ramifications of allowing love into one's life. It appeared that Shep was experiencing something similar. "You and Parvati. You got it bad, don't you?"

He ducked his head, trying to hide his soppy smile. "Yeah, maybe."

"If you got it for her like I do for Erik, then I suppose I can trust you."

Shep glanced up at me, his brows drawn with curiosity. "His scars don't bother you?"

"Should they?"

He studied my face like he expected my expression to belie my words. He could look as long as he wanted. *I know what I think. I know how I feel.*

He shook his head as if to loosen a thought. "I guess he's one hell of a fighter, and he sure seems to care about you. I hope we can work it out for you two to be together again."

"Aw, Shep," I said, thick and sweet as syrup. Irony was great camouflage to cover moments of vulnerability, feelings of unworthiness and doubt. "You keep this up, and I might start to like you."

The doorknob and lock rattled on the apartment's front door, and Shep and I froze while we waited for it to open.

"*Honey*," Bloom called in a singsong voice as she entered the room, "*I'm home.*" She carried a portfolio stuffed to the brim and studied another stack of papers in her hand. To better endure our forced cohabitation, Bloom and I had called a truce. I hadn't completely forgiven her for abandoning me, and she hadn't offered any more apologies. For the past few days, we'd coexisted in strained peace, mainly because we had no other choice.

My heart galloped in my chest, relieved that the intruder was only Bloom returning from work. Shep and I had kept our conversation quiet, but I took nothing for granted in that place. Sometimes I wondered if Moll had ears in the walls and eyes on the ceiling. She kept Bloom working most of the day somewhere in another part of the building. I only saw her when she came home to this apartment that had windows on the east wall looking over the roofs and broken faces of the buildings surrounding us. From this vantage point, I could see the river, and I imagined somewhere out there, Erik was waiting for me.

"Shep has come to make nice with me," I said.

Upon hearing that we had company, Bloom looked up from her papers.

"Hello, Corporal." She bent in a shallow bow. "To what do we owe the honor?"

He stood and ran a nervous hand through his short hair. "I've come to discuss something with you."

Bloom's eyebrow arched, and her gaze cut to me, possibly looking for a hint about what Shep was going to say. After I gave her a reassuring nod, she set her papers and case on the little dining table between the living room and kitchen. I put my finger to my lips, urging her to keep quiet, and motioned for her to join us.

"What's up, Corp?" Bloom asked.

"Moll isn't going to let your sister out of here as easy as trading for a little of her boyfriend's blood. So long as Moll keeps Sera, she knows Erik will keep doing whatever Moll asks."

Bloom's brows drew together. "What other choice does she have? I've asked Moll nicely. I've even begged. I've promised her everything short of my firstborn child. She won't budge."

"Sera's only other choice is to escape," Shep said.

Shaking her head, Bloom sank to her knees on the floor beside my ottoman and leaned in closer to us. "That'll never happen in a million years. Every inch of this place is watched by guards. There's no getting her out."

"I don't plan to get her out," he whispered. "At least, not at first."

"Then what?" Bloom asked.

"Yeah, what?" I echoed.

"What if, instead of getting Sera out, we let some of the dead in? More than some—enough to set this place in a panic. I can do it. Moll gives me that kind of freedom."

Mouth open, eyes wide, Boom recoiled. "You'd betray Moll but expect us to trust you?" She sucked a tooth. "Besides, it's too dangerous. Who's to say we won't end up fodder for the Rotters ourselves?"

Rotter fodder. Ha!

"I'm serious." Bloom frowned, noting my smile. "We should wait this out."

"Wait for what?" I waved at the city beyond Bloom's windows. "For Erik to bleed himself dry or get himself killed trying to come after me? I'm not waiting, Bloom. I don't need your permission. If Shep's willing to help, then I aim to let him." I poked her shoulder hard. Although Bloom had abandoned me, she hadn't actually *betrayed* me. Not yet anyway. She might have been selfish, but I had to believe she wouldn't actively sell me out to Moll. "All you have to do is keep your trap shut."

"We're all going to wind up dead or worse." With a grimace, Bloom rubbed her shoulder. "If you pull this off, who do you think Moll's going to come looking at first? You and Shep will be safely away while I'm left behind holding my hat in my hands and begging for mercy."

I was still mad at my sister, but I wasn't completely heartless. "Come with me then."

She jerked her chin up and looked down her nose at me. "I told you I don't want to go. I like it here."

"Well I *don't*." When Shep shot me a warning glance, I forced myself to calm down and lowered my voice. "This is a prison, and I did nothing to deserve it. If you expect me to understand why you want to stay here, then you've got to understand why I don't."

"We can do this without you, Bloom," Shep said. "We'll do it at a time when you have a perfect alibi, and there's no way Moll can pin it on you."

"You never told me why you'd risk yourself for Sera like this." Bloom leveled a menacing gaze at Shep.

Boldly, he returned her stare. "I got reasons for wanting out too. Sera trusts me. That's all that matters anyway."

Bloom looked at me, her annoyance carefully contained. "You trust him?"

Shrugging, I press my lips into a crooked line "I don't really have a choice, but... yeah. I do."

She sank back on her heels and wiped her face, brow to chin. "You two are idiotic and reckless." Inhaling deeply, she laid a hand on my shoulder. "I don't want any more bad things to happen to you, Sera. Are you sure you want to risk it?"

I opened myself to her, letting her see everything I felt. "Yes. More than anything."

She studied me for several more heartbeats, her eyes roaming my face. "What's your plan, Shep?"

He grinned and leaned closer, lowering his voice, so we almost had to touch noses to hear him. "First, I gotta round up some volunteers." He rolled his eyes over to me. "And I think I know just where to start."

Chapter 46: Blood and History

"Tonight's the night, huh?" Bloom asked as we looked at each other's reflections in her vanity mirror.

"Yeah, this is it." I put the finishing touches on her coiffure, pinning hot-ironed curls in place. Moll's people had found Bloom a clean skirt suit: a long, slim skirt, a lawn blouse accented with lace and pearl buttons, and a slim jacket tucked at the waist with long tails dropping past her knees. In it, she looked ready to command the world.

Side by side, we stood before her mirror, and the differences in our reflections were stark—her blond coloring contrasting my auburn shades. Bloom looked dashing. I looked a little less presentable, wearing my standard uniform of canvas britches and heavy boots.

This moment had taken a lot longer to arrive than I'd wanted, but we'd had to wait for an opportunity that would give Bloom an alibi. Such an occasion had presented itself when Moll announced she wanted Bloom to spend the evening with her, entertaining a group of bigwigs traveling in from other parts of the country. People didn't often make long-distance trips. The Resurrected weren't the only problem travelers had to worry about. There were thieves and bandits, wild animals, the weather—all the things over which mankind had falsely assumed we'd gained control. Also, most survivors were so busy trying to endure the day-to-day that they didn't waste energy worrying about events in other parts of the world. Visitors to our city were a huge deal, and Moll would do anything to make a good impression.

I can't wait to mess it all up.

Bloom and Moll's work crews had completed construction on the generator at the river, and tonight, they planned to crank it up and show it off. According to Bloom, they'd strung electric lights along the riverbank and planned to serve after-dinner drinks and smoke cigars under their artificial glow. The out-of-towners wanted to pay Moll to build them something similar in the cities where they lived.

I wouldn't have minded seeing the lights myself, but if everything went according to Shep's plans, then I'd be too occupied with dodging the undead and running away to worry about a bunch of flashy light bulbs.

"Shep already gave you the immunity serum, right?" Bloom asked.

"We have it under control. You just do your job keeping Moll away and distracted for as long as possible."

"How am I going to know if you're okay?" Bloom turned to me and gazed into my eyes. Her own eyes revealed what appeared to be genuine concern. Our relationship had fractured, but we shared too much history and blood to entirely give up on each other. I still loved her, but it wasn't the same naïve, guileless affection from our past, when I believed she could do no wrong. Now, I knew she was as imperfect and flawed as the rest of us, and loving her required an active choice on my part. I still believed she was worth it and hoped she wouldn't prove me wrong. Again.

"I'll get word to you one way or another," I said. "Dr. Dwivedi might help me."

Bloom inhaled and held her breath for a pensive moment. Then, exhaling, she rocked forward and pulled me in for a big sister bear hug. I hugged her back, hard as I could. Saying nothing, she dotted my forehead with a kiss, and then she was gone.

I glanced around the apartment, hopeful that this was the last time I would be locked within its walls. For Bloom, these quarters represented safety and purpose. For me, it could never be more than a prison. *It's finally time to make my escape.*

John Brown had taken most of my belongings before he locked me away in Bloom's apartment. Fortunately, I had left Erik's subway car that fateful morning with only my Colt revolver. I'd mourn its loss, but at least my rifles and other things were still stored safely at Erik's home. My home, too, I supposed. I had nothing to prepare or pack while I waited for Shep, nothing to do but pace and twiddle my thumbs.

It was the longest wait of my life.

A shout reverberated through the hallway, waking me from the trance I had fallen into. I'd been staring out Bloom's night-blackened windows so long, waiting for something to happen, that I'd nearly fallen asleep on my feet. Heavy bootsteps thumped in the hallway outside Bloom's apartment. I crossed her living room and cracked the door open. To my relief, it was unlocked. Part of our plan had relied on Bloom performing a pantomime of locking the door behind her, hoping to convince the guards I was still imprisoned inside.

A guard rocking anxiously on his heels spotted me peeking into the hallway. He stabbed a finger at me and scowled. "Shut that door, Blite girl!" Other guards scurried down the hall, their rifles seemingly primed and ready.

Ignoring him, I leaned farther out of the doorway. "What's going on?"

He huffed. "Security breach. Nasty rotten bastards all over the first floor."

Hand to my chest, I feigned shock. "But they aren't up here, are they?" I didn't have to fake the fear in my voice. The thought of fighting my way through the undead made me shudder and my stomach sour. Possibly, I hadn't fully recovered from my attack, and maybe I never would, but I intended to do whatever it took to get the hell out of Grimy Tower.

"Not yet. But get back inside before one of them comes to nibble your innards." Brow furrowed and teeth bared, he stepped toward me.

I ducked inside and shut the door before he asked again, hoping he was too distracted to think of locking my door. If he tried, I would have to fight him.

I wished I had my Colt, or, hell, even a sharpened butter knife.

A familiar voice somewhere beyond Bloom's front door barked a command. My pulse jittered. This was it. This was what I had been waiting for. Pressing my ear to the door, I listened to Shep ordering my guard to leave. "I'm here to secure the prisoner. Direct orders from the captain. You're to get down to the third floor and protect the other residents."

"Have you spotted any Rotters yet?" the nameless guard asked.

"No. They've been contained to the first floor. Now, go on and move out. Captain's orders."

"Yes, sir!" By the sound of his footfalls, the other guard had taken off running down the hall.

I cracked open the front door, and Shep gave me a worried grimace. "Let's go, Corpse Bait. I don't know how long it'll take for them to get everything under control downstairs, but we aren't going to get a better chance to escape."

"Is Erik here?" I stepped into the hall and pulled Bloom's door shut behind me.

"Him and a couple of other Solos I know from Livestock." Shep glanced down the hallway, obviously tense and eager to move.

I didn't know the details of how Shep had brought the dead into the building, but I knew he had needed a lot of help to do it, including Erik's. They'd had to find the dead, herd them, get them past traps and armed guards, then somehow entice them into the building. It had been quite the feat to arrange, and I was glad I hadn't had to participate in that part of the plan.

Shep and I paused in the hallway long enough to drink down a dose of immunity serum. From that moment, it would give us maybe thirty minutes of resistance to the Dead Disease. It tasted like death warmed over, but Dwivedi had guaranteed its effectiveness.

"I got you this." Shep offered me one of the standard-issue pistols all members of the Forces used. He dug into a pocket and pulled out a box of extra bullets.

I sighed with relief. Having a gun in my hand made me feel more like myself than I had in a long time.

"Ready?" he asked.

Chambering a round, I relished the satisfying click of gun parts engaging. I nodded. "Ready."

Shep shook his head, gave me a funny smirk, and pivoted toward the end of the hall. Together, he and I made it all the way into the stairwell before the gaslights went out. In the pitch black, Shep cursed. "Damn. That wasn't supposed to happen."

Chapter 47: Dying to Eat Us

"How many Rotters?" I whispered into the gloom.

"I can't tell," Shep said. "Damn, I need a lantern. Can't see a thing in this darkness."

Fear drip-dropped into my bloodstream. My heart battered my sternum. Dread puddled in my feet, then flooded up to my knees. My legs had frozen as solid as a marble statue. Nightmares pressed against the surface of my consciousness, clamoring to break free.

"C'mon." Shep tugged my forearm. "Nothing to do but fight our way through." He stepped forward but realized I wasn't following. "C'mon, Sera. That's the only way out."

"Sure, sure." I panted as panic clenched my heart. "Give me a sec, okay?"

"What's the matter?"

"Feet aren't moving."

"What?" He grunted an irritated noise in the back of his throat. "This is no time for jokes."

"Not joking, Shep." I grimaced. "I can't move."

He cursed again. "Dammit, Sera. You have no other choice."

Their smell preceded their attack. It was the only warning we got. One moment, I was standing there wondering if I should set up housekeeping in the middle of the hallway and settle in for a long stay, and in the next my survival instinct finally kicked in and I was exploding into action.

A bony hand grabbed my neck. Choking, I felt for the revenant's putrid face, avoiding its groping mouth. Shoving the barrel of my gun against what I hoped was its temple, I pulled the trigger, and the monster dropped without protest. After a burst of spark and fire from Shep's gun, another Rotter bit the carpet.

"Any more?" I asked, scanning the darkness as if I expected to suddenly develop night vision.

"I thought there was another, but maybe it ran off."

"They're not usually into self-preservation," I said as someone shouted, and a gunshot boomed from the end of the hall. Something groaned and thudded against the ground. "Guess that was the other one."

A soldier held up a bright lantern. "All clear up there?"

I shied from the glare and took the opportunity to study our surroundings and look over Shep, making sure he was okay. He seemed fine, a little panicky, but no obvious wounds. And, as far as I could tell, nothing else awaited us farther down the hall.

"All clear down here." Shep pointed at the body on the floor at the soldier's feet. "Thanks for taking that one down."

"No problem." The soldier's lantern bobbed. "Is that you Corporal Baumgartner? There's more down this way." He pointed down the hall in the direction from which Shep and I had just come. "C'mon, I'll lead you to them."

Shep shook his head. "No, I've got a civilian I need to secure first."

The soldier's head tilted as he scratched his temple with the barrel of his gun. "Then why are you taking her that way? Safe room on this floor is the other way." He waved in a general direction opposite the path to the basement door.

Shep gave him an embarrassed smile. "Got turned around in the dark, I guess."

"Well, come on then. I'll help you get her to the safe room, and then you can come lend a hand with getting these devils out of here."

Helpful Harry apparently wasn't going to take no for an answer. I gave Shep a wide-eyed, *what-do-we-do* look. He shrugged and started down the hall. "Sure thing." He grabbed my elbow, tugging me forward. "Lead the way."

As the soldier turned around to guide us forward, Shep lunged and, *thwack*, knocked him over the ear with his gun handle. The soldier grunted, but his eyes rolled back, and he wobbled to the floor like a pile of gelatin.

Shep knelt over the soldier's limp form. "Get his lantern."

"Is he dead?" My stomach sank. I'd been willing to risk myself—and Shep, too, if I was being honest—but I didn't want any human blood on our hands tonight if we could help it.

"No, but he's going have a helluva headache in the morning." Still kneeling, Shep rifled the soldier's pockets, taking a gun and extra ammo.

"We can't just leave him there." I gestured to our surroundings, which were clearly still unsecure and open to a resurgence of the undead.

Shep paused and glanced at me with one cocked eyebrow. "Why not?"

"What if a Crusty Critter gets him?" Lying there like that made him easy prey, and after the way he tried to help us, my conscience put up a fuss about leaving him like cheese on a rat trap.

Shep muttered something under his breath before yielding to my plea. "Bring him with us, then."

We heaved the unconscious body by his legs and arms, dragging him toward the basement access. Somewhere nearby, Erik was waiting, and so was my freedom. Knowing that made bearing the burden of the unconscious soldier much easier. As Shep and I tromped down the basement stairs, trying not to drop the lantern or bang the guard's head against the wall too many times, Shep called into the darkness. "Hey, LeRoux, you around?"

In the unlit cavern of the basement, a familiar voice answered. "Over here."

Erik stepped into the glow of our lantern, and I had never seen anything more wonderful in my whole life. My heart surged against my sternum as if trying to burst free and get to Erik before the rest of me could. I dropped the soldier's heavy legs and flung myself off the bottom step. Erik caught me and lifted his face to mine, greeting me with a relief-filled kiss.

"Um," cough-cough, "sorry to interrupt." Shep shined his light over us. "But could we save the romance for later?"

I hated that Shep was right. Getting safely away was our priority. There would be time to relish our reunion later.

"Who is that?" Erik let go of me and gestured to the insensible addition to our party.

"A roadblock," Shep said.

"What's he doing here?"

"Sera wouldn't leave him."

Erik clenched his jaw but nodded. "Okay. We'll dump him here. He should be safe once we secure the doors."

Shep folded the soldier's body into an upright, seated position against the wall and stepped away, brushing his hands together. After taking up the lantern again, he led us toward the exit. "What happened after I left you?" he asked Erik as we stepped into an alley behind Grimy Tower. "From the sound of it, it seemed like there were more in there than we planned on."

Erik snorted a wry laugh. "They just kept coming. We couldn't do anything to stop them, so we did our best to herd them while trying to stay out of their way."

The night wrapped around us in a humid cloak, and beads of sweat broke out along my hairline. We hurried through the streets of

Mini City while also watching for the undead and trying to maintain our stealth.

"Where are the others?" Shep asked, referring, I assumed, to the other Solo Practitioners he'd recruited to help.

"Keeping the guards busy," Erik said.

"Why would they help?" I asked. "Why take the risk?"

Putting a finger over his lips, Erik motioned for us to be quiet as we reached the corner of the building. He peered around and, finding the way clear, waved us on. "Immunity serum. Moll has a contract with Dwivedi to give her the only doses, but Dwivedi agreed to sneak some extra to the Solos if they would help."

I would have to remember to tell Dr. Dwivedi thanks. He deserved much more than that, but I had nothing else to give. "You had to give more blood?" I asked.

"I had to do it anyway. It was part of the agreement with Moll to get you back."

"Why do you suppose Dwivedi never gave us immunity serum in the first place? When he sent us out to get his lab rat, he should have given us some protection."

Erik kept his face averted. "First of all, immunity serum doesn't do *me* any good. I'm already immune. Second, he did offer it for you, but I told him I didn't intend to put you in the position of having to need it."

Stopping mid-step, I shoved my hands on my hips. "Why, you high-handed—"

"Not now, you two." Shep gave us both an angry glare "We don't have time for a lover's spat."

Again, I hated that he was right. "I'll never be able to pay you back for all you've done for me." I placed a hand on Erik's arm. "But all I ask is that you don't stop me from making my own choices."

He threw an arm around my shoulders, tugging me close to his side "Tell me you love me."

I rolled my eyes, but without hesitation I said, "I love you."

"I can't swear I'll stop being bossy, but I promise to never again prevent you from making your own choices." He plopped a kiss on my forehead. "Are we okay, now?"

I nodded. "We're all good."

Or as good as anyone could be in a city full of monsters who were literally dying to eat us.

Chapter 48: The Cost of a Sister

My escape seemed easy enough, right? If you had read as many dime novels as I had, then you'd know the moment you started thinking you were in the clear was the same moment everything went utterly to hell. Rounding the corner of the last building on the perimeter of Mini City, we came face-to-face with a horde of ravenous undead.

"*Shit*," Shep swore, oblivious to propriety. In fact, we each said our own share of four-letter words.

And then we started shooting.

I could've blamed our situation on a lot of things—the fact the Rotters had come upon us downwind, the belief we'd left our worst troubles behind at Grimy Tower, my eagerness to get alone with Erik and pull the safety and comfort of his train car around us. The reasons didn't matter, because regardless, there we were, surrounded by more of the putrid masses than we could possibly count.

"How much longer till the serum runs out?" I asked.

"I don't know," Shep said, worry evident in his tone. "Ten minutes maybe."

"Then we should probably count on only five more minutes, just to be sure." In all my previous encounters with the undead, I'd felt a healthy dose of respect and fear for them, but the emotions flooding through me that night felt like a million tiny ice picks, hammering at every nerve ending. Each pulse of fear screamed at me to shut down and curl into a ball, but I stomped down those urges and concentrated on shooting.

Pacing steadily backward, we retreated, keeping our guns pointed at the horde, aiming carefully but shooting as fast as possible. In the darkness, it was impossible to estimate the size of the crowd, but based on their stench, it smelled like hundreds. In reality, it was probably only several dozen. *Only? Ha!* The multitude pressed us toward the center of Mini City as though they knew we'd been trying to get away from that exact spot.

"Don't you know any secret passages out of here?" I asked Erik. "We could really use some of your Mysterious Rescuer skills right now."

"There's something about a block over." He gestured with his chin. "A grate that drops into the sewer. If we follow it a while, there'll be an access to the subway about two or three miles down."

"The sewer?" Shep asked, repulsion thick in his words.

I rolled my eyes. "You got a better idea?"

In the glow of his lantern light, I could see Shep wrinkle his nose and shake his head.

"Can we make it?" I fired two shots into the closest figures, taking down a man with a handlebar mustache and a nondescript fellow in work clothes that said he could've been a dockhand if not for the hole gaping in the side of his face.

"As long as the ammo holds out," Erik said.

Working together, we kept the fetid flock at bay as we backed down the street. Thankfully, the undead had only enough brains to walk and eat but not to plan and scheme. They couldn't use tools or fire guns. Their lack of awareness was the only reason anyone survived the Dead Wars.

Erik, Shep, and I were so focused on our slow retreat that none of us noticed that something had changed among the horde. The Rotters in front of us, including a shriveled man wearing a long braid and a quilted silk coat, kept shambling forward, but a larger group from the rear of the throng turned and shuffled in the opposite direction.

"Where are they going?" I asked between shots.

"Someone else is shooting at them," Erik said.

Relief surged through me. This was an unexpected break but also a very welcome one. "Who do you think it is?"

He craned his neck, searching in the distance, but either it was too dark or the shooters were too far away or both. "I can't tell."

We continued toward the sewer access, making faster progress once part of the undead crowd had been diverted. In the distance, shouts went up, followed by another volley of shots. On our side of the horde, Erik took out a small woman wearing the tatters of an evening gown.

"Shep, we're close," Erik said. "I think if you break and run, Sera and I can keep you covered while you open the sewer grate."

"Where is it?" Shep threw a look over his shoulder.

"About twenty yards back—it has a big iron lid."

"It's too dark. I can't see it."

"Okay, you cover me instead. I'll go open it."

The artillery on the other side of the horde sounded louder, closer. I could make out some of the words the shooters were yelling at each other.

"Sera," Erik said, "you keep doing what you're doing. We're almost there. You have to cover me."

A sour realization stirred in my stomach. "I'm almost out of ammo."

"If you give out, break and run, okay?" He squeezed my arm.

"Okay." I stopped and aimed for a boy, maybe thirteen or fourteen years old, his face sagging with decay, his pants ragged and torn. He lunged toward Erik, but I stopped him in his shambling tracks.

"Oy!" shouted one of the shooters from across the way. "Who's over there? You're heading to a dead end!"

That voice was vexingly familiar. I glanced at Shep to see if he agreed, and the look on his face told me I was right. John bloody Brown. *How does he do it?* He had a dreadful knack for showing up at all the most inopportune times.

"Don't answer him," Shep ordered in a loud whisper.

"I'm not an idiot." I jogged back a few steps before stopping to put a bullet in something that might've been a pretty young lady of means, judging by the style of her dress. Someone had bitten a chunk from her neck and ear, but she hadn't let that get her down.

"We're almost there." I gestured to Erik's dark figure huddled in the street behind us. "I have maybe two shots left."

Shep lifted his gun and pulled the trigger. Nothing happened. "Well, that's two more than I've got."

"Go help Erik then." I laid a careful round into a man who lurched ahead of the crowd. He might've been a blacksmith in a former life. His thick hair was dark, his beard bushy. He still had powerful shoulders and bulging forearms. My first bullet went wide and knocked him in the shoulder. He stumbled but didn't go down.

"Damn." I fired again, nailing him in the forehead. He took a few more uncertain steps before falling to his knees. He was going down, but if I'd had one more shot, I would've given it to him just to be sure.

"I'm out." I trotted to Shep and Erik's side and discovered they'd opened the sewer grate, revealing a gaping black hole that reminded me of a Rotter's mouth. Erik went down first to make sure the way was clear.

He called for me to come next. "I've got you, Sera. Just let yourself drop."

Crouching next to the grate, I lowered my legs into the hole.

"Serendipity Blite, stop right there!"

I looked up from my position halfway into the sewer to find John Brown holding a lantern and taking aim in my direction.

"C'mon, Sera," Erik said. "Don't mind him. They'll never catch us in here."

John read the decision in my face and whipped his gun around, pressing it against the temple of one of the members in his party. He raised his lantern, shedding light on the face of his unmistakable target.

My heart lurched into my throat.

Brown bared his teeth. "Make another move, Sera Blite, and it'll cost you a sister."

Chapter 49: No Pity

"Put down that gun right now, *Mister* Brown." An unfamiliar figure parted from the shadowy crowd, put her hand on John Brown's pistol, and pushed it away.

A brief sigh leaked from my throat.

"What's going on?" Erik asked.

"Shush," I said, not wanting to miss a moment of whatever was about to happen next. Shep was crouched beside me, preternaturally still and silent as if hoping to disappear into the gloom. John's shouting had drawn the dead's attention away from my party, and the small contingent of soldiers guarding my sister's troupe fired at the fray. Despite the soldiers' efforts, the dead continued their advance.

"You are replaceable, Brown," snarled the unfamiliar woman. She wore a glittery lavender frock that hugged her full bosom and complemented her golden complexion. Her black hair sat atop her head in a high pompadour. Shorter than all the others around her and small-framed, the woman still managed to exude power. "Miss Blite, however, is not."

If I were a gambling girl, I would've bet all of next year's crops that the small woman giving John Brown orders was none other than the notorious Moll Grimes.

"But Sera's gettin' away." John gestured with his gun in my general direction.

"That's not important right now." Moll motioned to the dead pressing in around them and the soldiers struggling to keep them back. "Your job is to protect *me*. We'll worry about the Blite girl later."

Bloom gave me a look, widening her eyes and nodding. She was telling me to go, make my getaway before it was too late.

"Shep, let's go."

I had just glanced away, preparing for the drop to the sewer floor, when a scream of pain and horror tore apart the night like a lightning storm. Every fine hair on my body stood up, and the ghost of a familiar pain ripped through me. That scream made blackness swirl at the edges of my vision, and a brief memory of being bitten sparked before my eyes. My stomach rolled, but I couldn't afford to swoon *or* vomit at that moment, so I sucked in a deep breath and held my composure with a sweaty, shaking grip. *Please don't let that scream have come from Bloom.*

"What happened?" Erik shouted from the sewer below me.

My vision strained against the darkness, but I could only make out a few dim figures huddled over a heap on the ground. Throngs of Crunching Corpses were filling in around them. Guns fired, people shouted, and fear for my sister lashed against my heart.

"We've got no time for this. Go, *now*, Sera." Without warning, Shep shoved me, and I swallowed a squeal as I fell through the sewer hole.

With a stumble and a grunt, Erik caught me. Moments later, Shep dropped down beside us, bringing his lantern with him.

"What was that scream about?" Erik asked.

"I think someone was bitten," Shep said.

Still in Erik's arms, I sobbed. "It might've been Bloom."

His embrace tightened around me. "You don't know for sure?"

"No, but I can't leave her." I squeezed Erik's arm, pleading. "We have to help."

"How?" Shep asked. "We're out of bullets. We'll make a fine corpse sandwich if we go back up there now."

A torrent of explosions and light suddenly rocked the street above us. The concussion blasted my eardrums and reverberated through my chest. Stumbling apart, our trio crouched, covered our ears, and waited for the attack to end.

"Shock bombs," Erik said when the silence finally returned. "Sounds like reinforcements have arrived."

"What do we do?" My ears were still ringing as I peered at the sewer opening above us and searched the small circle of night sky for a clue.

"*I'm* going to Dwivedi's college." Shep's head drooped, and he sounded worn and beaten. "I'm done with favors."

Erik patted his shoulder. "You've done more than anyone could have asked."

I couldn't disagree, but I also couldn't leave if my sister was in danger.

For several still moments, the three of us contemplated our next step.

"Sera?" A familiar voice shouted from the street. "Sera, where are you?"

"Bloom?" Heart surging into my throat, I sprang into the pool of gloomy moonlight streaming through the sewer opening. "Are you okay?"

Above me, Bloom's figure cut a black silhouette from the starry sky.

"Somebody screamed in a very bad way."

Bloom's shadow nodded. "It was Moll. She's been bitten. Badly."

"Where are the Biters now?"

"Ran off. Extra Forces showed up and scared them away, but the Biters tore Moll up pretty good first."

"Did she take any immunity serum?"

Bloom's shadow nodded. "We all did, at the first sign of trouble, but that was a while ago. Not sure if it was still effective when she was bitten."

I paused, giving myself a moment to digest that bit of news. Mostly, I was relieved Bloom had gotten away unscathed, but my pity for Moll Grimes was slow to appear. "What are you going to do now?"

Muffled voices argued above us for several moments before Bloom answered. "We need to get her to the College of Kimiyagari. Get her Dwivedi's cure."

Erik and Shep turned to me as if I somehow got to have a final say in the matter. "Why are you looking at me?" I threw my hands out and shrugged. "It's Dwivedi's decision."

"Should we even bother?" Erik asked. "Life would be easier without Moll."

He had a point—one I had a hard time disputing. Problem was, Moll served a purpose, like it or not. She kept order, and she produced hard-to-come-by products for trade—maybe at steep prices, but some people might've said it was worth it. As for her plans to bring the city back to life, who else had the resources and chutzpah to make it happen? Also, I'd already worn the pair of shoes Moll had just shoved her feet into, and I wouldn't have wished the curse of un-death on my worst enemy. Considering Moll Grimes probably *was* my worst enemy—not counting John Brown—well, then, I had answered my own question.

Taking Erik's hand, I gave him a beseeching look, hoping Shep's dim lantern provided enough light for him to see me. "No, we can't let her turn. Besides, if we save her, Moll Grimes will owe us. Big time."

"I'm not sure Moll keeps track of favors owed," Shep said. "She'd turn her back on you before she'd ever be in your debt."

"Maybe or maybe not. I can't have her death on my hands though. If nothing else, Dr. Dwivedi would appreciate having another test subject. It'll be repayment for all the help he's given us."

Giving me a grim smile, Erik nodded.

Shep sucked in a breath through his teeth, sounding thoroughly put out. But then he nodded. "Well, I guess I was going to Dwivedi's place anyway..."

Chapter 50: No Gods and No Miracles

Bloom, John Brown, and quite a few of Moll Grimes's personal guards met us several blocks away from Mini City at the first place where Shep, Erik, and I could exit the sewers. They carried the unresponsive body of Moll Grimes on an impromptu litter made of scrap plywood.

The light from several lanterns exposed the extent of her wounds. A rotting monster had bitten a chunk of flesh from her neck, and a large gash rent both the fabric of her dress and the skin beneath, exposing the tendons in her shoulder. She might've had more wounds, but I didn't need to see them to guess how she was feeling. Her countenance was haggard, and the hairs that had come loose from the pompadour fell lank across her forehead. She looked nothing like the queen of this fetid city but rather like and old, stained, and worn-out silk slipper.

She was quiet, as if sleeping, but it was likely she had passed out from extensive pain and blood loss. I doubted she'd survive long enough for us to deliver her to Dwivedi. If she woke up howling for fresh flesh, I vowed to myself that I'd be the first to put a bullet in her.

"How'd it happen?" Shep asked one of the soldiers supporting Moll's litter.

The soldier gave Shep a bleak look, eyes wide, pupils huge. "They came out of nowhere. One minute, they were under control, dropping like flies. Then, all of a sudden…" He stopped and swallowed. He coughed, clearing his throat. The memory clearly unsettled him. "All of a sudden, they were there, falling on us. More than we could fight off."

Our small troupe was hurrying through the city, moving as swiftly as a group could travel while toting an incapacitated body and staying on guard against further meetings with the undead. I couldn't see how another encounter could happen, though, because every living dead thing in the city had showed up at Moll Grimes's front door. There couldn't possibly be any more left. *If only that were true. There are* always *more.*

"Who threw the shock bombs?" Shep asked.

"That was us," said another soldier at Moll's legs. "I was with another unit. We came out of headquarters, chasing a group of Rotters out of Mini City, when we ran up on Moll and her folks."

"How'd this all happen anyway?" asked the first soldier, the one at Moll's shoulders. He gave Shep a curious glance. "We were down at the river at the generator site, and a couple of guys from the guard unit on duty at the perimeter of Mini City came flying up to the party, yelling about a security breach. We were on our way back with Ms. Grimes when we ran into you."

Shep shrugged. "It's a long story. Let's save our breath for the hike." When the soldier bobbed his head and turned his attention forward again, Shep leaned close and muttered in my ear, "I'm going to slip away and run ahead. Gonna give Dwivedi time to prepare for our arrival."

Nodding, I glanced at our companions, who could be as big a threat to us as the undead if they decided we might be the enemy. "Be careful."

John Brown had kept quiet throughout the trip, bringing up the rear and rarely taking his worried eyes from the wrecked figure of his esteemed leader. Erik and I walked together, separate from the main group but careful to keep them in sight.

"Will we ever have a moment of peace together?" He sighed sadly and gestured to our surrounding troupe and to our situation in general, I suspected. "Or will it always be like this?"

I shrugged. "I'm sure that soon enough, we'll be so bored with each other, we'll be begging for another adventure."

"No." He snorted. "I don't think you'll ever hear me wishing for a time like this again."

I poked his ribs, teasing, but he caught my hand before I could pull away and tugged me off-balance. I stumbled against him, and he threw an arm around my shoulder, holding me close as we marched on. "I don't want there to ever be another time when you and I are apart."

"I don't want to be away from you again either." His presence allowed me to breathe, big lung-sucking breaths, for the first time in weeks. Being with Bloom had never done that for me. Even in this strange moment, walking behind a dying Mell Grimes, I had absolute confidence that everything was going to be all right simply because I was with him.

Erik squeezed my shoulder. "I'm glad we finally found something we can agree on."

I could think of other things we could agree on, and they started with us being alone together, but I didn't have the guts to say such a thing out loud. He must have sensed my feelings, though. His mouth twitched, and he pulled me away from the group, taking us deeper into the shadows where passing lantern lights couldn't reach. Throwing caution aside, he backed me against the brick wall of a nearby building, pressing his weight against me. My fingers, my lips, even my ears started to tingle. My eyelids drooped, and my thoughts swirled similar to the way they had the night I drank too much Indian wine. Inhaling, I savored his sandalwood scent.

His low voice was almost a growl in my ear. "I swear to you that very soon, it's going to be just you and me. No more distractions or interruptions." He dropped his lips to mine for a soft, sweet moment. "No more undead. No Bloom, no Shep, no Moll Grimes or John Brown."

He pushed harder against me, his hands sliding over my hips and waist then roaming higher up to my throat. He pressed his mouth over the pulse in my neck, and a little whimper escaped me. Thoughts of immediate risk and danger slipped from my mind.

"Just you and me."

I couldn't think that far ahead because his hands and kisses turned me soft and warm like a ripe plum, and I was perfectly content to stay right there in that moment for the rest of my life. It was not to be, though. Not in this world. The ability to savor things, to take safety absolutely for granted, had died in the Dead Wars.

Before our group got too far ahead, Erik pulled away and hurried us into place behind Moll Grimes's funeral procession. At least, that was what it resembled. As we walked, Moll had expressed the occasional groan or grunt of pain, but nothing coherent. Now that we were nearing Dwivedi's college, I wondered if we'd come all this way in vain. Even if Moll had taken the immunity serum, and even if it had remained effective when she was attacked, her wound was severe and her blood loss massive. Dwivedi was clever and resourceful, but he wasn't a god, and I suspected Moll would need a miracle to survive.

Chapter 51: No Time to Waste

The College of Kimiyagari's lights burned a warm greeting, and a group of its inhabitants, including Dr. Dwivedi, welcomed us at the main entrance before ushering us into the safety of the lobby.

"The corporal has already explained what happened." Dr. Dwivedi jutted his chin toward Shep, who was standing among the college's residents as though he belonged there. "You were wise to bring Ms. Grimes here."

Dwivedi instructed the soldiers to relinquish Moll's body into his care and return to Mini City, but they balked. The wizened scientist raised a hand, silencing their objections. "I will not allow so many outsiders into my home at once. If you care for your leader, then you will leave her and let me tend to her. There is no time to waste."

"Do it," John Brown said, his voice tight and hoarse with desperation.

The soldiers deposited Moll's body in the arms of several people in white lab coats, who took her and disappeared into an awaiting elevator. Dwivedi searched the crowd until he found the person he wanted. "Cy, I will require another donation from you. I am afraid I will not have enough to treat her through a full recovery otherwise."

With puckered brow and lips pressed in a thin, dour frown, Erik turned to me. I understood his reluctance. While I didn't want Grimes to suffer, I also couldn't ask Erik to give more than he was willing. If he said no, I'd support him.

After several grim and silent moments, he exhaled and gave a slight nod. "The bare minimum, Dr. Dwivedi. I'm tired of needles."

Dwivedi clapped his hands together. "Of course you are. But for now, we must move quickly. Too much time may have already passed."

We started forward after Dwivedi, but Bloom grasped my shoulder and pulled me back. "One second, Sera."

I shook my head. "If it's more bad news, I don't want to hear it."

Her mouth screwed into a sympathetic grimace. "I'm going back to Mini City with the soldiers. The others will want a report, and someone has to keep the place running."

I blinked at her. "That someone is you?"

She shrugged and glanced away.

"What about John Brown?" I threw a dirty look at the subject of my question.

"He won't leave Moll, and he's no leader."

"He's like a devoted dog."

"That's not always a bad quality," she said in a way that made me wonder if she were referring to me instead of John.

Ignoring her potentially backhanded compliment, I took a step away from her, moving to Erik's side. "You might be too good for that place and those people, you know."

She rolled her eyes. "Thanks for the vote of confidence."

BY THE TIME ERIK AND I had descended into the laboratory, among the potions, experiments, and scientific clutter, Dr. Dwivedi's assistants had already chained Moll to an examination table and administered the first dose of curative. John waited in the corner, so meek and defeated he reminded me of a lost child. Moll didn't scream or flail. She merely stared, her dark eyes flickering over us with hunger and resentment.

It roused something dark and familiar within me.

If we had been in a Shakespeare play, that might have been the moment I lost it, when I fell to the floor, overcome with madness, tearing at my skin while shouting things like, "Out, damned spot! Out, I say!" Instead, I pretended to have all my demons safely stowed away as I continued my examination of Moll. My approach must have worked, though, because the stirrings of old nightmares never became more than bad memories. The monster inside me remained buried.

After leading Erik to a stool, Dwivedi prepped his arm, tying a rubber tube around his biceps and thumping a vein. I climbed onto a stool beside him while Dr. Dwivedi drew yet another vial of blood from Erik's weary body. Instead of sickening me as it had before, I found the scent of Erik's blood oddly soothing. *Better not think about that fact too much.*

"Did I look this bad?" I motioned toward Moll.

Erik turned a dark, troubled gaze on me. He seemed to be thinking along the same lines as I had, worried I was about to go all Lady Macbeth. "Are you sure you want to stick around for this?"

I waved away his concern and nodded at Moll. "Did I look as hateful as she does?"

He grimaced. "You slept a lot."

"But when I was awake, did I look at you the way she's looking at me?"

I watched as multiple unspoken answers passed over his face until he settled on which one to tell me. "You weren't hurt as badly as she is."

"That's not what I want to know."

"You *don't* want to know." He took my hand and grasped it to his chest. "Please don't make me tell you about it. It was horrible, and it's over. Let's not try to remember it."

Agreeing with the wisdom in his words, I dropped the subject.

When Dwivedi had finished his ministrations, he cleaned and covered Erik's arm. "I know you two are exhausted. Parvati has already prepared a room for you in the same apartment you stayed in before. Can you find your way?"

With a tired nod, Erik and I shuffled to the elevator.

"I don't want to do this anymore," Erik said as we waited for the doors to open. He looked sallow rather than simply pale, and his hair hung dark and limp. "I don't want to help that woman."

Wincing, I squeezed his free hand. "I know."

"I very possibly hate her." His whole body seemed to sag with fatigue. "Why am I giving my blood for her?"

I stroked his hair back from his brow. "Because you're a good person?"

"No, not that good."

"You did it for me." I rubbed his back as the elevator creaked and whined, announcing its approach. "Because I asked you."

"You didn't ask me." He flexed his elbow and rubbed the area where Dwivedi's needle had poked him.

"You knew it was what I wanted."

He lifted one shoulder and let it drop. "Maybe."

The elevator door opened, but as we stepped through, a thought flickered in my tired brain. I pulled Erik to a stop before he stepped inside. "Dr. Dwivedi?"

The scientist had returned to Moll's side and was pressing his fingers over her wrist, counting her heartbeats. He answered me without looking up. "Yes, Miss Blite?"

"How is Amity?"

His fuzzy brows drew together. "Who?"

"The girl we brought to you. The one in the cage." I tilted my head toward the silent, covered crate in the corner of the lab.

Dwivedi lowered Moll's wrist and gazed at me with big guileless eyes. "Oh, my dear. I sincerely regret to tell you she passed away several nights ago. There was no way to let you know. I am quite sorry."

The news hit like a punch. But why? I'd already accepted that she would never fully recover. "H-how?" I pressed my hand over my heart as Erik gathered me against his side.

Leaving Moll's examination table, Dwivedi approached, his hands open, arms spread in a posture of apology. "It had been several weeks since I gave her treatment. She lived for a while in peace. She never regressed, never turned into the monstrous creature she had been, but she never recovered her humanity. She died in her sleep without complaint."

"Where is she now?" She deserved mourning and tears, but I'd fought ghouls, I'd escaped Mini City, I'd given succor to my enemy, and I had nothing left for dealing with another emotional blow. Instead, I pushed my feelings aside. Perhaps, after a night of sleep, I could better deal with the grief of losing Amity.

"She has undergone an autopsy. I hope to study her further and maybe glean some knowledge from her death." Dr. Dwivedi, scientist through and through.

"I'd like to say goodbye to her."

Dwivedi thought about my request for a moment then nodded curtly. "I think that can be arranged if you will give me a little time."

Chapter 52: Lame Horse

Erik and I awoke to someone beating on our door. The dim light in our tiny bedroom gave the impression that the sun itself hadn't been awake for long. I wanted to roll over, put a pillow over my head, and ignore the knocking.

"*Sera. Erik.*" The voice belonged to Parvati. "Uncle sent me to get you. Something is happening in the laboratory."

Groaning, Erik slid out of bed and padded to the door in rumpled undershirt and trousers. Sluggishly, I followed, curiosity drawing me like a magnet. Erik turned the locks and opened the door. "What's happened?" He ran a hand through his messy bed hair, trying to smooth it over his scars.

Parvati radiated urgency in her tense posture and wide eyes. "It's Ms. Grimes. She has crossed over. She is... *undead.*"

Erik glanced at me, obviously curious about my reaction.

I arched an eyebrow. I wasn't surprised she had died. Her wounds had seemed to be the fatal sort. But crossing over to undeath... Had the effectiveness of her immunity serum run out? Or had something else happened? Hopefully, Dwivedi would have answers.

"What's being done with her?" Erik asked.

Parvati shook her head. She wore her hair in a thick, glossy braid, and silver earrings flashed around her face. Her yellow sari looked like a morning sunrise. "Uncle wanted to confer with you both before they made any decisions."

After we'd sent her away, telling her we'd come down shortly, we settled on the sofa and took a moment to absorb the news.

"We can't allow Moll to continue in that state," I said as I laced my boots. "Not even for Dwivedi's experiments."

Erik nodded as he finished buttoning his shirt and tucked in the loose tails. "I can't argue with that."

"Do you think Dwivedi will want to keep her?"

Erik paused. "That's a possibility."

"I don't want to do that to her. I think we should put her down." I cringed as soon as the words came out of my mouth. *Like Moll is a lame horse or something.*

"Are you ready?" Erik held out his hand.

I squeezed his fingers. "No. But I don't think we can avoid it."

In the cage that once provided a home to Amity McCall, Moll Grimes panted and whined. Along with Dr. Dwivedi, several other scientists in white lab coats stood around her enclosure. John Brown was there, too, like an odd brown duck among a flock of geese, and his mussed hair, sallow complexion, and red eyes said he hadn't slept at all.

Dwivedi waved us over without taking his gaze from Moll. "Good morning, Cy, Miss Blite. Come closer and tell me what you think."

I noted the death pallor coating Moll that hadn't been there only hours before. Her skin had lost its warm undertones and gained a purple shade similar to the color of her dress.

"When did she pass over?" Erik asked.

"Moments ago. Only moments ago." Dwivedi scratched his bristled jaw. "One second she was resting, breathing shallow with her heart beating weakly, then she let out a small groan, and everything stopped."

"How long did it take for her to resurrect?" I asked.

"Not long. I was able to give her a brief examination to verify her death before she woke again. We had some trouble transferring her to the cage, but she is secure now."

"Her immunity serum didn't save her?" Erik asked.

"I had a similar question, Cy. Mr. Brown here"—Dwivedi gestured to John—"has provided the vial that had contained Ms. Grimes's serum. I am running tests on the vial's residues as we speak. Likely, Ms. Grimes's situation comes down to a simple case of bad timing, but I would like to know for certain."

"What are you going to do with her?" I asked.

Moll rattled the cage's bars. When they didn't give, she shrieked and bashed her forehead against them until her skin split. One of Dwivedi's colleagues stepped up with a broom handle and poked it at her, forcing her to stop. She bared her teeth but backed into a corner and crouched, balancing on the balls of her feet. In her shredded, bloodied gown and limp pompadour, she looked ridiculous, pitiful, and terrifying all at the same time.

Part of me wished I'd had a chance to get to know her better before the events of the previous few hours. A larger part of me was grateful I hadn't. It made deciding what to do with her easier.

"I am asking for your advice, my dear," Dwivedi said. "I am always interested in pursuing the scientific answer, but I think your opinion will weigh heavily on me, considering your recent experiences."

Without taking my eyes from Moll, with no hesitation or uncertainty, I said, "Kill her."

Some of the others muttered unintelligibly, but John Brown wailed. He lurched to Dr. Dwivedi's side and grabbed the sleeve of his white coat. "You can cure her. You gotta cure her. Do whatever it takes."

Distaste crinkled Dwivedi's face as he pried John Brown's fingers from his arm. "Mr. Brown, please control yourself."

John turned to me, ignoring Dwivedi, and fell to his knees in front of me. "Sera, please. Have mercy."

I backed away. "Killing her would be a mercy. Letting her continue like this is torture."

"But you were cured," John said. "There's a chance for her too. Ain't there?"

"Miss Bite never made the transition from dead to undead," explained Dr. Dwivedi, who lamely patted John's shoulder. "She never died, and she never turned. Our experiments to this point demonstrate this is a crucial factor to recovery. Once the first death has occurred, I am not certain there is a cure."

Screwing his face into a visage of rage, John jumped to his feet. His cheeks flared red with anger as he jabbed a finger at Dwivedi. "Well then, you keep working at it until you find one. You ain't gonna let her die."

"She's already dead," Erik said. "And you can't bring her back."

"Don't say that!" John threw his fists over his ears. "You don't know that. You don't know." His whimpers turned into fits of anguish. He wailed like a child who had woken up to find someone had stolen him away in the night and abandoned him on a sidewalk in a foreign city. No one spoke his language, and he had no idea how to find his way home.

"It's your fault, Blite." He pointed a shaky finger at me. Tears and snot marred his beefy face, and he looked almost like one of the undead. "If you hadn't been trying to escape, none of this would've happened."

John's words and anger had no effect on me. We were not on his turf, and the authority behind his threats was dead.

Erik knocked John's hand away. "Moll Grimes is responsible for herself. She never should have kidnapped Sera in the first place."

Before John could raise another protest, Dr. Dwivedi stepped between us. "Mr. Brown, you are welcome to leave this place as a gentleman, or I will have you escorted out as a scoundrel. It is your choice."

John Brown's eyes turned hard. His jaw clenched. "This ain't over, Blite. This ain't the last you've seen of me."

Erik rocked forward, bringing his face close to Brown's, and spoke in a low, menacing voice. "If so, then it won't be the last you've seen of *me*."

"Go home, John." I shook my head, giving him a sad smile full of pity. "I'm not scared of you anymore."

Two younger men in Dwivedi's group approached John with the posture of confident fighters.

"I'm goin', I'm goin'," John told them, shaking off their grasps.

They followed him onto the elevator, and John disappeared behind the closing gate.

Exhaling, I leaned against Erik. He wrapped a comforting arm around me.

"Put Moll Grimes out of her misery, Dr. Dwivedi," Erik said. "I already told Sera I won't give more blood for that woman. She's taken all she's going to get from me."

Dwivedi nodded and gestured toward the space above us. "Parvati has breakfast for you up in the library. I thank you for your recommendations."

"What are you going to do?" I asked as Erik tugged me toward the elevator.

Dwivedi turned to his group of colleagues but threw a final reply over his shoulder. "I will send you word when we have made our decision."

Chapter 53: Marmalade

"So, what do we do today?" Seated at a low table in the college's library, Erik stirred sugar into a mug of tea before handing it to me.

I took a long, careful sip, relishing the sweetness. "I have to do something to keep busy, or else I'll worry about Moll and cry over Amity, and I'm not in the mood to do either of those things."

He bumped his shoulder against mine. "Want to go shopping?"

"Shopping?" I said, voice pitched high with surprise.

"Looting, foraging, trading, stealing..." Grinning, he shrugged. "Whatever you want to call it."

"What do you need?" I studied my toast, slathered in marmalade. My mouth watered, and I was dying to eat it. But once I did, it would be gone, and who knew when I'd get to have such a delicacy again?

"I'm almost out of food at my place, and Dwivedi's supplied me with some things to trade."

I tossed back the last swig of my tea, grabbed my toast, and pushed my seat back. "Let's go."

For our first stop, Erik took me to a family of Solo Practitioners who kept a quail coop on top of their apartment building. Quail eggs tasted like chicken eggs, but they were tiny, and it took three times as many to fill me up. I waited near the roof access while he bargained with a little girl around eight or nine years old. She wore her silky black hair in long pigtails, and I could tell she was giving Erik a hard time. At the end of their bargaining, Erik produced a crock of goat butter from one of his ubiquitous coat pockets and traded it for two dozen eggs. Before we left, an older woman peeked out from the coop and gave the girl an approving nod.

"She's quite the businesswoman," I said as Erik led us from the building.

"The woman watching from the coop is her grandmother. She's taught her well. They give me a harder time than other Solos, though."

"Why?" I was miffed on his behalf.

He motioned to his scars. "They think there's something unnatural about me that makes me immune. For anyone else, that crock of butter would have been worth at least another half dozen eggs."

"Why don't you make them treat you fairly?"

He sighed as we stepped onto the street into glaring sunlight. If we were lucky, it would keep the Non-Breathers hiding deep in their dark places. "Unnatural or not, I do have an advantage over most people. I've got immunity and blood to trade because of it. I get a lot more comforts with my currency than they do, and it's enough of a concession that I don't mind letting the wary ones jilt me a little if it makes them feel better."

I paused in the street, eyes wide with astonishment. "Do you have a single selfish bone in your body? I mean, do you ever do anything entirely for yourself?"

Erik kept walking. "I wanted you, and I got you, didn't I?"

Rolling my eyes, I hurried to catch up to him. "I'd like to think I had some say in it."

"I'm very selfish, if you want to know the truth, when it comes to the things I want." He gave me a sidelong glance. "I won't ever let go of you again. Not for any price."

With that said, we continued on, but I noticed he was leading us somewhere other than home. "Where are we going now?"

"I have one more thing I want to trade for."

"What is it?"

Grinning, he waggled his dark eyebrows. "A surprise."

He stopped us several blocks later at the edge of what used to be, and perhaps still was, China Town.

"Wait here." He stopped us outside of an empty dry-goods store. "You've got your guns on you, don't you?"

"Never leave home without one." From my apron pocket, I pulled out the pistol Shep had given me the previous night during our escape. That moment seemed like it had happened weeks ago rather than hours. I hoped it would be a long time before I saw that much action again.

He nodded. "I'll be right back."

The fact that I stayed behind said a lot about my trust in him. I leaned against the storefront and whistled a tune Bloom used to play on her harmonica, but after I'd run through it a few times, I traded whistling for pacing. I passed back and forth in front of the store maybe twenty times before I began to mutter unpleasant and unrepeatable things about Erik and his surprises. Patience exhausted, I turned for the doorway with the intent of going after him, but he happened to reappear at that same moment.

Reading the expression on my face, he snickered. "Getting worried, were you?"

"I was going to make sure no one had left any trace of your body before I took off to claim your train car for myself."

"Don't be ridiculous." He snorted. "It already belongs to you. What's mine is yours."

Ignoring the gale of emotions his words churned up inside me, I folded my arms across my chest and huffed. "Are you going to tell me what took all that time, or are you hoping I'll beg first?"

"Would you beg?" He waggled an eyebrow at me. "I might like to see that."

"I bet you would." I held out my hand. "Now, give it up."

Erik dug both hands deep into his coat pockets and brought them out, palms open and empty, giving me a look of confusion. He tucked his hand into one breast pocket then wrinkled his brow and rolled his eyes as if befuddled. His silly act worked. I was giggling with anticipation.

His eyes popped wide as if he had just remembered where he put whatever it was he'd been searching for. He reached into another interior pocket, but before he brought it out, it gave itself away with a high-pitched "Mew!"

Turning over his hands, he revealed a tiny orange kitten, barely old enough to hold its eyes open. "Mew!"

"A kitten?" I gasped, my voice squeaky with delight.

"His mom is the best mouser in the city, or so say the people who traded him to me."

"What did it cost you?" Taking the proffered kitten, I snuggled him to my cheek. He purred, and the sound went straight to my heart. I hadn't known I wanted such a thing until I saw its sweet, furry face.

"Not much," Erik said. "A jar of marmalade."

"Marmalade?" I laughed. "What a perfect name for an orange cat."

"It is, isn't it?" He stroked a finger over the tiny soft head. "I know you can get feral cats anywhere in the city, but this one came from a tame mother, so he should be good to you."

Romantic gestures aside, cats were useful agents for dealing with the other unpleasant critters infesting the subway tunnels—the pink-tailed, bewhiskered kind. He would earn his keep and be handsomely rewarded.

I cooed at the kitten. "Erik's a romantic sap, isn't he?"

"*Hey*," Erik objected, but laughter lit his eyes.

"It's a good thing we like romantic saps, isn't it, kitty?"

"Mew," Marmalade agreed.

For a whole day, Erik and I managed to stay safe and out of trouble. We traded half our eggs for a small packet of salt pork from a family of Italian ancestry. Then we traded one more container of jam—gooseberry this time—for a small jar of cream and a wedge of cheese from a family of goat keepers. We came home with talk of omelets for supper and found a note from Dr. Dwivedi pinned to the tapestry Erik used as a front door.

Dear Cy and Miss Blite,

I respectfully request your attendance at a ceremony to pay tribute to the life and death of your friend, Miss Amity McCall. I look forward to seeing you after sunup in two days' time. The event will take some planning and forethought.

We have decided Moll Grimes's people should deal with her death and interment. I have sent word to your sister, asking her to send a representative from Mini City to assist in the matter. Preliminary results from testing of the residue in the immunity serum vial supplied to Ms. Grimes revealed that she had been supplied with a counterfeit. The basis of the antitoxin in her vial was not formulated with Mr. LeRoux's blood but rather with the blood of unknown origin, but likely animal in nature. My hypothesis is that it was pig's blood.

Any further questions concerning Moll Grimes should be addressed to Bloomington Blite and Mini City's senior leadership.

I look forward to seeing you soon.

Yours most dearly and truly,

Dr. Anand Raj Dwivedi

"Moll was set up," I said, breathless with shock. "Who do you think was the culprit?"

Erik scratched his jaw contemplatively. "Dunno. A lot of people could've benefitted from her death. It's not a mystery I'm particularly interested in solving either way."

"Why do you suppose Dwivedi has contacted Bloom about all of this?"

"Why not?" Erik rifled his cooking area for bowls and pans. He cracked eggs and gave me a cutting board and a knife for the cheese. "Bloom is suited to take Moll's place, don't you think?"

I paused, knife blade hovering over the block of goat cheese. "Whoever sabotaged Moll might have something to say about Bloom stepping into Moll's shoes. Bloom is smart enough, but is she cutthroat enough? I dunno..." I tried to think of my sister in that role, living that kind of life. Surprisingly, it wasn't that hard to imagine, and I wasn't sure how I felt about it.

Erik poured a dollop of cream into the bowl of eggs and whipped them into a froth. Marmalade sat at his feet, mewing contentedly after having slurped down a saucer of goat milk mush. "I get the feeling the others will appreciate having anyone as long as that person is willing to take care of them. A woman like Moll didn't delegate power, and none of her people will know how to lead. They are too used to following.

"Bloom spent most of the last few years of her life taking care of you, thinking for herself, surviving on her own. That's more than most people in Mini City can say."

"I hope it doesn't turn out to be something bad for her." Having new authority and power could do funny things to people.

Erik set his whipped egg mixture aside. "She's your sister. You know her best."

"It's a lot of responsibility, but she's not a bad person. I think things will be better for everyone with her in charge."

He plopped a soft kiss on my cheek. "Mmmm, sweet." He drew me into his arms and brushed his lips against mine. "What do you say we have dessert before dinner?"

Just like that, my worries faded away, and for the first time since we'd met, Erik and I had no place to be and no one to distract us. No hungry horde, no demanding scientists, no supplies to scavenge. A warm tingle started in my toes and slowly crawled to my knees, then higher. I returned his kiss, opening fully to him.

Thoughts of omelets faded, overcome by a different and urgent hunger. A desire for something much more satisfying than food. Yes, I thought as Erik's hands skimmed over me, the omelets could definitely wait.

Chapter 54: Beginnings and Endings

Anticipating our arrival, Dr. Dwivedi met us at the College of Kimiyagari's front entrance rather than waiting for us to bang on the basement door. Parvati and Shep accompanied him, and Parvati, wearing all white, twiddled her fingers in a quick hello. Dwivedi ushered us into an atmosphere of hushed reverence, and the college's residents had obviously taken great care to treat Amity's remains with respect.

In the middle of the lobby, a burning oil lamp sat on the floor next to her body, which reclined on a simple palanquin. She was wrapped in linen, and a rose-colored kerchief covered her face. Tears swelled in my eyes and rolled silently down my cheeks as I gave in to grief.

Roses, jasmine, and marigolds adorned Amity's body, and I wondered where such a bounty of blooms had come from, but I had learned not to question Dr. Dwivedi's means and methods. The residents of the Kimiyagari College truly were alchemists. The fragrant flowers covered any smell of death and gave her an aura of royalty.

Dr. Dwivedi motioned to another man, one even older than him, who wore a long cotton tunic and matching white pants. Beads circled his neck, and a yellow scarf draped his shoulders.

He led the community in a series of chants in a language I didn't know. Quietly, under her breath, Parvati tried her best to explain the details. I appreciated her efforts, but I didn't need the words translated. The feelings and intent behind them were clear. My spirit understood what my conscious mind couldn't.

Later, after the ceremony, Parvati told us Amity's body would be cremated and her ashes taken to the river. Maybe Amity's family would have wished for something different, but the residents of the college had stepped into that role on behalf of a family that would never be found. There was no way of knowing for sure, but I thought that wherever Amity was, whatever happened to her next, for now, she knew peace.

AFTER A BRIEF STRUGGLE to arrange myself in a forest-green sari that Parvati had left in my room, and after Erik had dressed in attire similar to what he'd worn the night we last dined on the college's rooftop, we joined Dr. Dwivedi, Shep, Parvati, and the other funeral participants for a starlit feast. Also joining us, to my surprise and delight, was my sister.

I threw my arms around her. "What are you doing here?"

"Dwivedi asked me to come deal with Moll. At least he was nice enough to include me in his dinner plans first though." She looked tired. Dark smudges underscored her eyes, and her shoulders seemed to sag a bit under the weight of her new responsibilities.

"Is she *dead*-dead yet?" I asked.

Bloom squeezed her eyes shut and shook her head. "No. We're going to do the deed after dinner, I think."

My heart lurched with sympathy for Bloom. As much as I agreed with the decision to euthanize Moll, I understood the difficulties of executing it.

"You'll be there, won't you?" Bloom pleaded.

Regretfully, I nodded. "Sure, Bloom. If you want me to, I will."

"It's the right thing, isn't it?"

"Without a doubt." I squeezed Bloom's arm. "Moll's in hell right now, I promise. I know it."

"You know better than any of us." Her head drooped. "If you say it's right. I believe you."

We joined Erik and Dr. Dwivedi in line for the buffet dinner. I spooned a mound of something green—spinach, maybe—onto my plate and moved to the next chafing dish.

"How are things going at Mini City?" I asked.

Bloom stared absentmindedly at a pile of fried bread. Someone nudged her from behind, and she picked up a piece like a machine designed to fill a plate but not to feel any appetite for it. She looked at me and realized I'd asked her a question.

She shook herself. "What?"

"I asked how things were going at Mini City."

"As good as they can be, I guess. I've already called a meeting of the most influential people in Grimes's regime, and we're talking about turning the leadership into a structure similar to a corporate board of directors."

Bloom might as well have been speaking French. I blinked at her.

"They want me to be chairman of the board."

That much made sense to me at least. "You'll be in charge?"

"Sort of. We'll do things with voting. I'm trying to delineate the power structure."

Huffing, I shook my head. "Okay, forget I asked."

Bloom chuckled. "I mean I don't want there to be a dictator. I want people to have a say in the way things are run. Kind of like a democracy. Like the way they used to run the country."

"What about Moll's saboteur?" I asked. "Someone wanted her out of the way. Whoever it was might come for you next."

Color drained from Bloom's already-pale face. "I am aware. There will be a quiet investigation. In the meantime, I'll be looking over my shoulder. It sure would be nice to have you watching my back though."

"Hmmm," I said ambiguously. I worried for my sister, but the thought of living at Grimy Tower made me shudder. I didn't understand that world, didn't want to be a part of it. Not even for the sake of my sister. She'd made her choice—*she* had walked away from *me*. I no longer resented her for it, but I didn't feel obligated to her anymore either. They might occasionally intersect, but our paths were unlikely to converge again, and I had made my peace with it.

Once we reached the end of the buffet table, Dwivedi led us to the head of the table, where Parvati and Shep had already taken their seats. The food smelled wonderful, but I didn't have an appetite. It seemed I wasn't the only one. The mournful mood hovering around the dining table tonight felt like a visit from a distant, forgotten relative who showed up out of the blue, unexpected and unwanted.

The people around me had no knowledge of Amity as a human, as a girl who preferred cake over flesh and songs and walks in the park over a compelling desire to consume. The college's display of affection for her puzzled me somewhat. I hadn't known her well myself. We'd taken classes together. We'd spoken in passing and knew each other's names and faces well enough, but I could hardly call her more than an acquaintance. It didn't lessen the sting of her passing, though. Maybe I was merely grieving the loss of a connection to the Time Before, but I liked to think it was more than that, that I had come to truly care for her.

After they'd scraped the last bites from their plates, my fellow funeral-goers drifted off to their homes. No one brought out musical instruments or drew their partner close for a dance. Bloom dragged her fork around but never committed to eating anything. I glanced at my plate and noticed I'd made a similar lack of progress. Erik ate only a little more than I had. We made a sorry bunch.

Dr. Dwivedi had no such trouble. He pushed his empty dishes aside, patted his belly, and covered his mouth as he belched. "I would have never thought it possible, in this world, that anything could steal the appetites of the young." He leaned over to study my plate. "Was there nothing to your liking?"

I gave him a limp, apologetic smile. "Everything was wonderful as usual."

"And Ms. Blite." Dwivedi's eyebrows drew together with concern as he peered at Bloom. "Are you feeling unwell?"

"I feel fine," Bloom said. "Just not in the mood to eat."

"Well, I suppose that is reasonable, considering what is next on our agenda." He pushed his chair back and stood. "Let us not put it off any longer than necessary. Take a few moments to gather your wits and then please join me in the laboratory."

Bloom nodded without taking her sullen eyes from her plate.

"What will you do after?" I asked Bloom.

"Some of the Forces will be here in the morning to help me take her body back. There will be a ceremony. She'll be cremated."

"I'll come with you. Erik too." I glanced at Erik to make sure he agreed, and he gave a quick nod.

"We'll come too," said Shep, who sent a nervous look to Parvati. "Maybe you can give me my job back."

Bloom uttered a dry laugh. "I think I might have an opening. Do you want to move back to Mini City?"

Shep and Parvati stared at each other gravely for a moment. "Perhaps we could work something out."

"We'll talk about it later, Corporal." Bloom turned to me. "Sera, you're welcome to live at Mini City too. You won't be a prisoner anymore, and you can bring Erik with you."

Erik clamped a hand on my knee. I muffled a yelp. "I think we're happy where we are."

"Where are you anyway?" Bloom asked.

Erik squeezed harder.

I hesitated. "Um..."

Bloom raised an eyebrow and cut her gaze between me and Erik before letting out a snort. "It's fine if you want to keep it a secret. You know where I am if you ever want to get in touch."

MOLL GRIMES'S FUNERAL befitted a woman of her social stature, whether she deserved that kind of fanfare or not. Erik and I stood in the back of the audience with Shep, Parvati, Dr. Dwivedi, and a few others from his college while Bloom delivered a heartfelt speech on the front steps of Grimy Tower. John Brown was there, red-eyed and deflated. He shot hateful looks at me from time to time, but Erik and I brushed them off. Without the might of Moll Grimes's Forces behind him, John had about the same effect on me as a popgun.

Bloom looked relieved when the ceremony ended. She'd held her shoulders a little straighter and took the slaps on the back and hand-shakes offered to her by the residents of Mini City with aplomb. I was proud to be her sister.

Erik and I tried to get away unnoticed, but Bloom saw us in the crowd and called out to me. "Sera! Where're you going? Come give your sister a hug."

I obliged her, then Bloom shook Erik's hand and said, "Sure you don't want to stay for dinner? We're roasting a whole pig."

"Tempting." It really was. Barbecued pork was a rare delicacy, and maybe I was an idiot for saying no. I glanced at Erik to see if he'd changed his mind, but he shook his head. He hated crowds more than I did. "But I'm not comfortable in this place, around people who might still be loyal to Moll. I think it's best if Erik and I make ourselves scarce. Dwivedi and his people are leaving, too, and they offered to escort us home. Safety in numbers, you know?"

Nodding as though she understood, she held her hand out, asking for mine. "Please, Sera. No matter what's happened between us, I want you to keep in touch."

I slipped my fingers into Bloom's hand, and she squeezed them. "Of course I will." Pulling her closer, I threw my arms around her and held her tightly. "We're family. Not even undeath can take that away."

Acknowledgments

This book was a bit of an experiment for me and something a little stranger than my usual fare. So I owe a debt of gratitude to Lynn McNamee and Red Adept Publishing for being willing to let me explore this idea and for always changing, growing, adapting, and experimenting for the benefit of their authors. I've been so lucky to be a part of this publishing home for so long.

I also send thanks to Erica Lucke Dean for being a terrific writing partner and an even better friend. I might have given up this adventure a long time ago if not for you.

More thanks to Kim Husband, who invested a lot of time in sprucing up the early versions of this that ended up on Kindle Vella. Thanks for your open mind and encouragement.

Thanks to my "Fast & Furious Fam," Victor Catano, Mary Fan, and Christian Angeles. Y'all keep me sane on a daily basis.

Thanks to Felicia for tolerating all my fantastical nonsense and for making room for my dreams amid the day-to-day mundane.

To my family. We get this one life, and I'm so thankful I get to share it with you.

About the Author

Karissa Laurel always dabbled in writing, but she also wanted to be a chef when she grew up. So she did. After years of working nights, weekends, and holidays, she burnt out and said, "Now what do I do?" She tried a bunch of other things, the most steady of those being a paralegal for state government, but nothing makes her as happy as writing. She has published several short stories and reads "slush" for a couple of short-story markets.

Karissa lives in North Carolina with her kid, her husband, the occasional in-law, and a polka-dotted dog named Puzzle. She loves to read and has a sweet tooth for speculative fiction. Sometimes her husband convinces her to put down the books and take the motorcycles out for a spin. When it snows, you'll find her on the slopes.

Karissa also paints and draws and harbors a grand delusion that she might finish a graphic novel someday.

Read more at www.karissalaurel.com.

About the Publisher

Dear Reader,

We hope you enjoyed this book. Please consider leaving a review on your favorite book site.

Visit https://RedAdeptPublishing.com to see our entire catalogue.

Check out our app for short stories, articles, and interviews. You'll also be notified of future releases and special sales.